DEAD EVEN

A TRUTH SEEKERS NOVEL - BOOK SIX

SUSAN SLEEMAN

D1073345

Published by Edge of Your Seat Books, Inc.

Contact the publisher at contact@edgeofyourseatbooks.com

Copyright © 2020 by Susan Sleeman

Cover design by Kelly A. Martin of KAM Design

This book is a work of fiction. Characters, names, places, and incidents in this novel are either products of the imagination or are used fictitiously. Any resemblance to real people, either living or dead, to events, businesses, or locales is entirely coincidental.

1

Warning! Death Ahead. Land At Your Own Risk.

The boat pitched under Maya Glass's feet, and she grabbed the railing. She rolled her eyes at the sign.

Death ahead. Seriously?

Her friend Fletch's idea of a joke. Not hers for sure. A fellow scientist, Dr. Fletcher Gilliam, had positioned numerous signs warning of death on the beaches of his private island in the Willamette River near Portland, Oregon. No one found it funny except him. Just the kind of geeky and eccentric thing the near hermit was always doing.

The boat captain, a fellow with a heavy belly draping over khaki pants and wearing a nautical cap, stepped from his cabin and marched toward her in the August sunshine beating down on the boat. He'd idled the motor, now a steady hum, and without the breeze, perspiration beaded up on her forehead. She was starting to get cranky.

The captain swayed with the river's movement, his frown deepening. "I'm not landing there, Dr. Glass," he shouted to be heard over the thrum of the boat's idling motor. "Not with those signs. No way."

Maya waved his words away. "It's just my friend's idea of

a joke. He likes his solitude, and he had a problem with boaters who ignored his *private property* signs. They invade the place to picnic on his beach and explore the island. He put those up to curtail the problem."

The captain planted a hand on the railing next to her and lifted a bushy eyebrow as he faced the single-story concrete building that resembled a bunker. "What does this Fletcher guy do on his island? I mean, that building looks like a business, not a home."

Fletcher researched toxins and viruses for the government and private companies, but there was no way she'd tell the captain that. "He's a scientist."

The captain pursed his lips and eyed her. "A scientist who studies what?"

She shrugged lightly. "He's always changing his focus. But there's nothing to worry about."

"Right, nothing," He stared over her shoulder at the building.

"Hey." She forced out a smile. "Do you think I'd be visiting him if there was a problem?"

"No." He gave a heavy sigh. "I suppose not. But still, I don't think the crew will go for it."

Maya wanted to sigh like he'd just done. Let it go on and on. Why hadn't she chosen to rent a boat instead of renting a boat *and* crew? Because she was a landlubber and knew nothing about boating, that's why. She'd likely have killed herself if she'd tried to get to the island on her own. She'd visited Fletch many times before, but the boat tour company she'd always used had gone out of business, and she'd had to find a new one.

Now she was stuck explaining everything to this wary captain. "Have you ever heard of the Veritas Center?"

He swiped a handkerchief over his bald head. "Yeah, I think so. They're on the west side. Do DNA testing, right?"

She nodded. "And process forensics for law enforcement. I'm the toxicology and controlled substances expert and a partner there. So you can trust me when I tell you it's safe to land the boat and wait for me at the dock."

He bit his lip and looked back at one of his crew members. "I don't know."

"What if you dropped me at the dock and then came back out here to anchor where you can see me when I'm ready to leave? Would your crew agree to that?"

"Let me ask them." He spun, his rubber-soled shoes squeaking on the deck.

She wasn't one to accept failure, and she wouldn't today. Not with the cryptic voicemail Fletch had left three days ago. She got out her phone and listened to it again.

"Maya. It's Fletch. You won't believe what they're planning to do. I don't even believe it, and I need someone to confirm. Someone who knows how to keep their mouth shut and has top-notch scientific skills. That's you. Get here as quickly as you can. Please. It's important. Hurry."

The message ended, the silence feeling ominous to her.

She could easily imagine him in his lab, his curly red head bent over his lab table, his face covered in a scraggly beard because he wouldn't take the time to shower much less shave. His latest research in front of him. Maybe his assistant, Carson Delvalle, next to him or at another table. Likely another table, as Fletch really did need his space. Fletch's deep brown eyes would be narrowed behind thick glasses, pondering whatever problem he was working on.

That was typical Fletch. Leaving a message wasn't. They'd been friends for years, and she would've come running, but she was out of town testifying in court. She'd called him back. Multiple times. Got his voicemail and left messages, which he hadn't returned. If it was anyone else, she'd worry, but Fletch was scatterbrained and often

3

ignored calls. He probably didn't even need her anymore and thought that, by not calling her back, she would figure that out. But she wouldn't take any chances, just in case.

The captain marched back to her. "We'll do it. Drop you off, I mean. But anything hinky happens, and we're out of here and you find your own way home."

She smiled, though worry formed in the pit of her stomach. After Fletch's phone call, maybe she should consider something hinky was going on.

Didn't matter. She was here to help her friend, and she wasn't leaving until she knew he was all right. She pulled her shoulders back and came to her full five-foot-nine-inch height. "Let's go ahead and dock."

He gave a sharp nod and returned to the controls. The motor roared to life, and he piloted the boat to the long wooden dock. A young deckhand swung a rope into the air and captured a post on the dock to pull them in. He lowered a short gangplank and stood back, looking at her like she had the plague or something equally as deadly.

She resisted saying something sarcastic. He was uneasy, and she needed him to get back to the mainland.

"Go ahead, Doctor," the captain said. "No one's going to join you on that dock."

She picked up her backpack and shouldered it, taking her time moving down the dock where the odor of rotting fish rose up to assault her nose. She felt like she was walking the plank or being exiled, not going to visit a friend.

"You are so going to pay for this, Fletch," she muttered as she stepped onto the buoyant dock. She turned and waved at the captain, but he'd already returned to his cabin, and the deckhand was busy setting them free.

Listening to the revving motor on the boat fleeing to a safe distance, she strode down the dock. She glanced back to see that the boat was already a blip in the river, but the captain was true to his word, and the deckhand was tossing the anchor overboard.

She stepped onto firm ground, grateful to be on land since she often suffered from motion sickness. Today had been a good day, and her stomach was barely upset, but now that she was off the boat with a cool breeze, the sweltering temperatures wrapped around her like an unwanted blanket. She swiped a hand over her forehead and took the winding stone path toward the single-story building. Fletch was devoted to his work but had severe anxiety disorders that kept him confined to his own space. The very reason he'd had his own lab constructed with living quarters at the back of the building.

Weeds and perennials co-mingled along the path, but the weeds were winning and the path narrowing. Fletch needed to get someone out here to do his yard work, but landscape people had similar issues with the signs. Not to mention the difficult task of hauling their equipment in a boat. Maybe she could help Fletch out there. As the managing partner of the Veritas Center, she had a vast array of contacts with service businesses. Surely, she could get a landscape company to come out here. *If* Fletch would allow it.

She reached the door, pressed the bell, and looked up at the security camera so he could get a good look at her face and buzz her in. She waited, a soft breeze playing over the grasses that swayed in a feathery dance, but no one answered the bell.

"Seriously, Fletch," she muttered and pressed the button again.

She started counting. One, one thousand. Two, one thousand. Three, one thousand. At sixty, she jerked on the door handle. It came open under her touch. Shocked, she stood there for a moment. Nick, the Veritas electronics expert, had supervised the installation of top-of-the-line security just a few months ago. This door sure shouldn't be unlocked.

Feeling more unsettled, she stepped into the small foyer with a single chair and small table. The building felt cool after being in the bright sunshine. Silence greeted her.

"Fletch," she yelled. "Carson? Are either of you here?"

Her voice reverberating down the long hallway was the only sound. Fletch could easily be so wrapped up in his work that he didn't hear her. If the door hadn't been unlocked, she wouldn't be worried.

But she was worried. Very.

She reached into her purse for her gun. She'd carried for years and shot with Grady all the time in their small firing range behind their building, so she was very comfortable handling guns.

She eased down the hall and peeked in the window of the small lab with one stainless steel table and cabinets ringing the room. Fletch's assistant used this lab when Fletch wanted to be alone.

A microscope sat on the table, slides lying next to it, but no one occupied the stool. She continued farther down the hall to the next window, which overlooked Fletch's lab. He'd covered the window with white paper. Normal state of affairs. He didn't want onlookers. He designed the building, and when she'd asked him why he'd installed a window, he said it was expected. Then, the moment he occupied the lab, he covered it with paper, unnecessary as he rarely let any visitors into the lab.

Shaking her head at the memory, she reached for his door. Just like the front door, it was unlocked.

This was his kingdom. His life's work. And he'd left it unsecured. Even more disconcerting. Especially since the lab had to meet the Bio-Safety Level 4 laboratory standards, which were the strictest standard for labs working with toxins. And that meant the lab must have a locked door with limited and controlled access. Not an open door where anyone could walk in.

She poked her head inside, his office door standing open too. She didn't see him.

"Fletch," she called out, hoping he just hadn't heard her before.

No reply. Getting really worried now, she hurried down the hall, checking rooms. Small kitchenette. Bathroom. Storage closet. Still no sign of Fletch.

She raced to his apartment, the door ajar. "Fletch. Fletch. Where are you?"

The tiny one-bedroom was devoid of any personal décor and held very little furniture. She made a quick assessment of the place but found no sign of Fletch. The sink was filled with dirty dishes. A cereal bowl with milk congealed in Cheerios sat on the table. A half-filled cup of coffee sat next to it. She checked the pot. It was cold.

So, was this coffee from early this morning or days ago? What was going on?

She hurried to the bedroom. Found his bedding rumpled, but no one in the room or the bathroom. She looked in his medicine cabinet and found his toothbrush, toothpaste, and deodorant. His closet looked normal. A mess but normal. His small suitcase, which he used when he came to the city for the night, sat on the floor.

He hadn't packed a bag, but he wasn't here. He could've gone to the city, but she doubted that. In that case, he wouldn't have asked her to visit him and help out.

"His boat," she said, the thought popping into her brain. She ran down the hallway and outside. She wound through the tall grasses again to get to the boathouse. Water lapped at the building, and a soft breeze rolled in from the river, but it was still hot and muggy. She brushed her hand over her forehead and tugged on the door. Locked. She shifted to look through a dirty window. His speedboat wasn't on the rack. Did he leave the island in his boat? Leave Carson behind? She couldn't imagine him doing so.

A mosquito bit her leg, and she slapped at it. Panic starting to form, she moved out of the deep grass to the path. If he'd left the island on his own, why hadn't he locked up behind himself?

Maybe he'd left her a note.

She turned and raced back down the path and inside the building. She entered Fletch's lab, a large room with six stainless steel tables in the center and white cabinets circling the perimeter. On the countertops sat state-of-the-art science equipment. She was struck again by how quiet it was. Only the fans from the special air filtration system installed to comply with federal regulations hummed.

She glanced into his office, her heart pounding like a conga drum, and found his desk the usual jumbled mess of papers. She searched for a note but didn't find one. Hoping to see what he was working on, she turned back to the lab.

The tables were covered with a very fine clay-colored powder.

Odd.

She stepped in deeper and moved around the office wall. Her foot bumped something soft. She stuttered to a stop. Looked down. Gasped. "No. Oh. No."

A body lay crumpled on the floor. Male. Back to her.

Her heart sank, and she forced herself to take in the details. Lab coat. Jeans. A thick head of hair. Not the right color for Fletch. And too chubby. Fit Carson's build.

She rushed around his body to kneel beside him. Away from the air filtration system, the stench of death rose up to greet her.

8

She clamped her hand over her mouth and nose.

"Carson," she mumbled around her hand. "Carson. Are you okay?"

She turned him over, and bile rose in her throat. His face bloated and purple. His lips blue.

He was dead.

Still, she pressed her fingers on his neck. No pulse. Cold skin.

Dead. Honestly and truly dead, and had been for some time. If not for the strong ventilation system, she would've smelled the decay when she'd first entered the lab.

Now, the smell was thick and cloying. She wanted to hurl. To run. But she forced herself to take a good look at him. No knife or gunshot wound. Not even a bruise on his face.

What had he died from?

A vial lay next to his hand. She leaned closer to read the label.

Botulinum.

No. Oh no. It can't be. She jerked back.

Botulinum, or botulism, was deadly. Very deadly. Scientists agreed that it was the most toxic substance known to man.

Was this what Fletch had wanted to tell her about? The reason for the powder on the tables?

She scrambled back from Carson and looked around. The rat cages were silent, the animals all dead.

Had Fletch found a way to make the toxin airborne? She still had her hand clasped over her mouth and jerked it free. Had she inhaled some of the poison?

She looked at her knees. Fine powder covered her jeans.

If she had been exposed, and if she didn't get access to the antitoxin, she could have only days to live.

She tried to remember everything she knew about

botulism. Inhalation led to paralysis, starting with the eyes and working down the body. Obviously fatal. She'd once read that scientists estimated that one single teaspoon of the toxin was enough to kill over a billion people. And she might have been exposed to it.

She wanted to run screaming from the building, but she couldn't. Not when her clothing could be contaminated. She might have already carried some of it out of the building on her feet when she'd gone to the boat house.

Oh, dear, God, please no. Please don't let this be airborne. Don't let me have breathed it in. Or ingested it when I touched my face.

Tears wetted her eyes, and her mind clouded over. What should she do?

"Think, Maya, think."

Where was Fletch? Maybe he'd tried to go for help. Or maybe he was dead somewhere on the island.

No. No. He would have called the health department and arranged to get the CDC to the lab, along with the antitoxin.

She dug out her phone and tears started to fall. She didn't have the health department's number, but she did have a contact who could get them there faster than she could.

She dialed Hunter, a person she never thought she'd ask for help again.

"Special Agent Hunter Lane." His smooth baritone voice raised her angst, and her tears turned into sobs.

"Hunter," she managed to get out through the panic. "I need you. I need you now."

2

Hunter shoved a hand into his hair and dropped onto his desk chair at the Portland FBI office. "Maya? Is that you?"

"Y-yes," she said, her response clogged with tears, tugging at his heartstrings.

They'd dated for a year, but they'd broken up more than six years ago under terrible circumstances. No matter the time that had passed, the feelings that rose at the sound of her voice hadn't changed. He was still in love with her, and the pain in her single word cut him like a knife wound to his gut.

He snapped his chair forward. "What's wrong?"

"Botulinum or botulism. Fletch's assistant is dead. I might've been exposed and need help immediately." She gasped for a breath. "I know you can get a team from the health department to the island faster than I can."

Hunter tried to piece together the information she shared. "You're on Fletch's island?"

"In his lab, but he's missing. I'm worried the toxin is airborne, and I may have been exposed. Maybe he was too, and is on the island somewhere. Either very sick or dead."

Hunter's gut tightened around the cinnamon and raisin

bagel he'd just scarfed down for a late breakfast. "I'll call my contact at the county health department right now and call you back. Anything else they need to know?"

"Only to hurry and get the antitoxin from the CDC."

"They have one?"

"Yes. Hurry." The call went dead.

He stared at his phone for only a second before scrolling through his contacts until he located an old college friend, Dr. Isabelle Eller. He dialed her office.

"Dr. Eller."

"Izzy, it's Hunter. I need a favor. A friend thinks she's been exposed to airborne botulism. Can you get a team to her ASAP? Her friend, Fletcher Gilliam, is a research scientist. She's at his lab."

"Fletch," Izzy said. "You mean the island lab?"

"You know him?"

"We worked together years ago. Is he okay?"

"Don't know. Maya says he's missing. Maybe sick or dead." Hunter took a long breath. "She also said the CDC has an antitoxin."

"They do. The moment we hang up I'll give them a call."

"Perfect. I'll arrange for a boat, and you can meet me at the pier."

"No need. We have boats contracted for emergencies."

"Fine, I'll ride with you." Though he'd much rather be in control of his own transportation. "Just tell me where to meet you."

She didn't answer.

His concern escalated. "Izzy? What is it?"

"If the toxin is airborne, we'll have to quarantine the island. I'm afraid there's no way you can go in."

"I'm going in no matter what," he stated firmly. "Carson's dead. Could have been murdered. I'm going to protect the crime scene and make sure Maya's okay. Bring me a biohazard suit, or you'll be dealing with another exposure."

He hung up and charged down the hallway to his supervisor's office. Assistant Special Agent in Charge Nathan Adair sat behind his desk. He wore his usual white shirt and neutral tie, his black suit coat hanging on the back of his chair.

He looked up. "Agent Lane. What can I do for you?"

Hunter gave his supervisor a quick rundown. "I know we don't usually do homicides, but the botulism has far reaching consequences."

"Agreed." Adair ran a hand over a salt-and-pepper buzz cut. "But this doesn't fall under the cyber squad's purview."

Hunter knew Adair would bring up Hunter's squad assignment, and Hunter didn't have a strong rebuttal planned. "I know the players here, and that'll go a long way in progressing quickly in the investigation."

Adair jutted out his chin. "And you're willing to risk exposure to take lead and make an initial assessment?"

"Izzy—Dr. Eller—with Multnomah County is bringing a biohazard suit for me. I'll be fine."

"Suits can fail."

"I'll be fine."

"As long as you know the risks."

"I do."

Adair appraised him for long uncomfortable moments. "Report back as soon as you know what we're looking at, and I'll decide how to proceed from there and which agencies to loop in."

"Will do." Hunter turned to leave.

"And Lane." Adair met Hunter's gaze and held it. "I can tell this Maya is important to you. Don't take any risks. You can't help her if you're dead."

Maya breathed in through the respirator she'd located in the cupboard for emergency situations. She still wanted to run screaming from the room, but she curled her arms around her knees and watched the clock tick down instead. Her heart rate escalated with each second that crawled by.

Thirty-four minutes had passed since Hunter called back saying he was on the way with a doctor from the health department. Maya didn't want to just sit there and wait for symptoms to begin, but there was nothing she could do at this point other than wait. As a scientist, she knew enough to know symptoms could appear in a matter of hours or could take as long as three days. She could look on the internet for additional information about botulism, but why? Just to scare herself even more?

As much as she wanted to search the lab for leads on Fletch's whereabouts or even go looking for him, she wouldn't. If the toxin had been aerosolized and released in the lab, it could be on every surface. If she hadn't been exposed, she could easily become exposed. She didn't want to spread the toxin outside. Besides, Hunter promised he and the doctor would be here soon, and she knew he would be. He was a man of his word. Always. Honest. Trustworthy. A real Boy Scout.

Until, of course, it came to following through on love. There, he was a colossal failure. He'd lived a hard life. Lost every person he'd ever loved—except her when they were together. So, before he lost her, he'd bailed. He'd made up a lame excuse, but she knew he sabotaged their relationship because he feared that she'd somehow die too.

It was fine. Now anyway. Six years ago when he'd left, she'd been devastated. So she poured herself into launching the Veritas Center. Every moment of every waking day, she'd worked to create the lab boasting experts in forensic anthropology, DNA, trace evidence, ballistics, cybercrimes, criminal investigations, and her field of toxicology and controlled substances. Seven partners working in one lab to bring truth to individuals and law enforcement. She'd even chosen the center's name which meant truth in Latin.

She'd created a world-renowned lab. Something she was proud of. Now, she didn't have time for a man. She was far too busy at the lab. As their chief scientist and the managing partner, she was swamped now that they were working with law enforcement. She couldn't have both a career and a marriage. So, Hunter's need to bail on her had been fortuitous. Didn't mean it didn't hurt that he'd walked out on her, but she could deal now.

She heard a sound from the entryway and sat forward. She wished she'd taken down the paper from the window so she could see who was coming, but a blue-suited figure soon appeared in the doorway. Tall. Wide shoulders in a full-body biohazard suit. She searched the clear face mask. Found concern in Hunter's eyes.

She sagged in relief. For just a moment. Then she realized a woman was standing behind him, and she carried a field kit that likely held needles she would poke Maya with to draw blood.

Hunter crossed the room. The suit, gloves, and booties covered every inch of his body. He squatted next to her, which she knew was a challenge in one of those suits, considering he carried an oxygen tank on his back. It was connected to a respirator facepiece that covered his mouth and nose, so she couldn't get a good look at his face. He was going to have to talk loudly so she could hear him.

"How are you doing?" He raised his voice, as expected.

"No symptoms of the toxin," she said loudly.

The woman joined them. She carried a plastic container

that looked like a tackle box and set it on the floor next to Maya.

"I'm Dr. Isabelle Eller," she said, her voice raised too. "Call me Izzy. I'm glad to see you found a respirator. I'd like to examine you if I may."

"Sure," Maya said.

Dr. Eller leaned closer. "Look directly at me."

She used thickly-gloved fingers to touch Maya's eyelids.

"Not droopy," she said, her voice barely audible over the breathing apparatus. "Any double vision or blurred vision?"

"None."

"How about dry mouth or difficulty swallowing?"

"I feel perfectly normal."

"Your speech is clear. Not slurred or garbled." She sat back on her haunches. "Difficulty breathing or fatigue or any muscle weakness at all?"

"No. I feel fine."

"How long since your exposure?"

"I don't even know if I was exposed," Maya said. "I saw that Carson and the rats were all dead, and a vial labeled botulinum is lying beside Carson. That was about an hour ago. With all of them dead and the powder on the counters, I was worried it had been aerosolized. When I found Carson, I clasped my hand over my mouth and nose from the smell. I shouldn't have, I know, but it was instinct. I might've ingested some toxin. Or could have inhaled it, if it's still in the air."

Izzy's eyes narrowed. "It takes a very small quantity to kill someone, so it's a good possibility that you were exposed, if indeed it's been released in here. But don't let our full biohazard suits scare you. We're just being overly cautious. The toxin can't be absorbed through the skin unless you have an open wound. Any open sores?"

Maya shook her head.

"If it's not treated, how long after the symptoms appear before death occurs?" Hunter asked.

Maya gave him an incredulous stare at his blunt comment about death.

"It depends on the dosage and the patient." Izzy offered Maya a kind look. "We don't know a lot about inhalation botulism because it's very difficult to aerosolize, and we've only had a few cases to study."

"If Carson did die from inhaling the botulism," Hunter said, "would he have known what was going on?"

Izzy nodded. "And that's what I find odd. If he'd experienced the symptoms, he would know to seek help. He should never have died from this."

Hunter planted his hands on his knees. "Unless someone prevented him from getting help."

Izzy looked at him for a long time. "That would be the best explanation as to why he didn't call us or 911."

"Did you call the ME?" Maya wanted the medical examiner to get a look at Carson and remove his body so they could begin the investigation.

Izzy nodded, her head bobbing inside the suit's large hood. "Dr. Albertson's on her way."

"The sooner, the better," Hunter said. "We need to know what Carson died of."

"Don't worry," Izzy said calmly. "We'll find out how he died, but you should know testing for botulism takes forty-eight hours. We won't know for sure what we're looking at before then. And until then, Maya's our top priority."

"Of course. That's a given." Hunter met Maya's gaze and held it, taking her back to their time together, when that concerned look meant he would be there for her, helping her through whatever problems she might experience. But how long would he be at her side now? Was he planning on working the murder? Not likely. That was a job for local homicide.

Izzy sat back and peered at Maya through her face shield. "The CDC will have the antitoxin here soon. At this point, I say we hold off on administering it if you aren't showing any symptoms when it arrives. It carries side effects. There's no point in putting you through those if you haven't been exposed."

Maya didn't know how she felt about that. "What's the potential downside to waiting?"

Izzy leaned closer and raised her voice. "If we wait, the toxin can become bound to nerve terminals. The antitoxin can neutralize only circulating toxin, not toxin that has become bound to those terminals."

Maya was glad for her anatomy training or she might not have processed that, considering how stressed she was. "So I might sustain some nerve damage."

"Yes, but in most cases, people eventually recover all nerve functions."

"*Most* people," she clarified. "Not all."

"Yes."

Hunter shifted to face Izzy. "How long before Maya would start showing symptoms of exposure?"

Izzy had to pivot her whole upper body to look at him. "Four hours at the earliest. More likely twelve to thirty-six hours, but it could take up to eight days. As I mentioned, inhaling the toxin has only happened a few times, so we don't know a lot about it. But my gut says the time will be on the shorter end."

Hunter's dark eyes narrowed. "Aren't there any blood tests to confirm the exposure?"

"Yes, and we'll run them, but it takes the same amount of time to process these tests as the ones we'll run on the lab samples. So we're better off monitoring her symptoms and administering the antitoxin at the first sign of a problem." She met Maya's gaze through the clear face mask. "You should know. It's not known if the antitoxin will be effective against aerosolized toxin. We don't know that it won't either. We just don't have any data to suggest one way or other, and I want you to be prepared."

"Thank you for being honest with me." Maya pressed a hand on Izzy's arm. "I want to know everything as it unfolds."

Izzy gave a sharp nod inside her suit. "We need to get you decontaminated. My team is setting up the decontamination area, and I'll come back for you when we're ready. Until then, sit tight." She patted Maya's knee and looked at Hunter. "You want to stay here?"

He nodded. "I want to take a look around and see if I can figure out where Fletch might be."

"Fine." Izzy stood. "Remain inside only. You're not cleared to go outside before doffing your suit."

Hunter looked up at her. "Doffing?"

"Sorry. It's what we call taking off the suit in proper order."

"I assume someone will instruct me on that."

"The same person who helped you don the suit will help you doff it." She spun, slowly, and her suit crinkled with each lumbering step.

Maya watched her leave, her mind filled with disbelief. How was this happening to her? Had she really been infected? Might she die? And now that things had settled down in her mind, she had to wonder why she'd called Hunter of all people. Sure, he'd gotten Izzy here in record time, but a phone call directly to the health department would likely have done the same thing.

Was the call a subconscious plea to have Hunter at her

side? Someone who could hold her and tell her everything was going to be okay?

But would she even let him hold her? Not likely. No matter how much she would like that right about now, he'd hurt her so badly that the pain remained fixed in her heart.

Still squatting at her side, he shifted. "Are you sure you're doing okay?"

She nodded. She expected him to move the conversation to something personal, and she had to preempt that. "When you're clean again, can you go out and look for Fletch?"

He studied her carefully, likely wondering why she was acting so formal with him. Well, too bad. That was what he deserved.

"Well?" she asked.

"We already have people doing a grid search of the island."

"People as in agents or health department workers?"

"Health department," he said.

"And do you trust their searching abilities?"

"I don't have a choice. Izzy quarantined the island, and I'm the only one outside their vast team that they allowed on the property. I gave them instructions on how to do a grid search, so hopefully they'll follow through."

For some reason, the boat captain's face came to mind, and she laughed.

Hunter eyed her, his grayish-blue eyes above the respirator looking darker through the clear face shield. "What's so funny?"

"When I first got here, the captain of the boat I hired was worried about Fletch's signs and terrified to dock here." She shook her head. "Turns out he had a right to be worried. I can just imagine his face when you showed up with the health department and all of their gear."

"I don't have to imagine it. Because they'd docked to drop you off, Izzy quarantined them right along with us."

"Oh, no. He's got to be freaking out."

"He is. His crew too." Hunter frowned. "How are you really holding up?"

He wasn't going to let it go. She shrugged. "I keep looking at Carson and wondering when he died and if I could have saved him if I'd gotten here earlier. But we won't even know how long he's been here until the ME arrives."

He didn't say anything for the longest time, just sat there looking at her. Searching her gaze. "Sounds like you're blaming yourself when you shouldn't be. His death isn't on you."

She glanced at Carson. "My brain knows that. My heart not so much."

"Trust me, I get it." Pain that had often lingered in his tone rode on the words.

She knew he really did understand. His mom walked out on him when he was ten. Never saw her again. His dad started drinking that day and drank himself into cirrhosis of the liver and an early death. Hunter went to live with his grandparents, and they died in a house fire. After he and his older sister landed in foster care, she died of a drug overdose. And he lost a fiancée in a car accident. That was a lot of death for one person to recover from, and she didn't think he had—not really—or he wouldn't be running from commitment, nor would his tone be so pained.

He cleared the anguish from his eyes. "Would you like me to wait with you until Izzy comes back?"

She shook her head. "I'd rather you try to find a lead on Fletch."

She wished she could see the part of his face hidden under the respirator and read his expression, but his eyes had narrowed. "When did you last talk to him?"

"It's been weeks since we talked, but he left me a voicemail three days ago." She dug out her phone and played the message. "You know how paranoid he is. He doesn't like leaving voicemails. Just the fact that he did should've clued me in to get here sooner, but I was out of town, testifying in court."

"Any idea who he's referring to in the message when he says you wouldn't believe what *they're* doing?"

She shook her head. "No idea at all."

"Was he working for our government?"

"I don't know that either. I mean, he usually does, but he also takes on work for private companies too. So could be either one, but I don't know what a private company would want with the toxin." She twisted her hands together. "I don't have clearance, so he doesn't always share his projects with me."

"I'm sure I'll figure it out." He stood and peered down at her, seeming extra-large in his suit. "Hang tight. I'm going to look through his office."

"Okay."

He strode across the room, his suit crackling with each step and his breathing apparatus sounding eerie, like an invader from outer space had landed and taken over her world. *Yeah, yeah.* That was exactly what this whole situation felt like. Invaders from another planet had taken over the island, and she had no control over what was happening. Maybe they'd beamed Fletch up into their spacecraft.

She shook her head. Her mind was betraying her. Could it be a sign of the toxin having gotten into her body after all? Or was she just so dang terrified she wanted to think of anything other than that the botulism toxin had become airborne and threatened them all?

3

Hunter stepped into the messy office, the sound of his SCBA —self-contained breathing apparatus—as he inhaled a comfort to him in the very quiet building. The first thing he'd thought of when he'd entered the front door was how eerily quiet the place was. Fletch was a wannabe rock band drummer and loved music—if you could call headbanger rock-and-roll music. Hunter didn't, but Fletch often played it.

Hunter had visited the lab with Maya twice in the year they'd been together, and both times the music had been piped all over the island from speakers Fletch had installed to discourage visitors. And, as he said, "So I can rock out on my nightly walks when I commune with nature. And by communing with nature, I mean carrying my favorite rifle and chasing anything on two or four legs off my island." He'd grinned and laughed and now... Now the quirky, nerdy guy who was all blustery about island visitors—but who would give anyone the shirt off his back—was missing. And Hunter was at this point charged with finding him and figuring out who'd killed his assistant. Not to mention discovering if a bio-terrorism threat existed.

Hunter tried to sit in the black desk chair, but his oxygen tank prohibited that. So he found a stool in the corner and drew it up to the desk to look at the piles of paper. He didn't know where to begin. Maybe whatever Fletch was working on was on the top of the piles.

Hunter grabbed the closest stack and started thumbing through it. The task was made awkward with the gloves, but it didn't matter. He couldn't understand the information anyway. It was page after page of formulas. Hunter had taken high school chemistry but majored in criminal justice, so he hadn't needed much science in college. The data on these pages was way over his head.

He moved on to the next pile. And the next. No way any of this was going to help him. He needed Izzy or Maya to read it.

Maya. His Maya. No. Not his anymore. Hadn't been his for so many years that he had to wonder if she even thought about him. He sure thought about her. More than he should.

He looked through the window at her, curled up in a ball, anguish in her eyes. His heart screamed to go to her. To hug her. To love her. After all, wasn't that really why she wanted him here?

She'd called him when she needed help. Him! He could hardly believe it. If she wasn't sitting there, he still might not believe it. She could've phoned so many people. Even called the county or CDC directly.

Dare he really hope that she felt like she needed him? Nah. Impossible. They'd parted so badly. His fault. Totally. She'd gotten a terrible cold that turned into pneumonia, and she was hospitalized. It was touch-and-go for a night, and he'd felt so incredibly helpless.

He'd nearly had a meltdown. Seriously, a crazy catatonic mental collapse. He'd had too many losses in his life to lose her too. So when she'd completely healed, he'd picked a fight over the differences in their work ethics and broke up with her. He knew she didn't understand. That she was bitter, that she'd wanted more from him. But he couldn't give it to her. Not without caving and getting back together.

She looked up, and he jerked his gaze to the papers. He couldn't let her catch him drooling over her. Couldn't let her know how much he still loved her. That would only add to her pain, the last thing he wanted to do now. The very last thing.

If she didn't have any symptoms, she'd go home soon, and until then, he had to keep his head down and work the investigation. Because this case was a big deal, but he couldn't have her at his side. She would be too distracting.

He forced his focus to the desk, and he spotted a smartphone hidden under some papers. He wanted to wake it up and confirm it was Fletch's phone, but he couldn't do so before tech's imaged the device. Just waking it up could change the information on the phone, and that could jeopardize any criminal case when they found the killer, and he stood trial.

But it if was Fletch's phone—and the case holding a DNA helix symbol made Hunter think it was—Fletch would never have left the island without it. At least not willingly.

A discovery that didn't bode well for Fletch's safety. Hunter looked at Maya again and prayed he wouldn't soon be dealing with a double murder investigation.

Maya worked hard to calm her panicky nerves. To erase the crazy thoughts of invaders from outer space. She didn't even believe in such things. Was she trying to avoid thinking about Fletch? Or, more likely, about Hunter? About how good it was to see him? Even better, to see him under such dire circumstances because he could help her. He would figure out what was going on—of that she was certain.

She loved his get-it-done attitude. Matched her philosophy. Why sit around when there was work to be finished? Get to it. Get it done. Then rest. Problem was that, in her life, there was never a *done* stage. There was always more work to do, and she never had downtime. That was where they differed. With the many losses Hunter had suffered, he believed in working at full capacity during an allotted time, and then, when it was up, relaxing. Not always. Especially not on top-priority investigations, but in as much as was possible with his job. Which is why she hadn't come out here last night. She had urgent work to catch up on at the center. If only she'd let it go and come out here instead.

She glanced at Carson's body and imagined his last moments. If he'd died from botulism poisoning, his muscles would have gradually stopped working until he could no longer breathe. It would have been a frightening death. All alone in the lab with rats his only company. Or maybe Fletch had been here too. Maybe he'd gone for help.

Please, Father. Please let Fletch be alive.

She wished she knew if the powder was, in fact, botulism. Waiting forty-eight hours seemed like an eternity. When she got back to her lab, she would research the test and look for any experimental tests that she might be able to run in her lab to get faster results.

The outside door opened and closed, and Maya prepared herself for another visitor. Footsteps whispered down the hallway, and Izzy came into the room. She knelt in front of Maya. "How's the patient doing?"

"I'm fine," Maya said, though she was a basket case. "No signs of muscle issues at all."

"Excellent." Izzy reached for the tote she'd left behind.

"The decontamination area is set up. Let me draw your blood, and then you can get cleaned up."

"And then what?"

"Once we decontaminate you, you won't be contagious to anyone, but we'll want to monitor your health for a while. We've set up an isolation tent where the boat captain and his crew are being monitored. We'll want you to remain on the island too so we can monitor you as well."

Maya had hoped to help Hunter with the investigation, if indeed he was staying. "For how long exactly?"

"For the initial six hours. You can't infect anyone else, so after that you can go home and call me if any symptoms occur." She got out a syringe and tourniquet. She tightened the band around Maya's arm and inserted the needle, working deftly even with gloves. She extracted several vials of blood and then sat back. "Okay, ready to go?"

Maya had been waiting for this moment since she'd discovered Carson and quickly got to her feet. "Any sign of Fletch?"

Izzy packed up her kit and the vials. "Not yet." She stood. "Go ahead."

Maya took off and assumed that Izzy was watching her gait to see if she had any issues. Just knowing that made Maya trip over her own shoe. She looked back at Izzy. "Don't read anything into that. Just clumsy."

Izzy raised her eyebrows. "If you say so."

"Trust me," Maya said. "If I had even an inkling of a symptom, I would tell you to start the antitoxin."

"I'm sure you would." Her deep green eyes brightened. "Decontamination shower is just to your left."

Maya walked through a tunnel they'd erected and stepped into a dressing area. The air-filled vinyl structures, a loud generator keeping them inflated, reminded her of a bouncy house minus the bouncy fun.

27

"Discard your clothing here, bag, and seal it," Izzy said. "On the other side of the barrier, you'll find a shower. After you've scrubbed clean, you'll step through the other side and find hospital scrubs you can put on. Once dressed, wait there. I'll rinse my suit off in another area and then meet you. Any questions?"

"What about my phone?"

"Leave it on your bag of clothing, and my people with decontaminate it and get it back to you. Same goes with anything else you might have in your pockets."

"That's it. My other things are in my backpack in the lab."

"We'll take care of that too, but it'll have to wait until we complete gathering our samples."

"No worries. My phone is all I need right now." Maya stepped through the zippered barrier, then closed it behind her. She felt odd undressing out here, but she followed procedure and soon had her clothing bagged. In the shower, she made sure to scrub carefully so she didn't scratch her skin and give the botulism a place to penetrate.

In the next tent area, she put on the blue scrubs and vinyl scuffs. She sat on a plastic bench to wait for Izzy to escort her to her final destination and tried to keep her mind on anything but Hunter. But of course, that was where her mind wanted to go. Or more accurately, her heart.

"Ready, Maya?" Izzy shouted, but her words were still barely audible over the generator.

Maya pulled down the long zipper and stepped outside. She gulped in the air tinged with a decaying fish odor, thankful that she no longer had the possibility of botulism on her skin or clothing. That she'd likely escaped a terrible death. That she had a new lease on life. Even if she was infected, an antidote existed to take care of it.

Thank you, God. Thank you!

Izzy stepped out of another tent, still wearing her biohazard suit. She curled a gloved finger. "Follow me."

She whisked across grass and weeds that had been trampled into a wide path leading to a large tent. This tent was a regular structure with strong metal poles holding it up. Izzy held the flap open, and Maya stepped in, noticing a faint musty odor. Six cots dotted the canvas floor, and emergency medical supplies filled carts.

The boat captain was reclining in scrubs on one of the cots. He looked up, and swung his feet to the floor, his gaze turning cold and dark. "You! You said it was safe. Now look. We're all stuck here. Maybe dying."

"You're not dying, sir," Izzy said, her tone calm. "We have no reason to believe you were exposed to anything, and this is just a precaution for your safety."

He crossed his arms. "Then why are you wearing that suit?"

"Because I'm going back into the building, and it's easier to keep the suit on than to take if off and put it back on. But rest assured, I've been decontaminated from head to toe. Now, try to relax, and you'll be discharged soon enough."

He scoffed, crossed his arms, and shot Maya a look. "She better not be bringing anything hazardous in here."

"Dr. Glass isn't infectious." Izzy looked at Maya. "Go ahead and choose a cot. I'm going to get an IV started just in case I need to administer fluids."

Maya didn't want an IV, but the men in the tent had endured the needle stick, and she would too just to be fair.

The captain flicked a hand at the far corner. "Take that cot. As far away from us as possible."

She sat on the cot in the corner. The medical carts were located in the aisle between her and the other cots, so it would give her privacy from the men's angry glares. She felt badly about what happened to them, but she was paying them to wait for her today and would honor that commitment. And then, if they had to miss more work, she would compensate them for that too. They were certainly not going to take her back to the mainland, so she would have to count on Hunter or Izzy for transportation.

Izzy pulled a privacy screen into place and joined Maya. "Ignore the captain's bark. He's been like that since we brought him in."

"I wish you didn't have to hold him here, but I understand your caution."

Izzy leaned close. "Tell me truthfully. Do you think Fletch could've been working on aerosolizing botulism?"

"You mean weaponizing it?" Maya shook her head. "Absolutely not. He has a strong moral compass that he never deviates from."

"Then what do you think he was working on?" Izzy got out a needle and alcohol wipe and gestured for Maya to lie down. "And how did it all go wrong?"

"He's for sure on the side of good, not evil, so maybe he was developing a better antitoxin. One without the side-effects you mentioned." Maya reclined and put the extra pillow under her arm in prep for the IV.

Izzy sat on a nearby stool and rolled close to the bed. "I suppose with Hunter searching the lab, we'll know soon enough."

Maya wished that was true. "You know Fletch, right?"

Izzy nodded and opened an antiseptic wipe, the strong smell of alcohol filling the air.

"Then you know he's more paranoid than the average person." Maya didn't want to come right out and say he was a conspiracy enthusiast, but he was, believing there were conspiracies behind even the most innocent of happenstances. "As a result, he's very careful with his paperwork. He wouldn't leave anything behind that someone might use against him. We might need to get into his safe to figure what he was involved in."

"You wouldn't have the combination, would you?" Hunter asked.

Maya startled at his voice. She hadn't noticed he'd arrived at the head of her bed. She'd been too focused on the upcoming needle prick to sense his presence or even hear him approach in the big biohazard suit. She looked at him. "I take it you didn't find any evidence in the building."

"Nada."

"Sorry. I don't know the combination for the safe, but we could try a few different things that he might use."

"Let me locate a notepad," Hunter said. "You can write them down for me."

Izzy looked up at him. "One of the workers at the intake table by the dock should be able to provide paper and a pen."

He nodded and started to leave.

"Any word on Fletch?" Maya asked before he could go.

He shook his head. "And the workers have completed the grid search. He's not on the island. I put out an alert for law enforcement. They'll circulate his photo, and hopefully someone will see him."

"His boat is missing from the boat house. Can you add that to the alert?"

"Yes, if I can find the registration information. Or do you know the details?"

"Sorry. All I know is it's blue and white and has a big motor and really comfy seats."

"A little poke," Izzy said.

Maya ignored the sharp pain of the needle going into her arm and kept her focus on Hunter. "But where would he go? He surely wouldn't abandon Carson if he was dying."

"Agreed," Hunter said. "Did he know you were coming today?"

"Maybe," she said, doing her best to ignore Izzy moving the needle around in her arm. "I tried returning his call but he didn't answer."

Hunter shifted, looking like he couldn't get comfortable. "About his phone. I found it on his desk."

"I can't believe he'd leave it behind." Maya thought of Fletch wandering somewhere. Sick. In need of help. No phone. But if he was sick, he would know to go for help. "Are you sure it's his?"

"I can't be positive without waking it up, and I didn't want to do that without having an image taken first. But the phone case has a DNA helix symbol on it, so I figured it's his."

Her stomach clenched. "That's his case, all right. If he's sick and doesn't have a phone, he would go to the hospital."

Hunter nodded and got out his phone from a bag he'd tucked into a belt on the suit. "Let me text Piper to start calling them."

She waited while he texted his fellow agent who Maya knew from an investigation they'd recently worked with her, and she was now engaged to Nick, the Veritas cyber expert.

Hunter stowed his phone, and Maya looked at him. "We need to get the phone to Nick to image so we can look at it pronto."

Izzy taped the needle on Maya's arm. "Nothing's leaving the island without being decontaminated. At least not until we can prove that the toxin hasn't been released here."

Hunter took a wide stance. He was digging in his heels. "The decontamination process could destroy evidence. I can't allow that."

Izzy squinted at him. "I'd like to help but—"

"No buts." Hunter crossed his arms. "I won't risk compromising the evidence for any reason."

"Okay, fine." Izzy held up a hand. "What about bringing this Nick fella here? He'll have to be informed of the risks and sign a waiver. And of course, wear a biohazard suit."

"He's a thrill seeker, so I'm sure he'll agree," Maya said. "And if he doesn't, I'll talk him into it."

"Just one thing you're forgetting." Hunter moved closer to her bed and locked gazes. "Our agency doesn't have an unlimited budget, and we sure can't afford the rates you all charge."

She wanted to look away. Not because of the price issue, but because she was unable to think when he focused those big eyes of his on her.

She swallowed away the feelings. For now. "We'll do this pro bono."

"I can't ask you to do that." *Translated, I want this investigation, but I don't want to work with you.*

At least that was her take on his response. She wanted to cross her arms like he'd done, but Izzy was putting a clear covering over the needle. So Maya settled for gritting her teeth. "Fletch is my friend, and I want to help. We can bring Sierra in to handle the forensics too."

Izzy sat back and looked between them. "I don't have a say in this, but it sounds like a good idea to me."

"No!" Hunter narrowed his eyes. "This is an FBI investigation, and we can handle it."

"But I—" Maya said.

"I said no."

Frustration, maybe anger, was building in Maya's gut. She wanted to fire off a quick response, but she wouldn't have this conversation in front of Izzy.

Maya looked at the doctor. "Would you excuse us for a minute?"

Izzy shot a look between them, lingering for an uncomfortable moment before she stood. "I'm not going to start any fluids just yet, but be cautious with that IV. And let me know what you decide so I can plan the safety of any additional personnel you bring on board."

"You'll be the first to know." Maya kept her focus on Hunter. When Izzy was out of earshot, Maya swung her legs to the floor. "If this is about our past..."

He didn't answer, and she didn't like having to crane her neck to look up at him. She got up. "From where I stand, turning down the services of a top-notch forensic lab isn't the wisest of moves. We can get results before you can even ship the evidence to Quantico. And our staff's skills are on par or better than Quantico's lab."

He stepped closer, fire in his eyes. "We can't work together."

"Why not?"

"You know why not." He sighed out a long breath into his respirator. "Our past."

If he thought she was going to back down, he had another think coming. "I can overlook anything to find Fletch and the person who killed Carson. Even the way you bailed on me. Certainly, as the offender in our breakup, you can overlook it too."

He cringed. "But I—"

"You what?" she snapped. "Don't want to be near me? Fine. I don't want to be around you either. But please. Don't think with your emotions. Think with your brain. You'll see I'm right."

He let out a long breath, his gaze racing around the tent. Maybe he was grasping for another argument. Or maybe he didn't want to look at her. Be that as it may, she wasn't going to cave.

She lifted her shoulders into a hard line. "Be the FBI

34

agent I know you are. Strong. Assured. Confident. One who can overcome anything to resolve an investigation. Even your dislike for me."

He flinched. "I don't dislike you, Maya. Far from it. And that's the problem."

"What?" She stared at him. "But you broke up with me."

He gave her a wide-eyed look. "I can't get into that discussion here."

"Then say yes," she said quickly before he could argue more. "Our team can provide the backup you need."

"Fine. You win. I'll call my supervisor and get his permission to use your lab. Assuming he lets me stay lead on this investigation."

"Why wouldn't he?"

"It's not a cyber matter."

"Oh, right. Your squad assignment." She tapped her chin and thought about how she could connect this to a cyber-crime to keep him on the investigation, but she couldn't come up with a thing. She might not want to work with him, but he was very good at what he did and would be a strong leader for this case. Just what she hoped for in locating Fletch.

"You're persuasive," she said. "I'm sure you can convince him. And if you need to, you can tell him we're offering our services at no charge but only if we work with you."

"That should help." He locked gazes with her. "But know this. We will keep things totally professional between us. Is that clear?"

"Crystal," she said and offered a prayer that she could follow through and contain her feelings for this man.

He infuriated her while at the same time drawing her to him and she had no idea which emotion was going to win out.

4

Maya was right. Hunter knew that. Having the Veritas team working this investigation meant he would have top-notch support, and he'd made the call to Adair to get authorization to bring them on board, and while he had his supervisor on the phone, Hunter had also updated him. He was going to give DHS a head's up, but until the toxin was confirmed, they wouldn't be brought in. And he also agreed to let Hunter remain lead on the investigation.

Sierra and Nick came down the lab hallway wearing the same suits and respirators. Hunter was thankful for their willingness to help. It was perfect for the investigation, but personally? Bringing in the Veritas team meant spending more time with Maya and would be hazardous to his emotions. And distracting. Shoot, even dressed in a biohazard suit and standing next to him, he could see the sparkle of her eyes and remember when she'd fixed them on him with love instead of irritation.

And now she desperately wanted to find her friend. Before Hunter had met Fletch, Hunter had wondered if she had romantic interests in Fletch, but Hunter soon learned they truly were just friends, and he had no reason to be jealous. And now he had no reason to even know about who she was dating, if anyone.

Argh. Forget about her.

He turned his attention to Sierra. The last time he'd met her, she was wearing makeup, but today her face was scrubbed clean. She was a striking woman with dark blond hair that hung straight to her shoulders.

"Thanks for coming, Sierra," he said.

"Of course." Her eyes crinkled from behind the clear face shield.

"You too, Nick. Thanks for dropping everything for this." Hunter looked at Nick, who was more interested in looking around than focusing on Hunter. "I know the situation is less than ideal."

"Are you kidding?" Nick's brown eyes were wide with excitement above his respirator. "Living on the edge is the best."

Sierra rolled her eyes. "Speak for yourself. I'm happy to help out, but it's not easy picking up tiny specs of evidence when dressed like this. Plus, the suits are hot and sweaty and just plain uncomfortable."

Maya stepped closer to Sierra. "Sorry about that, but thanks again for coming."

Sierra shifted the shoulders of her suit. "I know. I know. Quit whining and do the job. Just point me in the right direction, and I'll get to it."

"That's the Sierra I know and love." Maya chuckled.

"Glad to see you can be so cheerful after...well, you know." Sierra stared at Maya. "You sure you're okay?"

"Fine so far. We're five hours in and no symptoms at all."

Sierra squeezed Maya's arm. "We're all praying that you don't develop any and that Fletch is found safe and sound."

"Thanks."

Nick finally focused on Hunter. "I called Piper to tell her

I was coming here. She wanted me to tell you she's phoned the ERs. No sign of Fletch. She'll start on urgent care facilities next."

"Thanks," Hunter said, but Maya frowned. He had to assume it was because she'd hoped Fletch had been at the hospital.

"Where do you want me to start?" Sierra picked up her kit, a large plastic box with a handle.

Reminded Hunter of a very big tackle box. Man, he'd love to be out on the river fishing for salmon right now instead of in the hot suit spinning his wheels. "I have a safe to crack. Can you dust it for prints first?"

"Sure thing." She shifted her kit to her other hand. "Lead the way."

"I'll help." Maya didn't wait for agreement from Hunter but hurried down the hall toward the office.

She probably thought he would say no to her help, and she wanted to see what, if anything, he found. Being an agent, he couldn't divulge every lead in the investigation to her, but, if they signed an agency agreement, he might be able to work around that. *If* he wanted to. He just wasn't sure what he wanted right now. Other than for her not to have any symptoms of exposure to the toxin.

If he was truthful, he also wanted to be the man she needed, but that was impossible. She would want even more in the future than they'd once had. A commitment. Marriage. Children. Both things he wanted, but he didn't have the faith he needed anymore to believe he deserved a family. Deserved happiness. The kind of happiness that God removed from his life until there was nothing but the deep, heavy loss.

The pain knifed through him like it always did when he thought of the people he'd lost. He swallowed it away and trailed the others down the hallway, passing a few of Izzy's techs, who were swabbing walls for the toxins. They were taking samples in every area of the building. Izzy had said they'd be done in an hour or so. Then there'd be a forty-eight hour wait to know if the samples were a harmless powder or a weaponized version of botulism.

At the office, Sierra blocked the doorway, her camera out, snapping photographs of the room. She'd once taken all of the crime scene photographs for Veritas Center, but they'd recently hired a photographer to help, a woman named Ainslie Duncan. Sierra hadn't wanted to expose Ainslie to the potential toxin, so Sierra had decided to take her own pictures today. She moved to each corner of the room and her camera shutter clicked repeatedly. Finally, she closed in on the safe and took several close-ups before putting the camera back in a bag.

"Okay, you can come in now." She grabbed the stool and rolled it to the safe. From her large field kit, she got out a swab. "I'll start with DNA samples then do the prints."

Hunter looked at Nick. "The phone's on the desk. Since the desk doesn't have the powder residue, it's looking like the door was closed when the toxin was released."

"At least not a heavy concentration," Maya said. "But it could still be there."

"No worries. Our space suits protect us." Nick chuckled. He moved to the far side of the desk and removed his equipment from a large tote bag he'd lugged into the room.

Maya looked up at Hunter. "We don't know how many digits are in the safe combination, so I can't be sure any of the ideas I gave you earlier will work."

"My safe at home is six digits." Sierra swiped a swab over the keypad.

Maya watched her partner work. "The one at our lab is only five. This one could be any number of digits."

Hunter had done some research since he first talked to

Maya about the safe and could put an end to their speculation. "I looked for the owner's manual online. This model comes with five digits preprogramed, and the owner can change it. I would expect a paranoid guy like Fletch to have customized his combination."

Maya nodded. "Absolutely."

Hunter looked at the paper where he'd written her suggestions. "All of your ideas are six digit dates, so you can rule them out."

Maya shifted her focus to Sierra. "If you fingerprint the keypad, maybe only five of the keys will have prints, giving us the digits we should be considering."

"You got it." Sierra grabbed a brush and a container of fingerprint powder. She dipped the brush into the jar and swirled it over all the keys. She placed a wide strip of tape over the entire keypad, lifted it carefully, and transferred the page to a card.

"We're in luck." She handed the card to Hunter. "Only five of the numbers have prints."

He showed it to Maya.

"Perfect." She looked up and smiled. "Now all we have to do is figure out what these numbers mean, and we'll have the combination to what will hopefully answer many of our questions."

"He was restrained at some point." Dr. Albertson spoke as if being tied up was an everyday event.

Maya was glad Dr. Albertson and her assistant had arrived to examine Carson, but Maya tried not to stare at the medical examiner after her shocking announcement. "You're sure?"

Dressed in biohazard gear like all the other workers in

the lab, Dr. Albertson nodded, her short bob of gray hair unmoving under her hood. She bent down and lifted Carson's hand then pointed at his wrist. "You can see the ligature marks on both wrists. He was definitely restrained."

Hunter looked at Maya. "Do you think he was used as a guinea pig to test the aerosolizing of the botulism?"

Maya hadn't considered that. "You mean like someone took over the lab, tied Carson up, released the toxin, and then observed him to see how well it worked?"

Hunter nodded, but he looked sickened at the thought.

Maya pondered his comment, but there were things that didn't make sense to her. "Where was Fletch in all of this, and if that's what was going on, why call me to come here? Why not call the police or 911?"

Hunter shrugged, the fabric of his suit crunching as he raised his shoulders. "He never was fond of authority, and he likely thought he could fix this on his own. Or with your help."

She could easily imagine what might have happened if she'd shown up the same day he'd left the message. She could be dead, too, or with Fletch, wherever he might be. "Since Fletch isn't at the hospital, do you think he went underground to get away from whoever released the toxin?"

"Maybe."

"Did you consider that maybe whoever did this took him so he could recreate the aerosolized version?" Dr. Albertson planted her hands on her slender hips. "It's very difficult to make, and they would need him if they wanted more of it."

"Because these people—whoever they are—are planning a terrorist attack?" Maya asked and worried her hands together at just the thought.

Maya had thought of terrorists possessing the toxin or having abducted Fletch. But there was no evidence pointing to terrorists or even abduction, and she didn't want rumors to spread.

She opened her mouth to say something, but Hunter said, "Let's not get ahead of ourselves here. We don't have any intel that says a terrorist organization might target Fletch's lab."

"You checked into it?" Maya asked.

He nodded. "I had Piper contact Homeland Security to see if they've heard any chatter at all about the lab or a toxin. Nothing."

"Lack of chatter doesn't mean it isn't happening." Dr. Albertson pulled her hand free inside her suit and ran a cloth over the fogged face shield. She must've skipped the anti-fog spray. "I know, I know. Keep my opinions to myself. I'm just a forensic pathologist."

"I appreciate your input," Maya said, but Hunter didn't speak.

"Josh and I'll just get the body ready for transport." The doctor slid her hand back into the sleeve and attached glove, then grabbed the special containment body bag used for transport of contaminated bodies. Heavy-duty, they were hermetically sealed, meeting the standards of Bio-Safety Level 4 laboratories.

Hunter stepped away from the pair and motioned for Maya to join him. "Now that we know Fletch didn't go to a hospital, we should talk about potential places he might have gone to ground. You know him the best of anyone. Do you have any ideas?"

"He doesn't go many places."

"He must do something other than work."

"Not much, but he does love escape rooms." Maya didn't explain to Hunter. She assumed he knew about escape rooms where a team of people gathered in a themed room and usually had an hour to escape the locked room. The people had to find hidden clues and solve challenging puzzles throughout the room, all related to the theme to unlock the door.

Hunter raised a hand to his head like he'd forgotten about the suit and was planning to shove his fingers into his hair, a gesture he often did when frustrated. He lowered his hand. "Sounds like Fletch."

"He also goes to Voodoo Doughnuts to get their bacon maple bars." She remembered their trip to one of the iconic Portland donut shops about a month ago. He'd devoured three of the doughnuts, his face beaming with bliss, but the vision was quickly replaced with him running scared and in danger.

"I can't imagine him hiding out at Voodoo, but we can look into escape rooms," Hunter said. "He might take sanctuary at one."

Another thought popped into her head. "I forgot. He's recently been going to Float Away. It's a shop that has float pods filled with salt water. People go there to float in the tank and relax."

His eyes narrowed. "You're serious? A business devoted just to people floating in a pod?"

"I thought the same thing when he'd first told me, but, yeah. He's really into that. I tried it once with him but didn't really see the benefit."

He met her gaze. "You probably laid there thinking about everything you could be doing instead of floating in water."

He knew her well. Something that at the moment didn't sit well with her. She was trying so hard to keep things professional.

"That and all the germs. They claimed they performed proper sanitation procedures, but still." She shrugged.

"With your scientific background, you doubted it."

43

"Yeah, and I don't get why the very skeptical Fletch didn't."

"Seems odd, all right. With his paranoia, he's not going to check into a hotel or motel using his own name and pay with a credit card. Which virtually makes it impossible to find him if he did. Still, I can ask Adair to assign agents to show his picture around at nearby motels and hotels."

Maya nodded. "He doesn't have any family, and I'm his only friend that I know of, so that's a dead end."

Hunter looked around the room, his gaze pausing on the body then coming back to her. "When we're finished with forensics here, I'll need to visit the locations you mentioned."

"I'm coming with you." Expecting an argument, she planted her hands on her hips.

He looked deep into her eyes and held her gaze. "You feel up to it?"

She glanced at the wall clock. "We passed the six hour mark and no symptoms, so yeah. I'm good to go."

He tilted his head. Emotions she couldn't name played across his face. "I don't know. Maybe it's not such a good idea for you to tag along. In addition to your health, this is an FBI investigation."

It was so unlike him to be uncertain about anything. But it worked in her favor. He didn't give an outright no, and that meant she could negotiate.

"No offense, Hunter, but you're kind of intimidating. You flash your badge in any of these off-the-wall businesses, and you're likely to get silence." She took a breath. "But I could approach the owners as a concerned friend, and I think we'll get more information that way."

"You could be right." His agreement came in a monotone voice that belied the words.

"I am, and I know you can see that."

44

"Okay, fine." He closed his eyes and took a long breath, then opened them. "We work together on these interviews."

"Perfect."

"But before we leave, I want to get that safe open. Which means we have to figure out the combination." They'd been interrupted when Dr. Albertson arrived and hadn't spent any time looking at the numbers Sierra had identified.

"Another thing I can help with," she said. "I know Fletch the best."

His fingers curled into fists. "Maybe with the potential toxin exposure you should rest."

He was concerned for her well-being and wanted her to take a break. Ironic, considering that was something that had been an area of disagreement with them. She tried to relax at times, but she'd grown up with taskmaster parents who didn't know the meaning of relax.

Her dad was a pharmacist, and they owned their own mom-and-pop drugstore. With that came the belief that the more they worked, the more the business would thrive. Which meant she spent a lot of time in the store when she was a kid. So much so that she'd actually learned how to walk leaning on a shopping cart. And family lunches and dinners frequently consisted of microwave meals in the break area.

Her first job had been to stock shelves and clean out coolers that had built up sour milk residue. Disgusting job, but she learned to work hard from her parents. And now? Now she practiced it every day, working sunup to sundown and beyond. In this case, maybe Carson would be alive if she hadn't felt the need to go back to the lab last night after days away.

"Maya?" he asked.

She looked at him. Assessed. Did he really want her to rest, or did he not want to work with her? Didn't matter which. If he balked at her help, she was going to dog him through the whole investigation. "You know I'm right again. Just admit it. I know Fletch, and I can help with the safe."

He let out a frustrated breath. "We should find a quiet place to discuss the digits Sierra found and come up with new codes to try."

Right. And that meant they would be alone together. But how bad could it be? They were covered from head to toe in the special fabric with loud oxygen tanks on their backs. And with the tension between them, it wasn't as if they were going to rekindle their lost romance.

"I think the techs are done in Fletch's apartment. We can go there." He held his hand out, motioning for her to precede him out of the room.

Maya took a few steps, still trying to get comfortable in this bulky suit. A short person dressed in the same garb marched into the lab.

When the woman stopped in front of Hunter, Maya could see she had gray hair and fire in her eyes. She fixed her focus on Hunter. "Are you Agent Lane?"

"I am," he said.

She stepped out of the doorway and gestured at it. "Please instruct your people to exit the building."

Hunter didn't move. "And you are?"

"Dr. Richards. CDC." Her tone held a good measure of haughtiness.

Hunter let out a breath. "Great. That means the anti-toxin has arrived."

Still watching Hunter, she narrowed her eyes. "We brought it, yes. But I'm still not going to risk civilian exposure, so remove your workers now."

The woman's request was ludicrous. Maya wanted to say something, but she had no standing here. It was up to Hunter to fight this battle.

"I can't do that," he said, his tone holding an undercurrent of iron.

Richards placed her hands on her hips. "Can't or won't?"

"Same thing," Hunter said. "I'm in charge of the criminal investigation, and we need to recover evidence before it's destroyed."

Richards moved closer to him and raised her shoulders. "Your evidence could be contaminated with the toxin, and I can't risk it being spread outside these walls."

This Maya should handle. She stepped forward. "I'm Dr. Maya Glass, toxicology and controlled substance expert at the Veritas Center, where the evidence will be processed. Our lab has proper ventilation and Level 4 suits. We work with toxins all the time, so we know the proper procedures. This botulism will not be spread with our handling of the evidence."

"No." Richards planted her feet, looking like she was trying to make herself taller. "I can't allow it."

Hunter glared at her. "The real problem here isn't how the Veritas Center will handle the evidence. They're *fully* capable of doing so. The real issue is the missing scientist and whoever might have killed our victim. Is the killer in possession of the toxin, and, if so, what does he plan to do with it?" Hunter widened his stance. "Are you prepared to find this person? To find a killer?"

"Of course not."

"Then my team and I will continue working the investigation, and we'll cooperate with you to address any concerns you may have. But in the end, finding the killer and the missing lab owner is top priority in stopping the spread of this toxin. And taking the evidence with us could be the key to achieving our goal."

Dr. Richards sputtered behind her mask but didn't argue. Maya was so proud of Hunter's determination and fortitude, and she wanted to give him a high five. But now was the time to try to pacify her and make nice.

"Now." Hunter's tone had softened. "What other concerns do you have that I can address so I can get back to work?"

Richards flexed and released her fingers. "I'd like to talk to the woman exposed to the toxin."

"That would be me," Maya said, making sure her voice didn't carry any hint of frustration. "How can I help?"

Richards shifted to face Maya. "Dr. Eller tells me you haven't shown any symptoms. Is this correct?"

"Correct." Maya gave her a detailed explanation of how she came upon the toxin. "It's been about six hours since the first exposure."

"And Dr. Eller informed you of the symptoms to watch for?"

"Yes," Maya said.

Dr. Richards gave a firm nod inside her suit. "Before I clear you to leave the island, I'll give you my personal cell number to call should any symptoms appear."

"Thank you." Maya smiled at the woman and hoped she could see it in Maya's eyes because the respirator covered her mouth.

Richards firmed her stance, once again trying to make herself appear taller. Maya could well imagine that, as a woman, and a short one at that, she often had to work harder to be taken seriously.

"And it should go without saying that you shouldn't leave the area without first consulting with me," Richards said.

"I wouldn't think of it," Maya said, pretending she was in awe of the doctor.

Richards shifted her focus to Hunter. "I will review all evidence before it leaves the grounds."

"No problem," he said.

Richards straightened her shoulders. "And just to be clear, Dr. Eller is no longer in charge here. I am."

"As it should be," Hunter said, but Maya saw him curl his gloved fingers again. "Now if you'll excuse us, we have a pressing lead to attend to."

Maya stepped around the body and past Josh and Dr. Albertson.

"I'm Dr. Richards," Maya heard the doctor say to the ME as if she hadn't been standing there for the entire conversation.

In the hallway, Maya looked at Hunter. "I think we have a control freak on our hands."

He nodded. "Which is a good trait to have in her job, but not when it interferes in my investigation."

"I think we can work around her, don't you?"

"Yes." He gestured at the end of the hall.

She headed for the apartment that was indeed empty and sat on the sofa. She had to perch sideways to fit her tank behind her, but it felt good to sit.

Hunter laid the paper with her combination ideas on his knee and then wrote down the five keys—12478—that had fingerprints lifted from them. "Is it possible the combination is less than five digits, and he pressed one of these in error? Maybe numbers that are next to each other on the keypad."

He shook his head. "The user manual said it had to be five digits. It *is* possible that he made a mistake while tapping the keys and the combination has a duplicate number in it."

"Okay, let me think for a minute." Maya studied the numbers and tried to come up with a logical sequence. Something that made sense with what she knew about Fletch. Nothing came to mind. "We could write them down in several different orders. Maybe that will jog something in my mind."

"I'll do it." He started writing on the paper on his knee. He usually had very precise straight up and down penmanship, but the numbers were misshapen, likely due to the thickness of the gloves. He wrote, and she studied the sequences.

"It could be an address," she said. "Or maybe it's a zip code. What else?"

"A custom license plate, maybe?"

She tried to shake her head, but the effort was too much with the hood. "Fletch doesn't even own a car, so I can't see that."

"Could it be the beginning of his social security number? Lots of people do that."

"If it is, I don't know it."

"Beginning of a phone number. You know, area code and next three digits. Or maybe, when Nick finishes with the computer, we'll find a password app, and Fletch will have it listed."

"I can't see Fletch keeping passwords on an electronic device. He'd more likely write them down and put them in the safe. Well, except for the safe's password."

"Right." Hunter sounded frustrated. "I could try to get a locksmith to crack the lock, but I doubt anyone would agree to come out here."

"Grady might know how to do it. He's a master at a lot of things." She tapped her knee and thought. "Or Nick might even have a suggestion on how to crack it."

Hunter met her gaze. "Then let's ask them, because I think the safe's contents could be the key to locating Fletch."

5

"Nah," Nick said, and looked up from imaging Fletch's desktop computer. "I don't know how to crack a safe. Never had to. You might not need to either, if the guy has a password app on his phone or computer."

"Maya thinks that's unlikely due to Fletch's paranoia," Hunter said.

Nick cocked an eyebrow. "Guy was paranoid, huh?"

"He was into conspiracy theories." Maya's hands were sweaty, so she shifted her decontaminated phone encased in a protective plastic bag from one hand to the other. "Not like obsessed with them, but enough that he questioned everything and limited his exposure to the outside world."

"Then I would say we aren't going to find a lot on his electronic devices." Nick frowned. "Or find anything in social media or the internet."

"Fletch definitely didn't do social media," Maya said, "but I know he used the internet for research. I also know he used a VPN and private browser windows to hide his location."

As IT experts, Hunter and Nick knew that Virtual

Private Networks routed internet logins through other servers so a website couldn't track a person's physical location.

"He probably doesn't use the same password in more than one place," Nick said. "And to remember them all, he must have them written down."

Hunter nodded. "We figure his list is in the safe."

Nick tsked. "Real catch-22, huh?"

"Exactly." Maya gazed around the room, hoping to find a lead of some sort, but she didn't see anything helpful. Fletch's whiteboard was covered in messy formulas that she believed were for aerosolizing the botulism, but the information disappeared in barely legible letters at the end.

"You see anything to help on that board?" Hunter asked.

She shook her head. "It's strictly about the botulism."

Hunter propped his shoulder against the wall. "You think Fletch did it? That maybe he's in the wind with the weapon?"

"If you mean do I think he's out there planning to release it, no," she said firmly. "But if you're asking if he succeeded in weaponizing it, then yes. If anyone could do it, it would be Fletch."

"You make it sound like it's a difficult thing to do," Nick said.

"I know that the government gave up trying," she said. "I read about it a couple of years ago. A bio-agent is a complicated, multi-stage process, and the final stage is the issue. You have to bind the bacteria to ultra-finely powdered materials. Things like silica gel or bentonite. Binding it allows the material to remain suspended and allows for a stable aerosol vehicle to disseminate it. This stage is particularly difficult with botulism."

Hunter pushed off the wall. "So, if someone wanted to

release this toxin, they'd be keen to learn Fletch's methodology or even get him to make the weapon for him."

"Yes, but first they'd have to know he was working with it."

"You've said how paranoid he is, so I doubt he was spouting off on what he was working on," Nick said.

She nodded. "We really need to figure out who hired Fletch for his current research and who else knew about it."

The device Nick had connected to Fletch's phone dinged.

"Image done." Nick unplugged the phone. "Now I can look at it to see what we have."

He set to work, and Maya turned her focus to Hunter. "I'm going to look through Fletch's desk drawers to see if there's anything helpful."

"I already did that." Hunter crossed his arms. "But go ahead. Maybe you'll see something that didn't mean anything to me."

Despite his frustration, maybe defeat, she sat on the stool, set down her phone, and pulled out the center drawer above her legs. It held pencils, pens, a ruler, rubber bands, and enough sticky notes in various sizes and colors to cover most of the walls in this room.

She moved to the top drawer on the side. Paper, envelopes, and labels. The next drawer—a plastic divider with a graphing calculator and colored paperclips in various sizes. She lifted out the divider and found a pink sticky note on the face of the drawer. She peeled it off. Fletch had written NiıAg.

"Did you see this?" She held it out to Hunter.

"Yeah, but I didn't think it was important. Do you?"

She shrugged.

"Well, this is a bust," Nick said, sounding disappointed. "The phone had nothing on it. I mean nothing. No contacts.

Call history. Voicemails. It's either been wiped or he didn't use it."

"What's the phone number?" Maya asked.

Nick clicked through files on his laptop covered in a large plastic bag for protection and rattled off a local number.

She checked her phone, thankful that tapping the screen through the protective plastic bag worked so well. "That's the number he used to call me and leave the message."

"So he must have erased his call log. The paranoia again, I suppose." Nick looked at his computer. "If he didn't use data removal software, and if the files haven't been overwritten, I should be able to recover them."

"Odds are good he would use such a program, though, right?" Hunter asked.

"Yeah," Maya said. "I would imagine he would."

"Give me a minute, and I'll know the answer to that." Nick's fingers flew over his keyboard, the plastic crackling with each hit of a key.

Maya turned her attention back to the sticky note.

Hunter looked over her shoulder. "Does that mean anything to you?"

"Seems like elements from the periodic table at the beginning and end. *Ni* is nickel and *Ag* is silver, but let me confirm." She still had her phone in her hand, so she surfed to the internet and located the periodic table. "I'm right, but what does the combination of the symbols mean?"

She stared at the table of colorful blocks with element abbreviations, looking for a clue. Didn't see anything,

Was she missing something?

Her gaze bounced between Ni and Ag on the large chart. "That's it! I should have thought of it right away. Each element has an atomic number. Ni is 28 and Ag is 47. Put them together with a 1 in the middle and you get 47128. Our numbers. Try it."

Hunter moved to the safe and squatted to tap in the numbers. The small light on the lock lit up, and she waited to hear a click, but the big suit covering her head blocked the sound.

He grabbed the handle. Pulled down. "Yes! We're in."

She moved closer, her breath held in anticipation.

He opened the door partway, a light going on in the safe's interior.

"Bingo!" He looked over his shoulder at her. "We've hit the motherlode."

Excitement burned through Hunter. He wanted to grab the items and get started reviewing them. He couldn't, though. Not without potentially contaminating things or obscuring DNA and fingerprints. He closed the door and stood.

"Wait?" Maya moved closer, her eyes narrowed behind the face shield. "Why aren't you taking the items out?"

"The toxin didn't get into the safe, and I don't want to contaminate them and then have to wait to have them cleaned."

"So what's the plan?"

"We'll have Sierra fingerprint everything and collect DNA samples. Then we wash our hands and have someone clean bring in evidence bags. Together we carefully load the items into clean evidence bags to prevent contamination. Worst case, we have to wash off the outside of the bags after we leave the building."

"But what's in there?" Maya asked.

"Several external hard drives, some paperwork, and a stack of cash."

"Drives? How many?" Nick asked, when if Hunter were in Nick's shoes, he would've asked about the cash.

"Ten."

Nick shook his head. "We'll need to image all of those drives."

"That can be done at your lab, right?" Hunter asked.

Nick nodded and glanced at his computer. "I'm not ready to leave. This computer image should finish in a few minutes, but then I need to look for other devices in the building." He frowned. "By the way, Fletch's phone data has been erased and overwritten. He didn't want anyone to see what he used it for, and that includes us."

Maya muttered something under her breath. "You know it's hard enough to work an investigation, but working one with a guy who's paranoid? I've never faced that before."

"Me neither." Nick's eyes lit with excitement. "But I love the challenge."

"You would." Maya shook her head. "I just want to find Fletch and whoever killed Carson and do it quickly."

"Then I suggest we head back to the lab with Nick when he's ready to go," Hunter said. "That is, if Dr. Richards will let you go."

"I'll convince her," Maya said. She was a real go-getter with powerful skills of persuasion. Hunter knew she would succeed even with the very tough Dr. Richards.

"We can review these drives," he said, thinking aloud, "and if we don't find anything actionable—or I guess even if we do—we'll get your partners together and come up with a game plan."

"You want us to work with you? Not just provide support?" She watched him closely, her expression hard to read.

He really wanted to know what she was thinking, but he suspected it was personal, and he didn't want to go there with Nick in the room. Shoot, he wouldn't want to go there even if he and Maya were alone.

"I want what's best for this investigation," he explained. "And that's having some of the top forensic minds in the country on my team. I'll call Piper and have her meet us there too."

"You know I'm all for that." A wide smile crossed Nick's face at the mention of his fiancée, who was also on Hunter's cyber squad.

"Then let's do it." Hunter tapped Izzy's number on his phone and lifted it to his ear, feeling odd about having a bag over the device.

When Izzy answered, he explained their discovery in the safe. "Can you send someone in with large evidence bags from my kit? It'd be great if you had a cart we could set them on to keep them clean."

"How can you be sure the evidence is clean?" Izzy asked.

"The safe was sealed."

"But that doesn't mean the stuff inside hadn't been cont-aminated before it went in there. We'll still need to process it."

"I didn't think of that." Hunter didn't want to waste the time, but he also didn't want to harm anyone who came in contact with the evidence. "I'm getting Sierra in here to dust for prints and lift any DNA first, but go ahead and send in the cart for transporting them to your people to process."

"That I can do."

He ended the call and explained Izzy's concerns.

"She's right to be cautious." Maya might agree with Izzy, but she sounded disappointed about the extra step. "I'll go find Sierra."

She lumbered out of the room in her big suit, and Hunter followed her with his gaze. On the one hand, he was thankful for the biohazard gear. It made things more impersonal between them. On the other hand, he wished they could shed the suits so he could give Maya a hug. Not that she'd want one from him. Of course she wouldn't, but it would make him feel better.

"You're worried about her," Nick said.

Hunter switched his focus and found the guy's gaze pinned to him. "She could start showing symptoms anytime."

"Which is really why you want to work with our team—you want to keep an eye on her. Am I right?"

He averted his gaze. "You guys are the best. I could use the help."

Nick wasn't buying it. He stood silently for a long moment. "What's the deal with you two? You date at some point?"

Hunter started to nod but stopped when he realized he had no idea what Maya would want him to say. "That's her story to tell you if she wants to."

"Yeah, you're right. If she wanted us to know, she would've said something that day you came to the lab. It's obvious you two have a thing for each other."

"*Had* a thing," Hunter corrected.

"Nah. It's obvious you're both still into each other."

Hunter didn't know how to respond to that, so he said nothing, and Nick went back to his work. Hunter laid his phone on the desk and headed into the lab to wash any contaminants from his gloves, his thoughts going back to Maya while the water ran. When they first met, he hadn't planned to get involved with her. With anyone. But she'd worked at the FBI Quantico lab back then and was dispatched to consult on a drug investigation he was working. He had to be hospitable to a woman in town on her own, right? Sure, she'd grown up in Portland. Had friends and family here, and it had just been an excuse. Even back then, simply looking at her set his heart on fire. Still did.

Her striking deep blue eyes and blond hair and that expression only she could muster up that showed such supreme confidence yet a soft vulnerability at the same time was totally captivating. But now, she was distressed. Hurt and hurting. And he was the last person who could offer comfort. She would reach out to her partners at Veritas Center for that. When he'd helped Piper on an investigation that involved the Veritas team, he'd witnessed firsthand how connected she was to them. Deeply connected.

His connection with Piper was similar to her relationship with her partners, but he never let it develop into something as intense, and he missed that kind of connection. But it wasn't his to have, and if what Nick said was true, Hunter needed to do a better job of hiding his feelings. Especially if his supervisor happened to see them together. Adair wouldn't be diplomatic. Far from it. He would question Hunter and pull him from the investigation. No way Hunter would let that happen. He needed to be near Maya to be sure she was okay.

She returned with Sierra, and Hunter shook the water from his gloves and held them out to air-dry. Maya joined him at the sink, tucked her phone under her arm, and turned on the water.

He looked her in the face to see if she was showing any signs of the toxin, like droopy eyelids, but her eyes were normal. The deepest of blue and beautiful. Striking even.

"What?" she asked, sounding irritated.

"How are you feeling?" he asked. "Any symptoms?"

"None." She angled her head to meet his gaze. "I promise to tell you if I notice even an inkling of a symptom, so you can stop asking."

He wished she would be okay with him caring for her,

but he could see why she wasn't. "I just want to remind you to think about it instead of getting wrapped up in the investigation like you're known to do."

She stopped washing her hands for a moment and held them under the running water. "You might have a point. I can't believe I could possibly forget about being exposed, but once we leave here and leave these suits behind, I might miss subtle changes. So fine. Go ahead and ask me."

"I'm going to set an hourly alarm on my phone to check in." He made a mental note to do it just as soon as he finished moving the items from the safe.

"I could do that on my phone too." She shook the water from her gloves.

"Maybe we both should set alarms."

She turned off the water and looked up at him. "It's not like we're going to be together twenty-four seven."

"I know, but I'd like to be with you as many of those hours that you're awake."

Her eyes narrowed. "Why?"

"To be sure you're okay."

She tilted her head and eyed him. "You know, this concern coming from a man who dumped me with a very lame explanation doesn't ring true."

"The lame explanation was just an excuse to leave." It felt good to finally admit that he had an ulterior motive for ending their relationship. Well, maybe not good, but honest anyway.

"No kidding," she said matter-of-factly, as if she'd figured this out years ago. "Things were really good between us. I just wish I understood why you wanted to end it."

"I—" He started to explain, but a tech entered the room pushing a two-tiered rolling cart.

"Where do you want this?" he asked.

Hunter waved a hand at the doorway. "Leave it there."

"You got it." He looked at the two of them as if he sensed the tension in the room, then turned and marched out.

"We should get the safe emptied." Maya wheeled the cart into the office.

Hunter hung back, his mind still on their breakup. She obviously knew he hadn't really been mad at her. What if he explained? Would she understand? Would she run the other way because he couldn't commit to her even after so many years apart? Shoot, what was he thinking? Would she even want him to commit? She'd likely moved on. But if what Nick said was true, she was showing her interest in Hunter.

So what? Interest and attraction didn't translate to wanting a lifetime commitment. He got that. Far too well.

No point in thinking about any of that until she was in the clear. Her health was the only thing that mattered right now.

He pushed off the counter and went to the office. Sierra had processed all ten of the drives and had started on the pile of papers. Maya was stacking the drives on the cart. "The only labels Fletch used on these drives were numbers."

Hunter frowned. "Probably made sense to him but means nothing to us."

Sierra looked up, her gloved hand resting on paperwork in the safe. "It'll take days for me to fingerprint each page here. How do you want me to handle that?"

Maya moved closer to Sierra and bent down. "Most of them are stapled in packets. So what if we only do the top and bottom page where someone would hold them in their hands?"

"That's a solid plan," Hunter said. "If we get to the point that we don't have any strong leads, you can do the rest."

Sierra nodded. "But it's still going to take some time. And you should know, so far I've only lifted one set of prints from inside the safe. It matches the majority of prints I lifted in the apartment. They likely belong to Fletch."

"It's still important to do," Hunter said.

"Then I will proceed." Sierra went back to work.

Maya moved away.

Hunter looked at her. "You never finished going through his desk. Or looked at the things on it."

"Right." She perched on the stool and opened another drawer.

"The desktop drive is finished." Nick stretched his back. "I'm going to go check for additional devices in the lab."

"There's a desktop in there," Hunter said.

Nick closed his laptop through the plastic bag and started gathering up his cords.

Hunter felt like everything was moving in slow motion when he was used to progressing quickly. The need to protect themselves and their equipment from contamination added to the delays, but there was nothing to be done about that.

"Hunter." Sierra looked up at him, a stack of papers in her hands. "You'll want to see this. I think it's the contract for Fletch's current botulism project."

Hunter stepped closer and looked at the top page. It was an official looking document from the U.S. government—specifically the Department of Homeland Security—notifying Fletch that he'd been registered as a select agent for researching this toxin.

"So he *was* working for the government," Hunter told the others. "Homeland Security, to be exact."

Nick looked up. "So how does a government program—one you have to assume is shrouded in secrecy—with a research scientist who's too paranoid to let anyone know what he's doing, wind up in the hands of someone who released the toxin and killed one of the workers?"

Hunter had no answer to that question, and when he did have one—because he would figure this out—he would be hunting down the person who put Maya's life on the line, murdered Carson, and could be in possession of enough toxin to kill millions of people.

6

Nearing seven o'clock, Maya stretched her arms overhead in her condo's bathroom and inhaled the fresh coconut scent of her shampoo and conditioner. It felt so good to have taken a shower—and not a decontamination shower—and to be out of the scrubs and biohazard suit. Free. And at ease to move around. Not to mention not overheated and sweating or carrying that heavy oxygen tank on her back.

She swiped her hand over the foggy mirror, also glad to be able to touch things around her. She never knew how much she'd taken that freedom for granted. Sure, she had to take precautions in her lab, and there were hot zones where she had to be cautious due to dangerous evidence, but only zones. Not her entire lab.

She didn't want to waste any time in getting down to Nick's lab, so she finger-combed her wet hair and decided to forgo drying. Already dressed, she stepped into the family room where Hunter waited.

He jumped to his feet, and the security card, their night-time guard, Pete Vincent, had issued to him swung around his neck on a blue lanyard. He ran his gaze over her from head to toe. She'd purposefully put on one of her boring work outfits of black slacks and royal blue button-up shirt. No reason to dress to impress him.

"Did you get ahold of your supervisor?" she asked, putting them on the work track and not the personal front.

He nodded. "He's looping DHS in on the situation, but holding off bringing them in until we confirm the toxin."

"I was thinking. New testing protocols are developed all the time and maybe there's a faster test out there. I'm going to look for one that I can run in the lab."

"That would be amazing. We really need to know if we're dealing with the toxin so we can proceed appropriately, and it would be great to confirm if you were exposed." He held out his phone. "My alarm went off. Any symptoms?"

"I'm fine," she was happy to report. "No symptoms, and we're twelve hours out now."

He shoved his phone into his pocket and watched her. She didn't like being the subject of his study, but she did like being able to see his entire face. The strong chin. Full lips. Reddish five o'clock shadow. She'd often thought she'd exaggerated his good looks in her memory, but he was truly a fine-looking man. She let her gaze run down his body, taking in the black knit shirt that displayed his sculpted chest and black dress pants that highlighted his long legs.

He cleared his throat. She snapped her gaze back to his face.

He was giving her an interesting yet pain-filled look. "Are you terrified about having been exposed?"

Interesting that he'd admitted such a thing when he was usually very closed down about his emotions. She didn't want to talk about this, but since he'd shared, responding in kind was the decent thing to do. "I was freaked out at first. You could probably tell that by my phone call."

He quirked a cute smile. "You were a bit nervous."

"A bit? Hah! I was totally freaking out." She met his gaze. "When did you get so diplomatic?"

He shrugged. "But how do you feel now?"

"Now I know that Dr. Richards is just a phone call away with the antitoxin, so I'm less concerned."

He frowned and clamped his lips closed. He was holding back now.

"What is it?"

"I hate to bring this up." He paused to draw in a long breath, raising her apprehension. "But Izzy said they didn't have any data to prove it works with aerosolized toxin."

And there it was in a nutshell. His very reason for breaking up with her years ago. His fear of losing her.

"That's the difference between us, isn't it?" She eyed him. "You're a glass-half-empty kind of person, and I'm a glass-half-full. I prefer to believe what she said about it having no data showing it doesn't work, either. So it could."

He shoved his hands into his pants' pockets. "I wish I could embrace the positive like you do. I really do. But when it comes to life and death matters? Let's just say I've had more than my share of the death part. You haven't."

She stepped closer to him and rested a hand on his arm, catching a faint hint of the musky deodorant that he'd always used. "I wish that you hadn't had to suffer so much. That you could trust God to protect those you love."

"Me, too, but I just can't." He shook his head. "History tells me to be cautious, and to me, that means I don't put myself out there to get hurt again."

She removed her hand. "But by bailing on me, you got hurt too. That is if you truly loved me like you said. If you did, it had to be hard to walk away."

"It was, but not as hard as staying together and seeing something terrible happen to you, which I was certain was going to happen." He jerked his hands out of his pockets and shoved one into his hair. "And that's why I need to keep these alarms going and stick by your side. I need to know you're okay. If you'll let me."

She took a moment to calm her warring emotions. It would do her no good to get upset. "Only because I know how you've suffered. Not because I've let go of how you hurt me."

A pained expression crossed his face. "I hope someday you can forgive me."

"Oh, I've already forgiven you. But the pain is still there." She pressed a hand against her chest, and she could literally feel the lingering emotions from the day he'd said goodbye. "The pain is still living right here in my heart."

He opened his mouth to speak but closed it again. Fine with her. There was nothing he could say to make things better.

"We should get down to Nick's lab. He might have found something." She rushed to the door and into the hallway, where she took long breaths until he caught up. When he did, she started toward the skybridge that connected the condo tower to the tower holding Veritas Center's labs.

She wished they were headed out to visit the places that Fletch liked to go in his free time instead of being cooped up together in a small room, but it was too late in the day. And besides, they hoped the hard drives might produce better leads.

Please, Father. Lead us to Fletch and watch over him until we can find him.

She reached the skybridge with its amazing view of downtown Portland and heard Hunter's footsteps behind her. What was he thinking about their lab, if indeed he was even thinking about it? Was he surprised by what she'd accomplished in the years they'd been apart? Sure, she'd had help, but the center was her baby. Her vision.

She'd inherited the six-story building from her grandfather, and that's when the idea for the lab came. He'd developed the two tower buildings with one holding condos and the other for retail shops. She'd converted the retail space into labs and recruited partners who believed in her vision, and they all moved into the condos. The skybridge connected the buildings at the top, and a lobby linked the ground floor.

"You really do have the best view from here," Hunter said as they crossed the bridge. "I'm impressed with what you've accomplished since we broke up."

She looked over the sparkling city lights in the distance and smiled. "I guess I should thank you for that. Our breakup motivated me to open the lab and work all hours of the day to make it successful."

He cringed. "I'm sorry about the motivation, but God really does work things for our good."

She almost turned to stare at him. His statement was at odds with his earlier comment. Seemed like he was selectively applying this belief to his life. She opened her mouth to ask how bailing on her worked for anyone's good, but she didn't want to take them back to the personal realm, so she snapped it closed. She continued on to the other tower and pressed her fingers on the reader to summon the elevator.

"I'm also impressed with your state-of-the-art security," he said.

That was something she would willingly discuss. "We need it if we want to be taken seriously by law enforcement. Wouldn't do to lose evidence due to lax security. Which is why we had to get you a pass when we first arrived."

The elevator doors whisked open, and she boarded to tap the number three.

"Does the lab take up all the floors?" He stepped to the back and rested on the railing.

She shook her head. "We continue to expand, but we still have some space on each of the lab floors and two empty floors in both towers."

The elevator dinged on three.

They stepped into the hallway, and she pointed at the doors to her right. "That area is for our investigator, Blake Jenkins."

She continued to the back of the building. "And this is Nick's kingdom. He had two labs. A large one for his growing team of techs and a small one he uses for top-secret investigations. That's where we'll find him tonight."

She continued down the hallway to the smaller lab, used her hand to gain access, and stepped back to let Hunter enter.

The small room was kept cold for the computers, and the chill set in immediately. The room had one wall filled with cabinets. Another had a long table holding three desktop computers. An empty pizza box sat on the counter, and the tangy smell of pepperoni filled the air.

Nick glanced up from behind the third computer, but turned his attention right back to his screen. "I've imaged half of the drives from the safe. He has years' worth of files here, and it's going to take weeks to get through it all."

"Only half?" Hunter asked.

"Passwords, dude," Nick said. "Took me some time to crack it. I got a clue from the safe and wrote an algorithm using the periodic table. Once I got it running, it worked like a charm on all of the drives so far."

"At least Fletch was predictable," Hunter said.

Maya shook her head. "He would hate to hear that."

"You can tell him that when we find him." Nick clicked on a file and opened it. "I've put a copy of the files on a secured area of the network, and we're the only ones with access. For network security purposes, I set up a login for each of you. I'll show you how to access the files and give you the passwords and logins."

"Go ahead and show both of us," she said. "I plan to review files, but first I'm going to start by researching tests that might be faster in confirming the toxin."

"Sounds like a plan." Nick grabbed two sticky notes and gave one to her and one to Hunter. "The passwords and logins. Don't share them. We don't want to compromise the security I work hard to maintain."

"That you do," Maya said. "And might I say you do it well."

"Aw, gee whiz. A compliment from the boss lady." He chuckled.

"I'm not the boss lady," she said, not sure why she felt a need to correct him in front of Hunter. If it had been another partner, she would've just laughed, but she didn't want Hunter to get the wrong impression. Each partner was on equal footing. Had the same voting rights. The same financial buy-in, minus the building, of course. The same legal responsibilities. She just managed their day-to-day operation. That was the only difference.

She stepped behind Nick and watched him run through the login steps. She made a mental note of how to do it so after she finished her research she could work on the files.

"Go ahead," he said. "You can use either of the computers. Just log into the network and start reviewing the files. We're doing this systematically by date. I created a log of the files and a place to check them off once you finish reviewing them. Find the log and start with the first file."

She sat at the computer next to Nick. "What did you name the drives you've imaged?"

"Wait for it." He grinned. "Drive1. Drive2. Drive3 and so on."

She rolled her eyes and swatted a hand at Nick then looked at Hunter. "Go ahead and start on the first file."

"Will do." He sat behind the computer on her other side.

She was acutely aware of him sitting so close in the small room. Not only that musky scent, but the heat emanating from his body and those strong arms reaching out to the keyboard. She managed to start her research and navigate down the list.

"From what I've seen, the drives hold daily backup files from his laptop and his notes for the botulism research," Nick said. "Based on the dates and times of the files, he must've kept the external drive connected to the computer and used it instead of the computer's hard drive."

"Then, at the end of the day, he unplugged it and locked it in the safe," she guessed.

"Looks like it," Nick replied. "I'll need to review the image from his laptop and the lab computer to confirm, but I wanted to get these drives imaged first so you could get started on them."

"Thanks for prioritizing them." She wanted him to know she appreciated him since she often had to rein him in for his outlandish stunts.

"Glad to." His phone dinged. "Piper's here. I'll run down and get her."

He bolted from his chair as if someone had set it on fire. Maya had to smile at his eagerness to see Piper.

"He's so infatuated." Hunter shook his head. "But then, so is Piper. She's changed a lot since meeting Nick."

Maya's thoughts went to Piper, who Hunter worked with on a daily basis. She was a super agent and very talented. Could be intimidating too. That's about all Maya knew about the woman. Other than the fact that she loved Nick and had been good for him.

"Why the frown?" Hunter asked.

"I didn't know I *was* frowning."

"You are. Big time."

She sat back and looked at him. "I was thinking about Piper. You and Nick both know her so well, but I don't. I try to be professional and I can work with almost anyone, but it might be awkward working together at first."

"Nah." Hunter waved a hand. "She's super relaxed and will make it comfortable for you."

"Relaxed?" She eyed him. "Are we talking about the same woman here?"

"Yeah, she can be aggressive, but she's still warm and friendly. You'll see." He turned back to his computer.

A bolt of jealousy struck Maya. Unreasonable considering Piper was head-over-heels for Nick, and she and Hunter had worked together for many years and never had a thing. They truly were just co-workers. Like Maya was with her team and Fletch. No reason to be jealous. Even more so because she had zero claim on Hunter. Like none. Nada.

She forced her attention to her computer and started searching for tests.

The door clicked open, and Maya shifted to watch Nick and Piper enter. She had black hair in a pixie cut and flawless creamy skin. She smelled fresh and looked fresh, too, like she hadn't worked all day when Maya knew the agent had. Maya would love to know how she achieved such perfection.

"Hey, Nash." Hunter smiled at her.

She fist bumped with him. "Some investigation you caught here."

He nodded, his expression sobering. "You ready to jump off the deep end with us?"

She grinned, and her chestnut eyes lit up. "You know it.

And on that front, no reports of anyone resembling Fletch at urgent care facilities either."

"I guess that's good news," Hunter said. "Means he's not likely sick."

"And if we are indeed looking at toxin, he probably wasn't exposed to it." Maya's phone chimed her alarm, and she reached out to silence it. Hunter gave her a questioning look.

"Still no symptoms."

Piper turned her attention to Maya. "I heard you might've been exposed to the toxin. That must be freaking you out."

"It helps not to dwell on it." Maya forced out a smile. "Thanks for dropping everything and coming to help."

"Glad to do it. You all did so much for me when Jinx tried to kill me, how could I not return the favor?" Not too long ago, Piper was trying to bring in a hacker named Jinx who turned her sights on killing Piper.

"Plus, she gets to hang with me." Nick grinned. "I mean, how could she say no to that?"

"Not even possible." She met his gaze, and a dreamy expression lit her face.

"So then," Hunter said, breaking the spell. "We're reviewing files Fletch stored on external hard drives. Fun times. You'll want to join in."

"Let me get a laptop and login set up for you." Nick rolled a chair from the corner next to his and held it while Piper sat. He looked like he wanted to do more than hold her chair, but he took a long breath and reached under the desk to pull out a computer case.

Maya didn't need to watch the lovebirds. All it did was make her wonder where she might be today if Hunter hadn't bailed. Would they be married? Have children? She wanted that. She just didn't have time for it. Not if she wanted to run one of the top forensic labs in the country while also heading up the toxicology and controlled substances unit. Vital work. Life altering work. Not her life, but it was to innocent people who found themselves on the wrong side of the law and guilty people who deserved to pay. She was on the frontline of those battles. How could she find time to seek a husband, much less ever raise children?

She snuck a quick glance at Hunter. Not even his children?

His sharp profile was chiseled and handsome. Not that he was perfect. His ears were a bit too big, his forehead high, and his nose a little broad. But still, it all fit together to make her heart beat faster. And a little boy with his features would be adorable.

He looked at her, his gaze confused. "You finding anything?"

You mean other than I'm totally still attracted to you. "Not yet. And you?"

"Fletch's introduction to his project. He says the Feds failed to successfully aerosolize this toxin, but terrorist chatter indicated that someone had succeeded. Homeland Security wanted to know if it was possible so they could be prepared for an attack. They'd found the most qualified scientist they knew—Fletch—and tasked him with the job." Hunter took a long breath.

"His contact at DHS is Dr. John Eberhardt, and he has a mile-long title." Hunter squinted at his screen. "Principal Deputy Assistant Secretary, Countering Weapons of Mass Destruction Office. It's part of Homeland Security in D.C."

"Man," Nick said. "That's got to be a mouthful when he introduces himself."

"We have to talk to him," Maya said. "But I'm not settling for a phone call. I want to see his expressions." She met

Hunter's gaze. "Means we'll either have to travel to D.C. or do a video interview."

"Travel would waste valuable time and money, but I agree we need a face-to-face interview," he said. "I'll call his office first thing in the morning and set up the video call. Hopefully he'll have some insight as to what went wrong at Fletch's lab."

7

Maya couldn't quit yawning, and the words swam on the screen in front of her. She needed to get some sleep soon, but she couldn't quit just yet. She'd hoped to find alternatives to the approved botulism mouse assay test, and she'd succeeded in finding a long list of quick tests for botulism. Tests that completed in far less time than the forty-eight hours of the mouse assay test.

She continued reading, carefully reviewing twenty different rapid detection tests that were in development. Four of them met the speed, sensitivity, and cost factors she wanted to see. They weren't yet approved by the FDA, but it would be wonderful if she could get the protocols needed to perform the tests, and then convince Dr. Albertson and Dr. Richards to allow her to run the quick test.

She blinked a few times to clear her dry eyes from staring at the computer so long and started to review the literature on each one. At the third test, her heart rate kicked up. She quickly read the text.

"Yes! Yes! This is it." She sent the information to the printer.

Hunter glanced at her. "What is it?"

She explained her findings. "I know one of the researchers. Kyle Larson. With instructions from him, I can perform this test right in my lab. I'll call him, and then we need to call Dr. Albertson and Dr. Richards to get samples so we can run the tests."

Hunter looked at his watch. "It's way too late to call anyone now. Tomorrow, I can talk to Dr. Albertson at the autopsy and call Dr. Richards."

Maya's heart sank. She didn't want to wait, but it couldn't be helped. "I'll come with you to the autopsy to answer any questions Dr. Albertson might have."

Hunter swiveled his chair to look at her. "She's not going to let you attend the autopsy."

"I can wait in the lobby."

"It'll be a long wait."

"No worries. I can review Fletch's files on my phone while I wait."

"That will work." He leaned back and stretched his arms overhead. "It's going on midnight. We should grab some sleep."

She didn't want to sleep, but he was right. She needed rest, though she would keep her alarms going to wake up every hour and check for symptoms.

He started to speak but hesitated and then took a breath. "If you don't mind, I'll bunk on your couch so I can check in with you on the symptoms."

What? On her couch? That was nuts. She didn't know how to answer him other than to put him off. "I can handle it myself, you know?"

He snapped his chair forward and curled his hands around the arms. "I know you can, but if I don't hear from you every hour, I'm not going to get any rest."

She met his gaze. Felt the warmth. Concern and caring. She had a sudden urge to say *Yes—I don't want to be alone.*

Please be there for me. And that was exactly why she couldn't agree. "I can text you."

"True, but what if you *do* have symptoms?" His intense gaze penetrated her brain. "I want to be nearby if that happens."

Really? He hadn't been there for her in years. He'd left her in a lurch. She wanted to tell him that, but if symptoms started in the wee hours of the morning, did she really want to be alone? She could call one of her partners but she didn't want to impose on them when they already had such taxing schedules. Besides, what harm would it do to let him sleep on her couch? It wasn't like she was agreeing to start a relationship with him again.

"Fine," she said. "You can have the couch but what about a change of clothes?"

"No problem." A glowing smile crossed his face, and he released the arms of the chair. "I never know what I might run into on the job, so I keep a bag in my car. I'll just grab that."

"You'll need an escort." She stood and fatigue threatened to pull her back down. She clasped the back of the chair.

"You okay?" He stood.

"Just tired." She shook it off and led him to his vehicle on the sixth floor of the parking garage. A tense silence settled over them, but she wasn't going to be the one to break it. The sharp westerly wind slapped her in the face and woke her up, helping her to realize she probably shouldn't be doing this. Too late now.

He lifted a large tote bag from his SUV and slung the strap over his shoulder. He'd barely slammed the hatch when she bolted for the building and hurried straight to her condo. She opened the door and stepped down a short hallway to the family room with the kitchen overlooking it. All of the team condos were set up in the same layout, but the colors and décor varied. She'd decorated in navy blue with bright yellow accents that cheered her up at the end of a long day.

"Set your bag down anywhere." She stepped into the kitchen to get a glass of water for her very dry throat.

He dropped it by the sectional sofa, and his stomach growled.

She looked at him. "You're hungry."

"No worries."

"Let me fix you something to eat." She didn't wait for him to respond but opened the refrigerator. She didn't keep it well stocked but did have eggs and bread. She could make scrambled eggs and toast. She took the items to the island and found him sitting on a stool there.

He looked up. "You don't have to cook for me."

"I don't mind." The truth. And more. Not only did she not mind, she liked having him sitting at her island while she cooked. Not something she was going to discuss or even think about.

She turned back to the cupboards before she said something she shouldn't and grabbed a bowl. She cracked eggs more forcefully than needed and ended up having to pick bits of shells out of the goopy mixture. So what? At least she'd kept her big mouth shut about her feelings.

"I like your place," he said.

She didn't look at him. "Thanks."

"Have you lived here since we split?"

"Yes," she replied and felt proud of herself for giving him one word answers in hopes that this wouldn't get too personal.

"I guess I deserve the almost silent treatment," he said. "But I was hoping we could talk and put our past behind us."

She eyed him over her shoulder, and at the pain in his

eyes, she could no longer put him off. "Easy for you to say."

He held up his hands. "I know. I know. I'm the one at fault. I don't deserve your kindness. I appreciate that you've forgiven me, but when you said earlier about how much I'd hurt you...well...I wish I could fix that."

She continued to look at him. "How?"

"I don't know. I was hoping you did."

"If I did, it wouldn't still hurt."

He winced. "Hurting you was the last thing I wanted."

"Was it? Because you had to know when we broke up that it would cause me pain." She shook her head. "We were almost engaged. Didn't it occur to you long before that day that you couldn't be in a relationship again?"

"Yes."

"So why not end it then? Before I was so deeply in love with you."

He took a long breath and eased it out. "I wanted to, but I just couldn't do it."

"But all of a sudden, you could?"

He rested his hands on the island. "Your pneumonia. It hit me hard. I could've lost you."

She'd never realized that her illness had spooked him. She'd been hospitalized, and it was tough, but she'd never been at death's door. He'd presented a strong front. In control and helpful. Still, she should've figured out that he was freaking out over it inside. "So that was it? What spooked you?"

He looked down at his hands. "That and I knew the next step was to ask you to marry me. I couldn't do that when I knew I would bail on you before the wedding. You would be humiliated. So that gave me the strength to walk away."

She tried to grab his attention but he wouldn't look up. "We could've talked about it instead of you picking a fight and running away."

"I know I handled it badly. But if I'd talked to you—explained—you would've convinced me not to go. In the long run, you would still have been hurt." He lifted his head. "Plus, the way I did it, I figured you'd be mad and that would help you get over me."

"You were wrong." She crossed her arms. "Nothing helped me get over you or what we had together. It was amazing. What I had always wanted in a relationship. Now, I keep too busy to date. No point in putting myself out there just to get hurt again."

He met her gaze, his eyes filled with contrition and sadness. "I'm sorry, Maya. So sorry. I didn't mean to hurt you so badly. Tell me how I can fix it."

"You can't." She turned back to the eggs and beat them hard, the whisk swirling in the bowl and frothing the eggs.

He came up behind her and rested his hand on hers, stilling it. "Don't."

She turned to look up at him and, despite her anger, being close enough to see the variations of blue and gray in his eyes, to feel the heat of his body, left her breathless. She could so easily reach up and draw his head down for a kiss. She would revel in it. In his touch. In the way only he could make her feel.

It had been so long since she felt any deep emotions resembling love for him. Oh, how she wanted that in her life again. But not with him. With anyone *but* him.

She slipped free and grabbed the bread to toss slices into the toaster. She glanced back, and he'd returned to his seat. Silently, she scrambled his eggs, plated the meal, and set it in front of him.

"I'll grab bedding for you." Despite the tantalizing smell of bread toasting that made her stomach rumble, she bailed from the room like he'd once bailed on her. Without a backward glance.

She opened the linen closet and pulled down bedding. The scent of her lavender and vanilla dryer sheets enveloped her. She was beginning to understand why he'd left the way he had. As he'd said, she would've done anything to keep him with her. Her reaction to him just now proved that. Because, even after he'd hurt her—hurt her deeply—it was clear she still loved him. She'd have to be on guard with her emotions every second she spent with him, or she'd get her hopes up for something that could never be.

~

At seven a.m., Hunter folded his bedding and went to the kitchen to make coffee. Maya made it through the night without any symptoms of the toxin invading her body. Not that she'd come out to tell him. She'd sent texts instead, proving how much she didn't want to see him.

Still, he wanted to celebrate her victory of remaining symptom-free. He should feel relieved. Revel in the joy of her health. But the tension of not knowing her long-term fate was bringing him down—that coupled with the way they'd ended things last night.

He deserved her response. Sure he did. No questions asked. Still, he'd hoped for something different. He wanted to be able to tell her he'd changed. That he was ready for a commitment and wanted to start their relationship again. That would be a lie, though. He wasn't ready. He didn't know if he ever would be, and he had to do his best not to lead her on.

Like last night. Taking her hand when she was attacking the eggs. What had he been thinking? She wanted to be beating him instead, and he couldn't stand by and watch. He'd needed to stop her. Maybe hold her until the feeling passed.

But she'd slipped away—running from him. He'd forced down the eggs and toast because she'd made them for him, but it all tasted like dirt. Dirt he deserved.

Father, please. Show me the way to help her forget about our past and move on so she can find the man she deserves in her life.

Even as he uttered the prayer, he didn't know if he really wanted God to provide his request. Sure, he wanted her to get over the pain. To be happy. But imagining her with another man? That had him seeing red.

Maybe You could help me work on my issues too, he added to his prayer.

He hadn't been successful so far, but things could change.

Right. And pigs could fly.

Shaking his head, he hunted for coffee supplies and found single cup pods to fit the maker on the counter. He located a mug and started a cup brewing, the nutty scent of coffee perking up his senses. He could make Maya breakfast, but somehow he didn't think she'd want a repeat of last night, so he held off and called Izzy.

Despite it being early, she answered on the first ring. "What's up, Hunter?"

"Maya discovered a rapid detection test for botulism that she can run in her lab. She's going to run her own sample, and we're going to ask Dr. Albertson for one from Carson. We were hoping you'd be agreeable to giving us a sample from the lab, too, just so we know if we're really looking at a release of the toxin in an aerosolized form."

"I have no objections to that."

The coffee finished, and he lifted the cup from the maker to set it on the counter, then discarded the pod. He inhaled the warm coffee aroma but left the cup until after his call. "Do you have a sample I can get from you, or do we need to go back to the lab for one?"

"I'll provide one. No sense in you having to take protective measures again to recover one."

"Carson's autopsy is at nine, and I'll be attending that. I can stop by afterward to pick it up." Hunter's gaze went to Maya as she entered the room.

She was dressed in her professional attire. Dressy black pants and a bright yellow blouse. She matched her condo. He wasn't big on wearing bright colors, but she was, and she knew how to wear them and decorate with them. She looked fresh and rested, but he suspected when he got up close that he'd see she'd applied extra makeup to cover up the lack of sleep.

"You still there, Hunter?" Izzy asked.

"Sorry. I was distracted."

"Text when you're nearby, and I'll meet you in the lobby with the sample."

"Perfect. Thanks." He ended the call and shoved his phone into the pocket of his cargo pants. "That was Izzy. She'll give us a sample from the lab for your rapid test."

"Excellent." She gave him a tight smile.

He tapped his cup. "I hope you don't mind but I made some coffee."

"Don't mind at all." She sounded as formal and professional as she looked. "Did you find something to eat, or can I make you something?"

"I'd rather not eat before the autopsy."

"Right." She retrieved a blue mug from the cupboard. "I've never been to an autopsy, but I can imagine it would be unsettling."

He didn't even want to think about it. "How are you feeling?"

"The same as an hour ago. Symptom-free." She sighed.

"I'm sorry to keep asking."

"No, it's not that." She set the mug on the coffee maker's

tray. "I keep thinking, as each hour passes, that I'll feel less stress over not knowing, but it's getting worse. I can't wait until I run the tests and get the results."

He picked up his cup and took a long sip of the dark roast. "Are you sure the guy who's pioneering this test will make time for you?"

"He owes me a favor. I'll give him a call while you're in the autopsy." She popped a coffee pod into the maker. It emitted fresh coffee, and she went to the refrigerator for milk.

He sipped from his cup and watched her fluid movements. She was a graceful woman and tall. Standing in the high heels she was wearing today, she topped six feet.

She poured in a generous helping of milk, and turned with her mug. She leaned on the counter and caught him watching her. She didn't seem bothered, but lifted the mug to her lips and took a cautious sip.

"Your shirt matches the condo," he said, at once feeling stupid for spouting off the first thing that came to mind.

She nodded and took another sip.

Okay, then. Try another tact. "With traffic, we'll need to leave in about thirty minutes."

She nodded. "I'd like to check in with Sierra on the way out if that's okay with you."

"Sure, fine."

She held up her cup. "I'll just pour this in my to-go mug. Would you like a cup for the road?"

He held up his mug. "I've got plenty here, and I can get the travel cups ready."

She held up a hand like a stop sign, her gaze telling him the kitchen was off limits now. Likely because she didn't want him nearby. Didn't bode well for being trapped together in a vehicle on their hour-long car ride. Didn't bode well at all.

8

At the morgue, Hunter shoved his phone into his pocket. He'd hoped that Dr. Eberhardt would have been available to schedule a video call, but he wasn't in and Hunter had to leave a message with Eberhardt's assistant. If he didn't hear back from the doctor by the end of the autopsy, he would call back and impress a sense of urgency on his assistant.

He stepped to the door and picked up the biohazard suit Dr. Albertson left for him in the hallway. He slipped a foot into the leg and swallowed hard. He'd witnessed his fair share of autopsies over the years, but they never got easier. Given a choice, he wouldn't be here, but it was procedure for the investigating officer in a murder investigation to attend the autopsy. A much faster way to get vital information.

He liked being with Maya. He really did. But he was glad she wasn't attending a procedure that stayed with you forever and made murder all the more horrific. And in this case, she knew the victim, and witnessing the cut would have been even worse. But she was waiting in the lobby to talk to Dr. Albertson about the botulism quick testing.

He closed the less restrictive suit than yesterday, put on a respirator and face shield, and stepped into the cold autopsy suite, his stomach unsettled. He'd hated wearing the respirator all day at Fletch's lab, but here, it kept out all the offending odors that came with the procedure.

He spotted Dr. Richards right off the bat, looming over the room like the control freak that she was. Today she was dressed in the same suit, as was Dr. Albertson and her assistant Josh who stood waiting for directions from the ME.

Dr. Albertson looked up. "External exam is done, and you're just in time for the Y-cut."

"Did you find anything on the exam?" Hunter made sure he spoke up so she could hear him over his respirator.

Her forehead knotted. "White powder in his nose."

"So not the clay-colored toxin. Could it be cocaine?"

"Likely. I used a field test that police often use, and it came back positive for cocaine, but I'll have to wait on blood tests to be sure."

Hunter was confused. "Isn't that proof, then?"

She shook her head. "The test has a ten percent risk of producing a false positive. Still, I think we're going to find out he snorted cocaine. I just can't go on record with that finding yet. Also, my examination of his nasal passages tell me he wasn't a regular user."

"Do you suspect an overdose?"

"Too soon to tell." She grabbed a scalpel from the tray and started her long cut at the neck.

Hunter's stomach churned. He looked at his feet. Counted to ten. Glanced up. She'd finished the cut and pulled back the skin. He swallowed hard but was able to keep his head up.

Dr. Richards moved closer to the table but Hunter remained at a distance.

"Let me know if I can help," Richards said.

"I'm fine." Dr. Albertson's tone contained a hint of irritation.

She reached into the upper abdominal cavity and removed Carson's lungs then handed them to Josh to weigh. Hunter sat back on a stool and waited for her to share her findings. She didn't say a word, but continued to remove organs.

She finally looked up at him. "No signs of a heart attack or stroke."

Hunter tensed. "Would you expect that in such a young man?"

"Cocaine users are at a higher risk for both," Dr. Richards said.

"So the cocaine didn't likely kill him," Hunter clarified.

"That's right." Dr. Albertson sliced open his lungs. "Significant lung tissue inflammation. Might be consistent with inhaled botulism. To be certain, I'll send off his blood and stool to be tested for the organisms of C. botulinum. And of course, I'll have that tox screen run for the cocaine."

Now would be a good time for Hunter to bring up Maya's request. "About the botulism test. Maya discovered a quick botulism test that she can perform right in her lab. It completes in a matter of hours, and she can determine if Carson breathed it in."

Dr. Albertson tipped her head at Richards. "I have to stick with protocols, and that means using the approved tests."

Dr. Richards met his gaze. "She's right about that."

Hunter was suddenly appreciating Izzy's easy agreement. "I understand that, but for our investigation, it would be great if we could get an earlier confirmation of the toxin in Carson's body." He held off mentioning if terrorists were involved, the sooner they could get DHS on investigating that aspect, the better.

Dr. Albertson narrowed her eyes. "I need to discuss this

test with Maya to determine what kind of sample she might need."

"She's waiting in the lobby to talk to you," Hunter said. "We can meet with her after you finish here if you have a few minutes."

She nodded.

Dr. Richards stared at Dr. Albertson. "Everything goes through me before releasing anything to this lab."

"You've made your position perfectly clear." Dr. Albertson kept her gaze pinned to the other doctor.

Hunter thought the women might come to blows, but when Dr. Albertson returned her focus to the body, he let out a breath. "So, are you offering an official cause of death at this point, or will you wait for the results?"

"The tissue changes aren't conclusive," Dr. Albertson said. "We'll wait for the results."

He nodded and sat back on his stool. No point in pressing her. Strong MEs never jumped to conclusions, and that was a good thing. They were dogged in finding the true cause of death.

"What about time of death?" Hunter asked.

"Forty-eight hours or so before we picked him up." Dr. Albertson put an organ that Hunter couldn't identify into a metal pan.

"So sometime on Monday, then," Hunter clarified.

She nodded and continued to work. She took slices of each organ and studied them but remained silent. He assumed that meant she didn't find anything to inform her decision on Carson's cause of death. She continued for hours, and Hunter's energy started to sag, as did his shoulders. After a very sleepless night, he feared that he might fall asleep. He took a few deep breaths and forced himself to sit up.

Dr. Albertson turned to Josh. "I'm finished here."

Josh nodded and started to return the organs to the body.

She faced Hunter. "Let's get cleaned up and go talk to Maya."

"Remember—" Richards started to say.

"Everything goes through you," Dr. Albertson said, a strong thread of sarcasm in her tone.

Hunter could only imagine what it was like to do your job with an exacting person like Dr. Richards looking over your shoulder the whole time.

Dr. Albertson marched across the room where they got cleaned up and went to the foyer.

Maya stood and pinned her focus on Dr. Albertson. "Cause of death?"

Dr. Albertson looked like she wanted to sigh. Hunter didn't know if it was because she was tired of them asking about the cause of death when she had no answer or if she was upset about not finding anything conclusive in the autopsy.

"Uncertain," she said. "His lungs could suggest the inhalation of botulism, but it's possible he also recently used cocaine."

"Cocaine." Maya's forehead furrowed. "I can't see Carson as a coke addict."

"I doubt he was an addict." Dr. Albertson frowned. "There weren't any signs of long-term use, but I found a white powder in his nose, and I did a preliminary test, which was positive for the cocaine. However, the test isn't infallible. I'll have to wait for the tox screen to come back."

"I can run it for you," Maya offered, her expression eager. "We can do the blood test or we can do a fingerprint test at our lab."

"Fingerprints for cocaine?" Dr. Albertson lowered her hand to her hip.

"I was about to ask the same thing." Hunter faced Maya. "I've never heard of such a thing."

Maya nodded vigorously. "It's a recent development, but commercial kits are already on the market. Not only can the test determine if the person has touched cocaine, but it can also tell if they have it in their system."

"Seriously?" Hunter asked.

"Sierra uses it all the time." Maya's enthusiasm rang through her words. "She could come over right away to recover the prints and run the tests. We'd know within hours if Carson used cocaine."

"Then let's go that route. I'm sure Dr. Richards will approve that process." Dr. Albertson shook her head. "I'm always amazed at the cutting-edge things your lab can do."

"I would still like to test the residue in his nose if you think I could get a sample of that," Maya said. "I might be able to trace the cocaine back to the source."

"I'll ask about that too," Dr. Albertson said.

Maya bit her lip in unusual uncertainty. "I did some research on botulism testing and discovered several rapid detection tests. With directions from one of the test pioneers, I can run one of them. I'm going to run my blood sample, but I'd also like to have a sample from Carson."

Dr. Albertson widened her stance. "It's highly irregular to do so."

"This is a highly irregular situation, right?" Maya argued.

"Yes." Dr. Albertson tapped a finger on her chin.

"Please," Hunter pleaded. "Time is of the essence here."

Dr. Albertson blew out a breath and gave a firm nod. "Josh is still suited up. I'll have him retrieve a sample for you, even if Dr. Richards doesn't agree."

Maya's face beamed with a bright smile. "Thank you."

"No thanks needed. I want the information as much as

you do." Dr. Albertson spun and marched down the hall like a woman on a mission.

Hunter looked at Maya. "I'm glad she was so amenable to the test."

"Me too." Her smile widened. "We can head right to my lab to get started."

"Any symptoms since I last asked?"

She shook her head. "Hopefully that will be the last time you need to ask me that, and soon we will know if my health is in danger and if botulism was indeed released in the lab."

Maya was glad to leave the morgue behind and step into the blinding sunshine. Sure, she didn't participate in the autopsy, but the place wasn't somewhere she wanted to spend a lot of time. On the way to the car, Hunter received a phone call. Listening in, Maya got the gist of the call that was referencing Dr. Eberhardt.

Hunter glanced at his watch. "An hour is fine. We'll make the call then."

He shoved his phone into his pocket and used his remote to click the locks open on his SUV. "That was Dr. Eberhardt's office. He can talk to us in an hour. I know you want to get started on the testing, but it's his only free time today. So I agreed to a video call in an hour."

He opened her door for her.

She slid inside. "You're right. I hate to wait, but interviewing him is top priority."

"If we're going to pick up the sample from Izzy and get to your office on time, I need to book it." He closed her door and ran around the front to slide behind the wheel.

She clicked her seatbelt into place, and she didn't want to distract him when he was getting the SUV going and maneuvering quickly through traffic, so she didn't speak. As a law enforcement officer, he'd taken defensive driving classes, but she still didn't like his dash over the heavily congested roads. She held onto her door handle until he reached the freeway with lighter traffic.

She relaxed then, and her mind went to the upcoming call. "Did Eberhardt give you any indication that he knew Fletch was missing?"

"No, and I didn't mention it," Hunter said, keeping his focus on the road. "I didn't want to tell him until I could see his reaction. Interviewing is as much about seeing what the interviewee isn't saying as it is listening to what they are saying."

"That makes me think of when you broke up with me," she said, trying to be matter-of-fact in her tone as she didn't mean anything negative by her comment. "You claimed one thing but it was another."

He flexed his fingers on the steering wheel. "Exactly, though I think I was pretty convincing."

"Honestly, I was too upset to look any deeper. I just took you at face value when you claimed we weren't as compatible as you needed in a long-term relationship. Sure, we didn't agree on everything, but we did on the big things in life. Faith. Family. Finances. Children."

"We *were* good together." He sounded pensive, maybe sad.

She hadn't thought about how he'd felt after the breakup. She'd honestly been too mad to care. He hadn't wanted to leave her, but his fears wouldn't allow him to stay. Still, he must have experienced similar anguish to what she'd faced.

She was about to say something to that effect when he tapped the button for his vehicle's speech to text program and sent Izzy a text saying he was a few minutes out. Izzy replied that she would meet him out front.

He navigated his SUV into downtown Portland and parked in front of the health department. "Be right back."

He took off running, and Izzy stepped out the door. Hunter snatched the sample from her hand and bolted back to the SUV to get them back on the road. Maya had always loved his sense of urgency—one of those many areas where they were compatible.

Once back at Veritas, she was the one who raced through the building to a small conference room on the same floor as her lab. He kept up with her, and they made it to the computer with only three minutes to spare.

"Let me log you in to our network and you can place the call," Maya said and dropped behind a computer at the end of the table.

Hunter made the call, and Dr. Eberhardt, who she put in his late sixties, came onto the screen. He had blond hair with a hint of gray above a wrinkled forehead, a long chin, and a bulbous nose.

Hunter introduced them.

"Nice to meet you both." Eberhardt had a broad yet cautious smile. "My assistant said this was about a botulism incident."

Hunter relayed the situation, concisely sharing all the details.

Eberhardt stared ahead for a moment as if digesting the information. "And you think this is a terrorist attack?"

"We're not sure," Hunter said.

Eberhardt leaned back. "I don't mean to be rude, but why are you contacting me instead of our investigative team?"

Maya was baffled by his reaction. "You're listed in documents as the project sponsor."

"I'm what?" His mouth fell open, and his eyes burrowed into her. "I have no knowledge of such a project."

"But you're on the paperwork," Hunter said. "And the email communications with project information came from your office."

He pressed his hands flat on the table and leaned forward. "Impossible. I haven't commissioned such a project."

Maya glanced at Hunter, who looked as confused as she felt.

Hunter turned back to the screen. "Give me a moment to find the emails."

He dug in his briefcase and pulled out a stack of papers. He flipped through them until he pulled out one of the emails Eberhardt had sent to Fletch. He held the page up to the camera. "This is your email address, right?"

Eberhardt squinted at the screen. "Yes, but I never emailed a Fletcher Gilliam. Of that, I'm certain."

Maya looked at the page then back up. "Then the emails had to be spoofed to look like they came from you."

Hunter shook his head. "Whoever set this up knew what they were doing. They told Dr. Gilliam that he'd be registered as a select agent and provided him with fake papers. Plus, they used a legitimate online service for everyone to electronically sign the fake agreement between you and Dr. Gilliam's lab."

Eberhardt frowned and crossed his arms. "We need to get to the bottom of this. Not only because of the toxin and murder, but because I can't have anyone impersonating me and getting away with it. Now that you advised me of the problem, I'll form a task force to look into it."

"I'm all for a task force as long as it doesn't interfere with my murder and missing person's investigation."

"I'll leave that to our investigative branch."

Hunter gave a sharp nod. "You should know. It's very likely that my killer is behind the spoofed emails, and I'll continue to investigate this matter."

Eberhardt eyed Hunter. "I'm still forming the task force. I can't trust an agent I've never heard of before to find the person responsible for sullying my name."

"Agent Lane is a top-notch agent, and very capable of finding this person," Maya said because she knew Hunter wouldn't brag about his skills and experience. "You couldn't have anyone more dedicated to his work. He has a stellar case close rate and has taken lead on many large and critical investigations."

Hunter gave her a quick smile. "I appreciate Dr. Glass's kind words, but what you really need to know is that I have the full support of my agency and the Veritas Center partners. They have experts in every area of the investigation. You'll find no one more skilled in cyber investigations than their cyber expert, and he'll figure out who spoofed those emails. You can count on that."

9

Unsettled by the call, Maya and Hunter entered her lab so she could get started on the tests. She looked at the space through Hunter's eyes. She kept the place spotless, but shelves lining the walls and filled with supplies looked chaotic. Not to mention the various equipment pieces spread around the area, taking up large portions of the room. The middle of the space looked neater with stainless steel tables where her lab assistants were hard at work.

They looked up as she approached them.

"This is FBI Agent Hunter Lane," she announced. "He'll be hanging out while I run a few tests."

He smiled, but it was forced. He was probably still thinking about the shocking development with Dr. Eberhardt. Maya could hardly believe anyone fooled Fletch, much less on such an important project. But then she and Hunter had been fooled by the documents too. They were perfectly executed. Now she wanted to know even more if they were dealing with botulism.

"You can take a seat at any empty table," she said to Hunter. He was going to review Fletch's files while she ran the tests.

She rolled a clean sheet of paper onto one of the free lab tables and placed Carson's, Fletcher's lab, and her own samples on top. She reached for a rack of test tubes. "I feel kind of selfish running my own test when the results won't help with the investigation."

"Will it take much added time to run yours?"

"No."

"Then don't even think about it." He stepped closer and lowered his voice. "Of course, I could be biased. I don't think I can separate my feelings for you from the investigation. I always thought of myself as being objective, but..." He paused and shook his head. "Your potential exposure has thrown me for a loop."

His distress seeped into her heart, and she felt sorry for him when she didn't want to feel anything but anger. "So I guess it will clear your head and let you function better if you know I'm okay."

"Yeah, that too."

"You don't sound convinced."

He took a long breath and let it out slowly. "Just seeing you again has distracted me beyond belief."

She should have realized he was fighting a similar battle to hers. They both seemed to be losing the fight. Big time.

Hunter sat at one of the long lab tables and watched Maya slide her arms into holes in a glass-fronted cabinet. Long, heavy gloves were attached to the holes inside the cabinet. She also wore a protective gown, face shield, and mask. She decided to test the powder in the lab first to confirm they were indeed dealing with aerosolized botulism, and if she or Carson had been infected.

If she confirmed the powder was botulism, Hunter

would need to call Adair so they could bring DHS into the investigation. The other agency might push to take over, but Adair would make sure the FBI kept control of the murder and missing person aspect of the investigation and let DHS work the terrorism angle.

For now, they just needed to keep moving forward.

He looked at Maya again. "There's a box like that in Fletch's lab."

She nodded. "It's a class 3 bio-safety containment cabinet. All the work with toxins must be done within the cabinet. We normally don't deal with class 4 toxins, but when we bought our cabinet, we decided to go to the extreme in case we needed it. Costs more, but you can't put a price on safety."

"I guess not." He wondered how much such a cabinet cost but thought it too unprofessional to ask.

She pulled her arms out and called her friend who pioneered the lab test she would run. She put him on speaker.

Hunter didn't understand what they were saying, so he tuned them out and signed into the network the way Nick had shown them. Hunter opened the log and noted that Nick and Piper had checked off quite a few of the files but there was a large number still to review. He started with the next file on the list, holding several emails, but kept an ear out while the guy walked her through each step of the testing procedure. Steps Hunter didn't understand at all, but she did.

Hours later, a timer dinged from across the room. Hoping that meant she had results, he looked up. She pulled her arms out of the cabinet and with her back to him, he couldn't see her expression. He waited for her to turn. To give him the results, but she went straight to the sink to wash up. Obviously protection against exposure was paramount, and he totally understood that.

She took off her face mask and goggles then removed her protective gown. She turned and started toward him. A wide grin crossed her face, and her eyes were gleaming.

His heart lifted. "You weren't exposed?" He held his breath for the answer.

"No."

His heart rate kicked up, and adrenaline flooded his body. He was in a professional lab with her subordinates sitting across the room, but he didn't care. He scooped her into his arms and swung her around. When she giggled like a little girl, he tightened his arms and held her close, inhaling her fresh scent and enjoying the feel of her in his arms again.

She squirmed to get free, and he set her down but didn't release her right away. "Sorry. I know this is your workspace, but..."

"I get it. I'm about to explode with joy. And thanksgiving. Thanks to God, I was spared."

Hunter couldn't get enough of holding her and locked eyes, imploring her to do...what? Forget how he'd hurt her? Let them have another chance? Why? So he could hurt her all over again?

He pushed back and shoved his hands into his pockets before his body betrayed his mind, and he kissed her. "What about Carson and the lab sample?"

"The lab and Carson's specimens were both positive. So the toxin was definitely spread throughout the room." Her expression sobered. "And it was bound to bentonite."

"Which means Fletch succeeded in aerosolizing the botulism."

"Yes." Her one word carried the heavy weight of her findings.

Hunter's mouth was suddenly dry, and he swallowed. "Makes finding Fletch and the killer even more pressing."

"Yes." Her one word again cut right through him.

"How, though?" he asked, his mind racing with the implications. "That's the question of the hour."

"I need to test the cocaine first, but then I can get the team together, and we'll help you come up with a plan." She grabbed her phone and tapped the screen.

He stood back and listened to her conference call where she stopped just short of demanding everyone meet her in the conference room in a few hours. When she ended the call, she looked at him. "We're a go on the meeting. Let me get the cocaine tested and we'll head down to the conference room."

He nodded. "I have to update Adair on the toxin. Is there somewhere I can call him in private?"

She pointed at the door in the corner. "You could use the storage room or I can take you to my office."

"Storage room is fine." He headed to the door and stepped into a room that smelled like the chemicals stored on the shelves.

He glanced back at Maya, who'd returned to her work then closed the door. He phoned Adair and didn't waste time on pleasantries. "We've confirmed the powder in the lab is botulism toxin."

Adair responded with a sharp intake of air. "I'll get on the horn to DHS and set up a meeting. I'll need you to be there."

"Of course," Hunter said, thankful that Adair didn't say he was pulling him from this investigation and handing it all off to their terrorism team.

"I'll text you with the time. I'll bring in our terrorism squad to work that aspect with DHS. We can get together an hour before the meeting so you can bring us up to speed on the details."

"Sounds good." Hunter took a breath. "How are we doing on the hotel search?"

"The team has visited all hotels and motels within a ten mile radius. No one has seen Fletch. But now that we've confirmed the seriousness of the investigation, I'll put more agents on the search and expand the radius."

"Perfect," Hunter said.

"I'll get back to you as soon as I hear from DHS." Adair ended the call.

Hunter took a few minutes of alone time to register the magnitude of this investigation. Sure, they still didn't know if a terrorist organization had abducted Fletch or stolen the toxin or formula. But they also didn't know that a terrorist group hadn't done so and that could mean a major terrorist attack.

Hunter's gut cramped. He'd worked big investigations before but not one with this big of stakes. A moment of panic hit him, but he remembered Maya's confidence in him and gritted his teeth to force it away. He could do this. He *would* do this.

With renewed energy, he went back to his computer. He passed Maya, who didn't look up from her work. He opened Fletch's files and an hour later, Adair texted with a meeting time. Hunter had plenty of time to meet with the Veritas partners before he had to be crosstown at his office, and then they could visit the places where Fletch had hung out.

Maya leaned back, her arms still in the cabinet. "Cocaine test done, but I didn't expect this."

"What?" Hunter asked.

"The cocaine is cut with botulism bound to bentonite."

Hunter's jaw dropped. "You're sure? It wasn't just mixed as he inhaled?"

"The composition makes me sure." She pulled her arms out of the cabinet. "This is very unique. Rarely do you find pure cocaine. It's usually cut with something. Most often caffeine, creatine, laxatives, or laundry detergent. But this only contains the botulism."

"So someone had pure cocaine—which would be pricey—mixed the botulism with it, and gave it to Carson," Hunter said. "Now the big question is, why aerosolize it *and* lace the cocaine too?"

She arched a brow. "They needed it in the powder form to add it to the cocaine. So maybe this was another test of some sort?"

"Perhaps, but if whoever has the toxin planned to kill a large number of people with botulism-laced cocaine, they would need a lot of money to buy the pure cocaine."

"So we're looking at someone who's well supported."

"Makes sense, I guess," he said, thinking it through. "Especially with the elaborate way they set up the contract with Fletch. This is an organized, well-funded person or group. It's surprising there wasn't any chatter about it."

She nodded. "Let me get cleaned up, and we can head to the conference room."

He'd been in that very room not too long ago when he'd helped Piper on her investigation into Jinx, and he knew the room was located on the first floor. She told her staff where she was going and stepped out the door.

In the hallway, he looked at her. "You must be so relieved."

"I am." She pressed her fingers on the reader to open the stairwell door instead of the elevator. "But I'm still very worried about Fletch. I really think someone abducted him."

"Seems like a good possibility. After the meeting with DHS, we'll get going on visiting the places you said he hangs out." He followed her down a flight of stairs to the large room with a glass wall and a long table.

Maya stopped at the whiteboard at the head of the table, and he went around the table.

Nick and Piper entered together. Hunter hadn't even known she was in the building.

"Hey." She looked at Maya. "How are you doing?"

"I'm in the clear. No exposure."

"Man, that's great news," Nick said, a ready smile forming. "I'd be lost without you. I count on you to keep me in line."

Maya smiled. "I might just give that job to Piper now."

Piper held up her hands. "I'm too smitten to do it."

"Smitten, huh?" Nick grinned at her and took her hand. "Right back atcha."

If this had happened before Hunter had spent time with Maya again, Hunter would have mocked gagging, but at the moment he was jealous of the relationship these two shared. He wanted the same thing. Had always wanted it. But the fear of loss was just too strong.

Maybe it was time he found a way through that fear. But how? He'd tried just about everything. Except counseling. He didn't need counseling. That was for other people.

"Something wrong?" Maya asked him.

He shook his head and cleared his thoughts. "Nope. All good."

He looked around to discover the other team members had arrived while he'd been lost in thought. Emory, whose baby was due any day now, lumbered in front of her husband, Blake, who strode into the room like the confident former sheriff he was. He pulled out the chair for her and helped her to sit.

Hunter's jealousy rose up again. He swallowed and moved his gaze to Kelsey and Sierra as they took seats on the other side of the table. Kelsey was wearing one of her usual feminine skirts and blouse while Sierra wore tactical pants and a polo shirt with the center's logo embroidered on the chest. Grady, a big guy with an intense look, entered behind them. He was dressed much like Sierra.

Surprisingly, Piper and Nick split up, sitting on opposite sides of the table. Hunter sat next to Piper.

"I'm really glad Maya's okay," she said.

He nodded.

"You're still not going to tell me what's going on between you, are you?"

"No," he said and fixed his focus on Maya.

She jotted the heading *Action Items* on the board with a black marker and turned to her team. "First, I need to tell everyone that I wasn't exposed to the toxin."

Applause broke out in the room and heartfelt best wishes were offered, reminding Hunter of the closeness these partners shared and how they cared for one another.

"I also confirmed that Carson was exposed and that the toxin was aerosolized in the lab," Maya added. "And our biggest discovery to date is that the government contract we all thought Fletch was working on wasn't a government contract at all."

"But I don't understand." Sierra narrowed her big brown eyes. "I read it when I processed the pages. It was clearly a federal document."

"It was actually a spoofed federal document," Hunter said.

"Spoofed?" Nick set down his Dr. Pepper can. "Do tell."

Maya recounted their conversation with Dr. Eberhardt.

Nick gave a low whistle. "We're dealing with some slick operators here if they could pull this off and fool a paranoid guy like Fletch."

Hunter looked at Nick. "Smooth or not, you'll be able to track them, right?"

"Normally I'd say yes, because we all know I'm amazing." He chuckled. "But with the way Fletch saved his files, I don't honestly know. I might need you to get a warrant for the files from his email provider. Just in case."

"I'll do it the minute we break up," Hunter said.

"Make sure we get access to the electronic files," Nick said. "Not just some printed document."

"I'll do my best," he promised, but he knew gaining access to electronic files would pose a bigger problem. Very few email providers allowed such a thing.

Maya wrote Hunter's name along with the item on the board. "We've worked several government contracts in the past, and though I did most of the paperwork, you all know it's a laborious process to finalize these contracts."

"Laborious is too tame of a word." Grady rolled his eyes. "More like torturous."

The team laughed, and so did Hunter, as his job involved far too much paperwork that he often thought was a waste of time.

"Right, well," she said over their laughter. "We're not just dealing with someone who has electronics skills here. Whoever is behind this has to be familiar with the process, have access to the right government documents, and also be familiar enough with botulism to convince Fletch of the legitimacy."

Maya's smile evaporated. "I think the real question we should be asking is who would want aerosolized botulism?"

Blake's dark gaze narrowed. "The obvious answer would be terrorists."

Grady nodded. "Or someone who wants to sell the product *to* a terrorist and make a tidy profit along the way."

"Could be someone with a grudge not only against Fletch but against the scientific community," Sierra said.

Blake leaned forward to look at her. "What are you thinking?"

She rested her hands on the table. "What if we have a person who got called out for an error. Maybe they published a paper but their research was faulty. The community turned against them. They want revenge."

"Sort of like disgruntled workers who come back with a gun," Blake said.

Sierra's eyes lit up. "Exactly. Though they would have to be very angry to go to these lengths instead of just going postal and taking Fletch out."

Hunter thought this was a viable lead, and Maya's bright expression told him that she did too.

She looked at Nick. "Can you look for any situations in the scientific community of late where something like this happened?"

"Will do." He jotted a note on a legal pad. "And you should know, I've got my staff working on a deep dive on Fletch's and Carson's backgrounds."

"Perfect. Just what I was going to ask you to do." Maya added the information to the board and ran her gaze over the group. "Any other ideas of who might want this toxin?"

"Could be someone Fletch collaborated with or worked with." Emory rested her hands on her large baby bump, and Hunter hoped she wouldn't suddenly go into labor.

"Like a fellow scientist, maybe," Blake suggested. "Maybe even someone who he worked with who's holding a grudge and released the toxin to get back at Fletch."

"That sounds possible." Maya tapped the marker against her hand. "Problem is, I don't know all the people he might have collaborated with in the past."

Hunter figured that could be a large group of people.

"We need to look for contact information from associates on Fletch's hard drives."

She added it to the board and turned. "Okay, we also learned that it looks like Carson used cocaine right before he died. Dr. Albertson said there was no evidence of long-term use. Factor that into your thoughts and see if it brings anything else to mind."

"I stopped by the ME's office and got his prints." Sierra explained about her procedure, likely for Piper's benefit, because the team and Hunter knew about the fingerprint test. "We can assume he snorted the cocaine, but I'll process the prints this afternoon, and we can verify it."

"Perfect, thank you," Maya said. "FYI, I confirmed the cocaine was cut with the toxin."

Grady's high forehead furrowed. "But why cut it with the toxin when he was already exposed to it via the air?"

Kelsey faced Grady. "If it was a dealer, the toxin would kill the users, and the drug dealer would lose clients. And I doubt he would go to these lengths just to kill one person like an enemy or a client who didn't pay. Or even a client who double-crossed him in some way."

"That's true," Maya said. "But the cocaine use *is* related somehow. The cocaine was pure before it was cut with the toxin, so we might be able to trace the cocaine purchase."

"I can look for known drug dealers who might have had contact with Carson or Fletch," Blake offered. "And ask if there's word on the street about the pure stuff."

"Thanks." Maya added that to the board.

"What about Fletch's banking info?" Nick asked. "He might've checked into a motel, and we can track him that way."

Maya shook her head. "He's too paranoid to have a credit card. He's cash all the way. Which is why there was a stack of it in his safe. I know he even pays his bills with cashier's checks. So, no tracking him that way. And you have his phone, so that's out."

Hunter looked at Nick. "Agents from my office have been canvassing motels and hotels within a ten mile radius of the island. No sighting. But my supervisor is adding additional agents and expanding the radius."

"So he hasn't gone to a medical facility or a hotel," Kelsey said. "What does that leave? Friends, family?"

"No to that, too," Maya said. "No family and as far as I know, I'm his only friend."

Kelsey frowned. "He sounds like such a hermit."

"He really is," Maya said. "I've never been sad about the way he lived because he chose his lifestyle. He likes it and doesn't want more."

"I assume with his paranoia he doesn't have cameras inside his lab," Blake said.

"Correct," Maya said. "His paranoia is going to make it very hard to find him."

"That could be a good thing, right?" Emory shifted in her chair, looking like she was trying to get comfortable. "If he's running from someone, and we can't find him, then they likely can't either."

"Good point," Maya said.

Blake looked at Maya. "He would have to flee the island by boat and could've landed at one of the main docks on the other side of the river. If so, there could be cameras at the dock."

"I can check into that," Nick offered. "And if we catch him on camera, we might be able to see if he's alone or if someone forced him to leave."

"His speedboat is missing so I think he might have left in that," Maya said.

Hunter imagined the scene in his mind. "I would expect if he'd been coerced, that the abductors wouldn't use the main dock but pull in somewhere private. Even alone, Fletch could've done the same thing."

Nick frowned. "You're probably right, and that area of the riverfront is pretty secluded so there won't be many cameras."

"But if he *was* abducted, wouldn't they leave in their own boat instead of his?" Maya asked.

"That would make sense," Grady said. "Maybe his boat is in for repair."

Maya pursed her lips. "Could be, I suppose."

"I can track that down," Piper offered. "See what I can find."

"Thank you." Maya smiled and wrote it on the board.

"You all should know that my supervisor called DHS in on the investigation," Hunter said. "I'm meeting with them right after this, and they'll handle the terrorism aspect of the investigation."

"That's a good thing, right?" Piper asked.

Hunter nodded. "As long as they play nice and don't try to take over the investigation. If they do, they're in for a fight."

10

Maya and Hunter drove to Float Away, located in Portland's trendy Pearl District. Hunter's meeting lasted for an hour, and Maya found herself missing him. Odd when they'd been apart for so many years. He'd come right back to the lab with nothing to report other than he updated the DHS agent who seemed to be cooperative. They would both publish updates at the end of the day and call if anything major occurred.

Still, he seemed bothered by something he wasn't willing to talk about. Just walked her to his SUV and drove in silence to park in front of the small shop. Clouds obscured the sun, mimicking her mood as she pushed open the glass door for the business. The smell of lavender lingered in the air. The plush waiting area held a comfy blue sofa and lime green chairs. The ceiling was covered with sailcloth in matching blue and green. The checkout counter was shaped like a large boat, and a thin woman stood behind it. She had frizzy blond hair and a narrow face and wore a loose paisley blouse and a big gold cross on a thick chain.

"Welcome," she said, her tone soothing. "Do you have an appointment?"

Maya smiled. "I'm looking for my friend Fletcher Gilliam. Have you seen him lately?"

"I remember you." She tipped her head and eyed Maya. "Maya, right? You came with him that one time, and I thought you were his girlfriend."

Maya had forgotten that part. "An honest mistake."

"You probably don't remember me. I'm Peggy, the owner."

"Yes, of course," Maya said, though her memory of the woman was fuzzy. "You showed me around."

She nodded, but shifted her gaze to Hunter, her expression wary. "And you are?"

He reached into his pocket, and Maya knew he was going to display his ID. That would stall the conversation and ruin the rapport Maya had going with Peggy.

Maya shifted closer to him and slid her arm around his waist. "This is Hunter. My *real* boyfriend."

He cast her a surprised look, and she tried to convey in one look to go along with her.

He nodded and put his arm around her shoulders, his hold possessive. Maya had to admit to liking his touch. Admit to feeling at home under his arm. At peace. She looked up at him.

"I'm helping find Fletch." He smiled that megawatt smile that always melted Maya's heart.

"Find him?" Peggy's blueish-green eyes narrowed, emphasizing the deep crow's feet lining her eyes.

Maya could make up some story, but it would be faster to just come right out with the problem. "He's missing, and I need to find him."

"Missing?" Peggy's hand rose to her chest, and she fidgeted with the giant cross.

Maya met Peggy's gaze. "He called me a few days ago and left a message, but when I went to his lab, he wasn't there."

"Oh, gosh." Peggy frowned. "Have you tried Voodoo? He loves their—"

"Maple bacon bar, I know," Maya said. "When was the last time he was here?"

"He hasn't been here for...hmm... I don't know how long. Let me look."

Peggy moved to an iPad lying on the counter and tapped the screen. "Gosh. It's been three weeks." She looked up, her eyes narrowed. "Normally, I would've noticed, but we're doing some renovating, and I've been swamped. He never goes this long without a float. Is he in some kind of trouble?"

"He's been busy with a special project," Maya said, trying to downplay the situation. "He's probably doing an escape room."

"Yeah. Yeah. He loves those. Which is odd to me, because they cause all kinds of stress, which he then comes here to offload it all in the water." Peggy shook her head.

"It makes sense to him," Maya said. "Is there anything you can think of to help me find him?"

"Nah," Peggy said. "We're not close or anything."

"Do you know the people he does the escape rooms with?" Hunter asked.

"Not most of them, but Greg—he works here—goes with him sometimes."

Hunter's arm tightened on Maya's shoulder. "Is he here now? Can we talk to him?"

Peggy shook her head. "He's on vacation until tomorrow night."

Greg could be just the lead they'd been searching for. Maya smiled at Peggy to disarm her. "Could I get Greg's last name and contact information from you?"

"Sorry." Peggy lifted her shoulders into a hard line. "Privacy laws and all. But if you have a card, I can have him call you."

"Could we at least get his last name?" Hunter asked.

She shook her head. "With all the identity theft these days, I'm overly cautious on employee privacy and prefer not to give that out."

Hunter pulled out his ID. "I'm investigating Fletch's disappearance."

"But I thought..." She looked Maya in the eye. "You were lying to me. You're not a couple."

Guilt heaped itself on Maya's back, and she eased out from under Hunter's hold. "I'm sorry. We once were together. But yes, we thought if I asked the questions you might be more forthcoming."

Peggy gritted her teeth. "I don't appreciate that."

"We apologize for misleading you," Hunter said. "But we still need Greg's last name."

"And I still won't give it to you."

"I appreciate you wanting to protect your employee's privacy," Hunter said. "But I can get a subpoena to compel you to provide the information."

Peggy crossed her arms. "Then you're going to have to do that."

Maya wished they could go back and start over, but honestly, she believed they would be in the same place. She fished out her business card. "I'll add my cell number so he can call at any time."

Maya picked up a pen in the shape of a shark and jotted down her number, nearly laughing at the fact that the tip of the pen poked out of a shark head.

Maya laid the pen on her card. "Thanks for offering to give this to Greg."

Peggy gave a sharp nod. "I hope you find Fletch and he's okay."

"Thanks, me, too," Maya said and started for the door.

Outside, Maya gave Hunter a stern look. "You didn't need to keep your arm around me all that time."

"Hey." He unlocked the SUV. "If you don't want to play, then don't start anything."

"I didn't think you'd take advantage of the situation."

"I wasn't. Just doing my part to be convincing. Now if I wanted to take advantage, I would have done this."

He slid his arms around her waist and drew her close. He met her gaze and held it, locking on with such intensity that it made her heart flip-flop. She gasped at the true interest burning in his eyes. He was still interested in her. Still cared. He was so dangerous to her heart, and yet, she felt safe. Completely and totally safe.

"Honestly, I wasn't acting at all," he said, looking like he wanted to kiss her. If he did, she would be powerless to stop him.

And with that, he lowered his head, but paused and looked her in the eye as if asking permission before kissing her. She let her emotions rule and pulled his head down. He pressed his lips against hers. The touch of his warm lips sent shock traveling through her body, and she was paralyzed in his arms. His kiss grew insistent, and she thawed. She let herself respond in kind. Deepening the kiss. Twining her arms around his powerful neck. Pulling him closer.

He tightened his arms around her back. Drawing her to him.

She reveled in every touchpoint. Every nerve ending tingling. She wanted this kiss to go on and on. She couldn't even consider withdrawing from his arms, where she felt at home for the first time in years.

A horn honked nearby, bringing her to her senses. She couldn't be kissing Hunter out in public. She couldn't be kissing him at all.

Hunter expected Maya to be quiet on the ride to the escape rooms, but he didn't expect her to turn her back to him, stare out the window, and not say a word. Sure, he shouldn't have kissed her. It was wrong on all kinds of levels. But man, when the opportunity presented itself, how could he not take it? Especially when he was still in love with her.

But it wasn't fair to her. He'd taken advantage of the situation. Not that she seemed to mind. Quite the contrary. She'd been into it. No question about that. Didn't matter. He needed to apologize.

"I'm sorry, Maya." He glanced at her. "I shouldn't have kissed you."

She didn't turn. Didn't move at all.

"I hope you can forgive me," he added.

"Nothing to forgive," she finally said. "I'd be a hypocrite if I said I didn't enjoy it."

"I noticed."

She spun and fired him a testy look. "That doesn't mean that I'm ready to get back together or anything."

"I didn't think you were." He pulled up in front of the escape room company and parked.

"I just wanted to make it clear."

Anger started rising in his gut, and he should probably just get out of the vehicle and leave things alone. But he'd done that once. Hurt her badly. Wouldn't do it again. "It's clear."

She took a long breath and eased it out. "I'm sorry if I sound mad at you. I'm not. I'm mad at myself."

"Because you don't want to like kissing me?"

"Exactly."

"Is it such a terrible thing?" He turned off the engine.

She eyed him. "You hurt me, Hunter. Badly. I can't just

forget that because I liked one little kiss."

"I understand. But just know if I could go back and have a do over, I would do things differently."

She met and held his gaze. "But you'd still leave, right?"

"Yes," he said and the word echoed around the vehicle like a bullet looking for a victim.

"Then we'd be at the same place." Her words came out on a choked breath.

Her sadness ate a gaping hole in his gut. "Would we? Even if I'd taken the time to explain why I had to go?"

"I would still be hurt."

He wasn't handling this well. Not well at all. He had to do a better job of explaining. "Yeah, I know, but you would've at least understood that my reason for leaving was out of my control."

She held his gaze, something raw and vulnerable in her eyes. "Is it out of your control, or is it a choice? A reason to hide away because you're afraid to get hurt?"

He had to look away and turned to clench the steering wheel, putting all of his frustration into his grip. "Trust me. If I could let it go, I would have six years ago. I would never have left you. I loved you—love you—Maya. I will never stop. But as much as I want this whole fear of losing others to go away, I can't make it happen."

She let out a long breath. One that went on and on, as if sighing out years of pent-up emotions. "Then maybe it's time you let God handle it for you."

Like it was that simple. It hurt that she thought it was. He eyed her. "Like the way you're letting Him handle the hurt from the careless way I left you?"

She jerked back as if he'd slapped her. He opened his mouth to apologize.

She held up her hand. "You're right. I'm doing the same thing. I may have forgiven you, but haven't let go of the hurt and put up a similar barrier. Maybe we should agree right here that we'll both turn the hurt and fear over to God and let Him take care of it."

He loved how she could find the positive here, when he couldn't even begin to. "You know it's not that simple, right?"

"Laying it down is exactly that simple." She held his gaze. "The hard part is not picking it back up again."

"Yeah." He jerked the key from the ignition and got out of his vehicle. He was done. He had no rebuttal for that comment. None. She'd nailed him. It was exactly what he'd done for six years. Told God that He had this. Had control of Hunter's life. And then something would happen to remind Hunter of how easily people close to him could die, and he would redouble his efforts to shut down so he didn't get hurt.

He didn't know if it would be worth trying again.

He took a long look at Maya as she marched up to the business's front door. If he could get over his fear for anyone, it would be for her. And that kiss? It reminded him of all the wonderful times they'd had together. Of the life they'd built together until he'd bailed.

He wanted that again. But even if he managed to get over his issues, she'd made it clear that she would never want to get back together with him.

She opened the door and looked back at him. "You coming?"

"Yeah," he said, but his feet dragged while he made his way across the sidewalk and trailed her inside the older building with glass door and storefront window advertising six thrilling escape rooms.

The place smelled like popcorn and dirty socks. He could explain the popcorn from the small concession stand connected to the registration counter, but the socks remained a mystery. They were greeted by a teenage guy with a bad case of acne and stringy blond hair. He stood behind a scarred Formica counter. Maya stepped up to the kid, who stared past her as if not seeing them.

Maya cleared her throat. "Hello."

"Hi," the kid said.

"I'm looking for my friend. Have you seen him lately?" She showed him a picture of Fletch on her phone.

"Hey." His expression perked up. "That's Fletch."

"Yeah," Maya said. "You know him?"

"Know him, are you kidding me?" He blinked. "He's got like the record time for all of our escape rooms. No one beats his time. Ever."

"Has he been here in the last few days?" Maya asked.

The kid shrugged. "I've been off. You'd have to ask our manager."

"Is he in?"

"Her and yes." He picked up a handset from a desktop phone and pressed a button. "Someone here to see you." He nodded and set down the phone. "She'll be right out."

"Thank you," Maya said.

Hunter looked around. If he'd come here to do an escape room, he'd have his choice of rooms. He figured Fletch would choose *Mission: Mars,* where their spacecraft had crashed and cosmic radiation was heading the team's way and would kill them all if they didn't figure out how to escape their spaceship. He could totally see Fletch enjoying that room.

He looked at Maya, who was reviewing the room descriptions too. "Looks like fun."

"It really does." Her voice was flat.

"Which one would you choose?"

"I'd have to do *Mission: Mars*. I'm sure Fletch would join me." She looked up at him, her expression still tight.

She hadn't let their discussion go, something he understood. Maybe he could lighten the mood some. "I'd have to do the Special Ops room. Totally up my alley."

"Yeah, I can see that."

A thin woman hitching up dark-washed jeans and pulling down the tails of a white blouse stepped up to the desk. She wore thick black-framed glasses and had blunt cut pink hair. "I'm Lucy Karl, the manager. How can I help you?"

Maya faced the woman. "I'm looking for my friend Fletcher Gilliam and was wondering if he's been here in the last few days."

"Haven't seen him this week," Lucy said, her eyebrow with a small piercing cocked.

"Do you run these rooms every night?" Hunter asked.

"Nah, we're closed Monday and Tuesday unless we have a business with a special party that fills most of our rooms." Lucy crossed her arms—why, Hunter had no idea, but he would keep an eye on her for signs of duplicity.

"So he could've come in yesterday?" Maya asked.

"Could've." Lucy considered Maya, her mouth tight. "But like I said, he wasn't here."

"You're sure."

"Positive. We all know Fletch here." She shot the kid a look. "Don't we?"

The kid nodded. "I already told them that."

"How can you be so positive he didn't come in?" Hunter pinned his focus on Lucy. "Do you work all the hours the rooms are open?"

She tightened her arms. "I review the reservations every day, and he didn't make one."

Hunter still didn't get why she was irritated with them, but he wouldn't let this go. "Could he have joined someone else who made the reservation?"

"If he did, he would have to sign a waiver." Lucy dropped

her arms and shifted her feet, her gaze bouncing around the room. "And he couldn't have broken a time record, which he always does. He's done all these rooms at least once, and we have new rooms starting next week. He would wait for those."

"He would totally wait," the teenager agreed.

Lucy lifted her chin. "Is he in trouble or something?"

"He's missing," Maya said.

"Oh, man, that's rough." Lucy bit her lip and glanced at the kid then back at Maya.

"What about his friend Greg? Has he come by in the last few days?"

Lucy shook her head. "He never comes in without Fletch."

"Never," the kid confirmed.

Lucy laid her hands on the counter. "Is there anything we can do to help?"

"Can you think of anywhere else he might go?" Maya asked.

"Yeah, sure." Lucy tapped her chin. "He loves Float Away and Voodoo."

For being a shy guy who respected his privacy, Hunter thought people seemed to know a lot about Fletch. "What about other escape rooms?"

Lucy mimicked pulling a knife from her chest and laughed, the first real sign that she wasn't wary of them. "Not that he's ever told me. Except in the early days. He tried them all but said our special effects and actors are better."

Maya handed over a business card. "Call me if he shows up or if you think of anything else."

"Sure. Sure. Glad to." Lucy pocketed the card.

"Thank you," Maya said and they exited the building.

"You believe her?" Hunter clicked open his SUV's locks.

"I do." She looked up at him. "And you?"

"Yeah, she seems to be telling the truth."

"So, what do you want to do?"

"Head back to the lab and dig into Fletch's files again." Hunter got the SUV pointed in the right direction, and the tension between him and Maya returned, filling the vehicle like toxic smoke. He felt like he should say something, but what? He'd already declared his love—and his unwillingness to do anything about it.

He'd likely hurt her even more by that admission. Another rejection by telling her that her love wasn't enough for him. That he needed something more to make a commitment.

She swiveled to face him. "You know what you said earlier about me still letting the hurt control me from our breakup? I didn't realize how much I was letting it impact me. And I don't want it to anymore. I really am going to give it to God and do my very best not to take it back."

He nodded, but didn't say anything. He knew he couldn't do the same thing. He'd tried it enough times and failed before. Why would now be any different?

"And that starts right now with accepting the past and leaving the hurt behind so I can work with you and have no hard feelings." She clutched his arm. "Maybe we can even be friends."

"Friends?" *Really, friends.* He worked hard not to stare at her. How was that going to work when he was still in love with her?

She smiled at him, and his pulse started racing. He wanted so much more with her, and that was how giving his fear to God could work. Hunter could remember the goal and why he should let God take charge of his life. God saw the big picture. Everything. Not just Hunter's little view of the world. And God would work this out for Hunter's good. Maybe, anyway. If that was what God wanted.

11

Maya looked out the window and ignored the strain between her and Hunter. She didn't know what to say to him. He clearly still didn't believe that he could let go of his fear, and now that she'd committed to let go of her bitterness toward him, she was aware of everything he did. Like shifting his hands on the steering wheel. Strong hands. Long fingers. Hands that had gently touched her face in the past. And had urgently drawn her toward him for a kiss today.

If he gave up his fear, could she truly forget the hurt and be with him again? He'd been an amazing partner. Kind. Appreciative. Supportive. Sure, he had his faults. He was aggressive and wanted things done his way. She was the same, and they'd had to compromise on the things they disagreed on. Surprisingly, there weren't many of them. She was smart enough to know if they ever married, they would clash on a lot more things that living together would bring.

She let herself think about marriage to him. A life together. Children.

"Maya, did you hear me?" His insistent tone broke into her thoughts.

"What?" she was surprised to see they were idling in front of the gate to the Veritas parking garage.

"I need your fingerprints to get in."

"Sorry." She leaned over him and reached her fingers toward the keypad. She couldn't touch it. She unbuckled her seatbelt but remained a few inches shy. Hunter clasped her waist and helped her make the final stretch.

His touch brought her back to her daydreaming. She wanted a future with him. She really did. No matter how badly he'd hurt her. He was as much a prisoner to his fear as she'd been in not being able to help let go of her hurt toward him.

She pressed her fingers until the gate opened. Then, she lurched back to her seat, releasing her body from Hunter's hands.

He took a long look at her before driving into the structure. "You were a million miles away."

"Yeah." She left it at that and focused on the investigation. She needed one of their leads to work out. Something —anything—to turn out in their favor and show them where Fletch had taken shelter. If indeed he was on the run and some terrible terrorist group hadn't kidnapped him.

She got out of the SUV and looked at Hunter. "What do you really think happened to Fletch?"

"I honestly don't know." He joined her at the front of the car. "It's looking like he didn't go to ground. At least not with any of the people we know about."

Maya searched her brain for additional ideas. "It's odd that he hasn't called me back. I doubt he would want to hide from me."

"Probably not, but he might not be calling you to protect you from what's going on."

"You could be right." She unlocked the door.

Hunter's phone dinged. "It's a text from Piper. She got

the warrant for Fletch's emails and internet history. She's emailing it to his internet provider as we speak. Let's hope she gets them to act quickly."

"She's very convincing. If anyone can manage that, it will be Piper."

Maya got the door open and held it for him but when his fingers brushed against her, the shock of his touch had her nearly running down the hallway to the elevator. This was so unlike her. Running from anything. She was normally a *run toward and embrace things* kind of person.

She got him signed in with a security pass and hurried to Nick's small lab. He sat behind his usual computer and Blake leaned against the wall, his ankles crossed. Hunter caught up to her and stepped into the room behind her.

Blake came to his feet. "Did you find Fletch?"

She shook her head and updated the pair. "I don't think the owners are people we need to be concerned about, but it wouldn't hurt for us to run a background check on them."

"And we need to find a worker from Float Away," Hunter added. "The owner will only give us his first name. Greg. But supposedly he's friends with Fletch. I'll request a subpoena to compel her to turn over the guy's information, but Nick, maybe you can find it faster."

"I can try," he said. "But with only a first name, and a common one at that, finding anything on Greg might be a challenge."

"I can request that subpoena for you," Piper offered. "And then serve Peggy when it comes through and get the information to you."

"Great," Hunter said.

"And FYI, I heard back from Fletch's internet provider," she said. "They're cooperating, and we should have all of his files tomorrow."

"That's my girl." Nick flashed a smile at Piper then

looked back at Hunter. "You have to know that tracking that spoofed email is going to be a challenge."

"You can do it." Maya tried to sound encouraging. "I have confidence in you."

"You sound like my own personal cheer squad." Nick grinned at her.

She returned his smile, and it felt good to smile again. They'd only been looking for Fletch and trying to figure out who killed Carson for two days, but it felt like weeks. "What's happening with your other assignments?"

Nick leaned back in his chair. "There weren't any video sightings of Fletcher docking a boat. I went back to a week before he called you through the day you found Carson. Nothing."

Blake looked at her. "I took a drive along the river. Found a canoe abandoned in a public area. Nothing to indicate the owner, but Sierra's dusting it for prints now. Do you know if Fletch owns a canoe?"

Maya shrugged. "I've never seen one, but that doesn't mean anything. We spent most of our time in the lab when I visited him. And even if he did, would both his canoe and boat be away from the island?"

Blake tipped his head at Nick. "I thought maybe the wonder boy here might be able to get satellite photos, so came up here to ask him."

Maya looked at Nick. "And can you?"

"I'll try, but no promises." He looked up at Hunter. "You should have connections to get that information, right?"

"I can check into it," Hunter said, but he didn't sound optimistic.

"We finished our background checks on Carson and Fletch." Nick leaned back, his chair groaning. "I emailed the report to you, but there was nothing of interest. Two pretty clean guys. Carson does have a boatload of college debt, but otherwise, no issues. And nothing to suggest drug use."

"The debt could be motive for Carson to try to sell the toxin," Hunter said.

"If so, why did he end up dead?" Maya asked.

"Could be the buyer turned on him or never intended to pay him," Blake suggested. "Would be a common enough response from someone who's up to no good."

Blake's phone rang. He pulled it from his pocket and glanced at it, his expression tightening. "I have to take this."

He stepped to the other side of the room. He worked many investigations at one time, and the call might not be about their investigation, but Maya's gut tightened at Blake's serious expression anyway. As a former sheriff who served for years in that capacity, he knew how to hide his feelings. But he wasn't hiding his worry well enough at the moment.

He ended his call and pinned that serious focus on Maya. "The police have a report of someone matching Fletch's description entering a known crack house in Northeast Portland."

"Crack house?" she asked. "As in crack cocaine?"

Blake nodded. "The abandoned building is frequented with drug users."

"Fletch didn't do drugs." She crossed her arms. "Would never do them. They'd make him lose control, the very worst thing that could happen to him. So if he's there, it has to be about the cocaine and Carson."

"Sounds likely," Blake said.

"Was he alone?" Hunter asked.

Blake shook his head. "Eyewitness says he was out of it and being supported by another guy."

"When was this?" Maya asked.

"Earlier this afternoon."

"He could still be there." Maya swiveled toward the door. "We need to get down there now!"

~

Maya and Hunter drove through the night, the skies gray and overcast. The scent of coming rain drifted through Maya's open window in Hunter's SUV, and the warm breeze blew over her body. The air might be warm but when she thought about Fletch in a crack house, maybe under the influence of drugs, a coldness seeped into her body. He would hate every minute of being there. She hated it for him. She shivered.

Hunter glanced at her. "You want me to turn the heat on?"

Maya shook her head. "I'm just afraid of what we might find when we get to the house. The witness said Fletch was out of it. What if someone injected him with drugs and dumped him there? Anything could happen to him in a place like that."

"But why would someone drug him?"

"I don't know, and that's adding to my worry." She paused to gather her thoughts instead of focusing on her feelings. "We know Carson snorted cocaine, but I know that Fletch would never do drugs. He'd once blown out his knee and refused all narcotics. So someone drugging Fletch is the most logical explanation."

"Assuming you're right about Fletch."

"I am. That I know for sure." She looked out the window, taking in the run-down neighborhood.

"The person who reported seeing him to the police could be wrong. Eyewitnesses often are."

"I hope so." And she really did but couldn't actually dredge up enough hope to believe it.

Flashing red lights glowed deeper in the neighborhood.

"What in the world is going on?" She sat forward and squinted.

"It's likely police arresting someone for drug possession," Hunter said. "Or maybe someone overdosed, and it's an ambulance."

Maya looked at him. "What if someone stole the toxin from Fletch and then gave him an overdose of drugs to kill him and make it look like an accident?"

"Sounds possible."

She didn't like that answer. Not one bit.

Please don't let it be Fletch.

Hunter turned the corner and drove toward the red light coming from a fire truck.

She craned her neck. "Please don't let them be at the house we're going to."

"They're on the right side of the street." Hunter slowed to a crawl, likely to avoid hitting neighbors who'd gathered to watch.

She looked at the house numbers and clutched Hunter's arm. "It's the crack house. They're at our house."

"Let me park, and we'll check it out." He found a space and parallel parked.

Maya didn't wait for him to turn off the ignition but bolted out and ran down the street, watching the last few house numbers. She drew closer to the truck, and her stomach roiled. The firefighters had put out the blaze, but the crack house lay in black charred smoldering ruins.

"Fletch!" She ran toward the thick acrid smoke rising into the muggy air.

A burly police officer dressed in a navy blue Portland Police Bureau uniform stepped in front of her. "You can't go any closer."

"But Fletch! He was there." She tried to push past him,

but hands circled her upper arms from behind and held her back.

"Let's calm down and find out if anyone was in the house." Hunter drew her back, and his logical voice should have calmed her panic, but it only angered her that he could be so composed when Fletch might've died in that fire.

She spun on him. "How can you be so calm? Fletch could be in there. Could've died."

"If so, there's nothing we can do for him now." Hunter circled his arms around her and pulled her against his chest. After two days of fear and frustration, she had no fight left in her, and she relaxed against Hunter's broad chest to let her tears fall. She tried to control them, but she'd managed to hold them back since finding Carson and this just broke the dam. She heaved out deep sobs and tears ran down her cheeks.

"It's going to be okay," Hunter whispered and stroked her hair.

At his gentle touch, the flood burst, and she sobbed with abandon. He stood strong. Holding her tight. Whispering to her. When her tears subsided, she grabbed a tissue from her jacket pocket and cleaned up her face.

She looked up at him. "Sorry about that."

He used his thumb to swipe away the last of her tears. "No need to apologize. I'm glad to be here for you."

She was glad too. She didn't want to be alone if they learned Fletch had indeed died in the fire.

Hunter gave her a tight smile. "Are you good now so I can talk to the officer?"

"Yes."

He dug out his ID but kept his arm around Maya's shoulders as he introduced himself to the officer, who was watching them with narrowed eyes.

"Were there any victims?" Hunter asked.

"All but three people made it out safely," the officer said. "We're waiting on the ME to recover their bodies."

Maya gasped, and pushed out of Hunter's arm to look up at him.

"We believe a friend of ours was in the house," Hunter told the officer.

The officer widened his stance. "I'm sorry. If he was here, it's going to take some time to ID him. There was a huge explosion, and the fire burned hot. The fire investigator suspects arson."

Maya imagined Fletch lying there. Drugged. The fire starting. Maybe awake and unable to move. Knowing he was going to die. An agonizing groan found its way out of her mouth.

"Hey," Hunter said, taking hold of her arms. "We don't know Fletch was here."

"And we don't know he wasn't." She hated to be negative, but she had to be realistic. She turned to the officer. "Can we talk to the investigator?"

He locked gazes, transmitting his authority in his look. "Only authorized personnel allowed beyond this point."

"Then find someone to authorize us," Hunter said. "We have knowledge that could help with this investigation."

The officer evaluated Hunter, but Hunter held the officer's gaze and stood strong and tall.

The officer stepped back. "Wait here."

Maya waited for the officer to move out of earshot. "We don't know anything that can help. At least nothing other than a person saw someone resembling Fletch being led into this house."

Hunter frowned. "If the bodies are as badly burned as the officer claims, we can offer Kelsey's help to recover the victims, right?"

"Yes. Yes. Of course. The ME will likely need a forensic

anthropologist to recover the bones. There's one at the state forensic lab, but Kelsey would probably get here faster and do a better job."

Maya shifted her attention back to the property and took a better look at what was left of the two-story house. She took in the charred timbers. The smoking ruins.

She could barely handle the thought that Fletch might have died in this fire because they hadn't figured out what was going on with him.

Maya moved closer to Hunter, not only so no one would overhear them, but also because she wanted to feel his presence. "The officer said this was arson. Do you think the person who set the fire drugged Fletch and left him here to die?"

"It's possible, but until we confirm he was in the house, it's all speculation. The fire might not even be related to him."

"Yeah, you could be right," she said, but her gut didn't agree.

She moved her focus to the officer who was talking to a tall, thin man with a thick head of black hair, his pen poised over a clipboard. He glanced at them and nodded.

The officer spun and picked his way through firehoses and equipment on his path back to them. He lifted the yellow tape. "The investigator will talk to you."

Maya didn't waste time but slipped under the tape, and Hunter followed.

The investigator turned and watched them advance toward him. His face was contorted with anger. She wanted to talk to him, but she dreaded hearing what he had to say.

Hunter held out his credentials and introduced himself.

"Arson Investigator, Thompson." He tucked his clipboard under his arm. "Didn't expect the FBI to be interested in a crack house fire."

"We have reason to believe the person we're looking for might be one of your victims."

He cocked a bushy eyebrow the same intense black color as his hair. "Is that so? What's he wanted for?"

"He's not wanted," Maya snapped.

Thompson shot her a questioning look.

She regretted her testy response, but she wouldn't explain. Just control her tone from now on. "He's a missing person."

His brow rose higher. "And you are?"

"Maya Glass. Toxicology and controlled substance expert at Veritas Center."

"Ah," he said and watched her for a moment. "That fancy lab on the other side of town. Heard about your work. Could never afford your services though."

"Help us identify these victims, and we'll provide services to you for free," she said.

He sighed. "As much as I'd like to take you up on your offer, I have no control over the victims' disposition. It'll be the medical examiner's office you'll have to talk to about that."

"Do you know who's responding from their office?" Maya asked.

Thompson shook his head. "With multiple victims, I wouldn't be surprised if Dr. A. herself didn't show up. She's conscientious like that."

As if talking about the ME's team summoned them to the scene, two vans pulled up to the fluttering yellow tape and parked. Maya watched, praying that Dr. Albertson stepped out. Josh exited the first vehicle with another man. Dr. Albertson slid out of the second one and stopped to look at the house.

Maya hurried over to her. "We need your help. We think

Fletch might be one of the victims, and we'd like Kelsey to recover the bodies."

Dr. Albertson frowned. "I'm sorry to hear about Fletch. If the bodies are in the kind of condition I suspect from the looks of the dwelling, we would call in a forensic anthropologist anyway. We'd be glad for Kelsey's help. Assuming there's no price tag attached to it. You know my budget doesn't stretch to include your fees."

"Pro bono all the way," Maya assured her.

"Then let me do an initial assessment and get back to you." She turned to her team. "Wait here."

Dr. Albertson donned a protective suit and gloves, then slipped under the yellow tape to talk to the investigator. Together they stepped into the ruins and paused a few feet in. Dr. Albertson squatted and shook her head then stood and followed the investigator in a bit further and to the right. She shook her head again and then a third time in the back left of the building. She took one last look and then picked her way out of the remnants of the house.

She marched straight to Maya. "Call Kelsey. Tell her she'll have three bodies to recover, and it's going to be a very difficult recovery."

12

Hunter was glad Maya listened to him and waited in his SUV while he accompanied Investigator Thompson and Kelsey through the charred building. As lead on the investigation, he had to see first-hand what had happened in the fire. For once, Kelsey wasn't wearing a skirt or dress but had arrived wearing jeans and a T-shirt, which she immediately covered with a Tyvek suit.

She walked lightly, slowly picking her way deep into the house, and Hunter tried to follow suit, but with ash and charred debris scattered like a tornado had whipped through the building, it was difficult not to disturb the scene.

They reached the first body, and if Thompson hadn't pointed it out, Hunter wouldn't have distinguished the charred bones from the other debris.

"Fire started back here," Thompson said.

"So this person took the brunt of the fire." Kelsey squatted next to the charred remains.

Bile rose up Hunter's throat. He didn't know how Kelsey could handle working with burn victims. Shoot, how did she handle working with bodies in the condition she found them at all? The autopsy Hunter had attended was bad enough, but this scene? The inferno that destroyed this person. Destroyed them so badly, Hunter couldn't even tell if it was a man or woman? Horrific.

Thompson looked at Kelsey. "Gonna be a chore to get the remains out of here without leaving anything behind."

Kelsey, still looking at the victim, nodded, but she didn't look daunted by the task.

Hunter couldn't get beyond the fact that they had no idea who this person could be. "Can you get DNA from the remains so we can ID the victims?"

Kelsey stood, planted her hands on her hips, and continued to stare at the victim. "Fingerprints and DNA are destroyed in temperatures of more than two-hundred-fifty degrees."

"This building likely sustained four times that heat," Thompson said.

Kelsey nodded. "Teeth are the most resilient part of the body. In cases of high-heat fires like this one, dental remains are the fastest and most reliable way to ID a victim."

"Figured as much," Thompson said. "But getting everything out intact is gonna be a challenge here, right?"

She nodded. "Take me to the other victims, please."

Thompson led them to the middle of the building, where another incinerated body was barely discernible. Kelsey took a good look then moved on to the third person, who lay near the door and had suffered less damage.

"Looks like he or she almost made it out." Thompson tsked. "If only the firefighters had gotten here earlier."

Hunter's thoughts were more along the line of *If only someone hadn't torched this place*. "Have the police canvassed the neighborhood looking for witnesses?"

Thompson nodded. "The sergeant in charge said

someone saw a man fleeing the building shortly before the explosion."

Hunter would talk to that sergeant after they finished looking at the scene. He turned his attention to Kelsey. "Do any of these bodies fit Fletch's build?"

"The other two are too damaged for me to tell at a quick look, but this person looks to be about the right height. And that's all I can tell you at this point."

"It's a start."

"I've seen enough to start my recovery." She stood and looked at Thompson. "No one can enter the rubble until I'm finished. Can you make sure that's taken care of?"

"Of course."

She gave a sharp nod and started out of the building and down the street toward her white van with the Veritas logo on the back.

Hunter caught up to her. "Any idea of the victims' sexes?"

She opened the back door of her van. "My preliminary observations say a male and female at the back. The one up front is male. But that's subject to change."

"How long before you can ID them?" Hunter knew he was pushing her, but he wanted an answer. Not only for the investigation, but for Maya.

Kelsey shook her head and let out a long breath. She reached into her vehicle and pulled out a spray bottle. "It could take days, but this should help."

"And this is?"

"A spray glue developed in Australia for recovering bodies."

"Glue? For bodies? Never heard of such a thing."

She shoved the bottle in a field bag. "It's a recent development. Using the stabilizing spray on the victim could help me preserve dental remains intact so we can ID the victims faster."

"I'm glad you're on the cutting edge," he said. "Because I know Maya won't sleep until you tell her if Fletch is one of the victims."

Kelsey glanced at Hunter's SUV. "She looks pretty shaken up."

"She is." His heart broke at the dejected look on Maya's face. "I'll go check on her."

Kelsey grabbed his arm. "It's no secret you have a thing for her, but she's extra vulnerable right now. Please don't hurt her."

"It's never my intention to hurt her." He walked away before Kelsey asked for an explanation.

He circled the van, and a woman wearing a black pantsuit stepped into his path. She pushed the jacket back, and her hands landed on her sidearm and hip. "So, you're the Fed."

Hunter figured she was a local detective, so he displayed his credentials. "Special Agent Hunter Lane."

She shoved out a hand. "Detective Alisha Barry. PPB. What's your interest in *my* investigation?"

She was staking her claim. Not an unusual move for a local detective to take until they determined how cooperative a federal officer might be.

"I believe one of the victims might be a person of interest in my investigation." He gave her a very brief summary of his case but didn't mention the toxin. "Someone fitting his description was seen entering this house this afternoon, and I have no idea if he left or not. The anthropologist confirmed that one of the victims fits the build of my guy."

"Are you the one who suggested this anthropologist instead of the state expert?" Her tone held a measure of accusation.

He didn't think she'd be upset about the choice of anthropologist, but it was likely a territory thing again. "I'm working with the Veritas Center on my investigation. Seemed appropriate to have the best anthropologist in the area to do the work. Wouldn't you agree?"

"I would, but I also think it gives you an unfair advantage here."

"I haven't really given it any thought. I just wanted the best person for the job."

She eyed him, likely trying to find out if he was telling the truth.

"I can introduce you to Kelsey," he said. "And we can ask her to update us both at the same time."

"I'll take care of that on my own." Her expression hardened.

Okay. She was still ticked off, but he wasn't going to back down. "If Fletcher Gilliam is one of the victims, I'll continue to investigate this fire and ask for updates from you."

She folded her arms over her chest. "And at the same time, you'll update me on your progress."

She wasn't going to like his answer. "To the extent that's possible, yes. This is a classified investigation, and you need clearance for many of the details."

She scoffed. "I figured you'd pull that."

"I'm not pulling anything. Just stating a fact."

She glared.

He got out his card and handed it to her.

She reciprocated, eyeing him all the while.

A large SUV pulled up to the crime scene tape, taking Hunter's attention. The vehicle had a government plate, and Hunter knew a Fed of some sort sat behind that wheel. The door opened, and a guy that Hunter put in his early thirties slid out.

He wore khaki tactical pants and a blue polo shirt. He

reached inside the vehicle and came out with a windbreaker, even though it wasn't cool enough for a jacket. When he slipped it on, Hunter read the back with Police and ICE written in large white letters on it.

"ICE." Hunter looked at the detective. "You called them in?"

"No." She followed Hunter's gaze. "Great. Another Fed."

The ICE agent strode their way, confidence in his steps, and Hunter felt certain he was going to do battle with this guy. He was a couple of inches taller than Hunter and had thick black hair and a penetrating look.

He held out his credentials. Hunter noted his last name was spelled the same as Sierra's before she got married. He knew she had brothers in law enforcement. Maybe this guy was one of them.

"ICE Special Agent, Clay Byrd," he said, his voice deep and rumbly. "One of you in charge here?"

"I am. Detective Alisha Barry. PPB." She held out her hand.

Clay briefly shook her hand, his attention shifting to Hunter. "And you are?"

"FBI. Hunter Lane." Hunter didn't like the stare he was getting, so he widened his stance and tipped his head at the house, where Sierra had joined Kelsey and was looking at the scene. "You related to Sierra?"

"My sister."

This ought to be interesting. "And what brings you to our crime scene?"

He arched a dark brow, likely at Hunter's reference to *our* scene. "One of my informants often hangs here. When he didn't show up for a meet, I thought I'd come looking for him. Heard about the fire on the way." He shifted his focus to the house. "Guess since Kelsey's here we have a badly burned victim."

Right, he would know Kelsey. "Three, actually."

He grimaced. "Male or female?"

"Too early to tell," Barry said. "I'll be glad to share the IDs when we get them."

"Thanks." He kept his gaze on the house. "Place is totally destroyed. Arson?"

"The fire investigator says it is, but we'll have to wait for his report to be certain," Barry said.

Clay got out a business card and gave it to Barry. "Call when you have any information. I'm gonna go say hi to my sister."

He didn't wait for Barry to give him permission to access the crime scene, but slipped under the tape, and he really didn't sound like he cared if Barry called him or not. Why would he? He had an inside source in his sister, and he'd likely get information from her even before Hunter did.

Clay approached Sierra. She gave him an air fist bump to protect her gloved hands from contamination.

Barry looked at Clay. "He's even more of a pain than you are."

Hunter had no rebuttal for that. "We'll be in touch."

He walked away, feeling the barbs of her pointed gaze on his back. He wished his conversation with her had gone better, but he wasn't at liberty to share details of his investigation. And he wished Clay had been more forthcoming as well. Clay showing up here said his investigation might be linked to Fletch. Hunter wouldn't give up on getting the guy to talk. He'd take him aside and try to get something out of him. After he checked on Maya.

He opened the driver's door and slid behind the wheel. Maya sat in the passenger seat.

"Anything to suggest one of the bodies is Fletch?" she asked before he got his door closed.

He turned to her. "One of them is the right height, but

141

there was nothing left of the victims to use as an obvious identifier."

She stared at the rubble, and tears filled her eyes.

He didn't want her to focus on the fire. "I'll do a door-to-door canvass and look for witnesses. Maybe they can tell us if Fletch left or not."

"But if he was killed..."

"Even if he died here—which we don't know—we have to figure out who started the fire so we can bring Fletch's killer to justice. But again, we don't know Fletch is dead," he added to try to keep her spirits up.

She gave him a trembling smile. "Thank you for the repeated reminder. I don't know why I'm so set on thinking he's dead."

Hunter wanted to take her hand and comfort her more, but he resisted the urge. "Because that's what most people would do. But we can't think that way or it will skew our actions."

"You're right." She gave a sharp nod. "We'll think he's alive until proven otherwise."

"That's the way to go," he said.

"What's Clay doing here?"

Hunter explained.

"Do you think his informant might have something to do with Fletch? Last I heard Clay was working with the terrorism unit, and with the toxin, we could be looking at a terrorist attack."

Hunter's gut tightened at the confirmation of his earlier thoughts. "I wanted to talk to him again without the detective present. Let's do that now and then knock on some doors." He reached for his handle, but Kelsey waved at them and stepped out of the building, her mouth clamped closed while she marched in their direction.

"I wonder what she wants," Hunter said.

"It doesn't look like good news." Maya's voice trembled. "Not with the look on her face. Do you think she identified Fletch?"

He gestured at Maya's side of the vehicle where Kelsey was fast approaching. "Open your window, and we'll find out."

Maya took a deep breath and pressed the button. The window whirred down, and Kelsey joined them. She leaned inside. "We need to get Grady out here. The victim by the door sustained a gunshot wound."

Near Hunter's SUV, Maya wanted to think about anything but the fire and the potential loss of Fletch. She looked at Clay beside her and then, in the distance, at Sierra. Maya was always taken aback by how different Sierra looked from all of her brothers except Erik. Sierra took after her mother with brown eyes and blond hair, and Clay looked like his father, with nearly black hair and blue eyes. Not surprising as it turned out that his father wasn't Sierra's biological father. Something she'd recently discovered and had to come to grips with. But she had. With God's help.

It struck Maya then. If Sierra could accept such a huge life-altering shock, couldn't Maya let go of her past with Hunter?

Clay planted his hands on his waist, eyeing Hunter. "I don't see how our investigations could be linked. Neither of the names you mentioned are on my radar."

Maya met Clay's intense gaze. "Maybe your informant was going to tell you something about Fletch or Carson or what they were doing in their lab."

"Could be, I suppose." Clay ran a hand over his hair, and his gaze traveled around the space like he wanted to get going. "I'd like to be notified the minute these guys are identified. Is that possible?"

"That would be up to Hunter," Maya said. "We're contracted to work for him."

"Fine by me," Hunter said. "And if you hear our guys' names mentioned on the street, let us know."

"Will do." Clay looked at the crime scene. "I've always wanted to catch an investigation that involved the Veritas Center, but never happened."

"Maybe this is the one, then," Maya said.

"Yeah, maybe. Keep me informed." Clay gave a sharp nod and walked away.

Hunter turned to her. "Do you know much about him?"

"He's a good guy from what I know. And he comes up with really great ideas. Which is why him not thinking these investigations could be related seems odd."

"You think he's playing us?" Hunter's gaze drifted to Clay, who was climbing into his vehicle.

She looked up at Hunter to gain his attention. "I think he might have reasons not to share all of his information with you, just like you didn't share everything with him."

"Yeah, but the big question is, does he have information we need to figure out our investigation?"

"If he does, there's not much you can do about it."

"Actually," Hunter said as he got out his phone, "there is."

He stepped away from her, and she had no idea who he was calling. But that fire that said he was going to succeed here burned in his eyes.

Maya approached Sierra, who was standing by Grady's pickup. He was just climbing out, dressed in his usual black tactical pants and T-shirt. He grabbed a pair of rubber boots from behind his seat and leaned against the vehicle to change from his tactical boots.

"Clay was awfully quiet," Maya said to Sierra.

"He wouldn't say much about why he was here. Figured it was top-secret spy stuff." Sierra laughed.

"Is he still working terrorism?"

Sierra's smile fled. "I don't like it, but yes. I think it's one of the most dangerous areas he could choose to work in. Never know when a terrorist will retaliate, and when they do…" She shrugged as if she couldn't even say the words.

When Maya had been dating Hunter, she worried about him every day. She didn't know how Sierra survived with worry about five brothers putting their lives on the line every day. "Your brothers should give up law enforcement and form a protection or investigation agency. That's where the money is these days, and it's safer. Look how well Blackwell Tactical is doing."

Sierra nodded, as they often used the protection and investigative agency owned by Gage Blackwell out of Cold Harbor. "I'd love that, but I can't imagine my brothers would go for it."

"But why not?" Maya asked. "They'd still get to have all the fun toys, and they would be their own bosses like us. It's the best."

"It is indeed." Sierra's eyes narrowed. "Maybe I'll suggest it to them. We all worry about Aiden still working as an ATF agent and getting hurt after he gave his kidney to Dad, and this might be a solution to that. If I mentioned it that way, maybe they'd at least consider it."

"Why not suggest they partner with us?" Maya was just thinking aloud here, but she was growing to like the idea. "With the situations we've run into lately, we could use them."

Grady tugged on his last boot. "That would be great."

"They could even work from our building," Maya said. "And live in the empty condos. We have plenty of space."

"That would work," Sierra said. "Though I don't know if I want my brothers so close by."

Grady closed his truck door and looked at Sierra. "Now that you and Reed are married, will you want to keep living at the condos?"

"I don't know. Maybe. At least until we have kids." She shook her head. "I can't believe I'm even talking about kids. Do *not* tell my mother. Please. Not a word. Or she'll nag me more than she does already."

Maya smiled with Sierra.

"As much as I love our girl talk..." Grady rolled his eyes. "...it's time to get to work."

Maya swatted her hand at him. "Back to Clay. I think Hunter's going over his head to be read in on Clay's investigation, so things might get tense. Thought you'd like a heads-up on that."

Sierra frowned. "Another reason for my brothers to get out of law enforcement. So I don't have to wonder when and where I'm going to run into them at crime scenes."

Maya squeezed Sierra's shoulder and followed Grady. She really didn't want to see the incinerated victim, but she felt a need to hear firsthand what Grady had to say.

He picked his way inside and squatted by the body. He grimaced, ran a hand over his hair, and looked away for a minute. Maya didn't blame him. She stared at the burn victim, her stomach churning. And if a big strapping guy like Grady, who'd served our country in Delta Force, was unsettled by what he was looking at, she knew she had a right to be too.

The charred bones couldn't be Fletch. It just couldn't be. He was such a wonderful man and didn't deserve to die this way.

What was she thinking? No one deserved such a death.

Why, Father? Why did this have to happen?

146

She asked the questions but she knew there would be no answer. God didn't have to explain anything to her. She didn't need to know His reasons. Just needed to know that He was all powerful, and He was in control.

Kelsey squatted next to Grady and pointed at the victim's spine. "Bullet entered the back and went clean through. I suspect, however, at this level, that it would have severed the spinal cord, and the victim would've been unable to move."

Grady bent even closer, peering at the bones, then he stood and looked around. "If I find the bullet, it's going to be impossible to get a trajectory. I need two points of impact, and the structure it might've lodged in has been destroyed."

"But you think you can find the bullet?" Maya asked.

"I'll give it my best shot, but I can't begin until Sierra and Ainslie finish up." His focus drifted to his fiancée, Ainslie, who was snapping photos in the front yard, and the horror that had been in his eyes evaporated.

Maya had seen every one of her partners find a loving, committed relationship in the last few years, and she was happy for each of them. Even with them all finding a mate, she hadn't thought anything was lacking in her own life until Hunter came back into it. Now, she didn't know what she wanted. Was she happy alone? Did she want someone in her life? Children?

Marriage would surely change her life. She'd have to give up being managing partner, and they'd have to hire someone for the job. Could she let go of control for the business she founded?

Man, that was a big thing she'd never seriously considered. But if she was to take this leap with someone, she had to be all in. Just like she would require of her partner. All in or nothing. And hopefully, this time it would end up with her potential partner being all in with her.

"We'll get out of your way, Kels." Grady linked arms with Maya to walk her out. "You're worried this is Fletch, right?"

She nodded.

Grady grimaced. "If it is, hopefully that gunshot wound killed him before the fire started."

"I can't bear the thought of him being paralyzed by a bullet and a fire blazing around him, knowing he couldn't get out."

"If what the eyewitness said is true about him being helped into the house, maybe he was drugged and out of it."

"True, but I still can't see him using drugs, so we need to try to find the person who brought him here."

"Nick can look for CCTV in the area," Grady suggested.

"And Hunter and I are going door-to-door to ask if other people might've seen something."

Grady looked around. "In this neighborhood, people aren't likely to trust law enforcement."

"Which is why I won't let Hunter say who he is. I'll ask the questions as a concerned friend."

"That might work." He sounded so skeptical that Maya wondered if their canvass of the area was doomed to fail before they even started.

13

Maya sat back and laid her phone on the desk in her lab, the heavy morning rain beating against the windows and keeping temperatures in the seventies today. She never thought she would have to call a dentist to ask for Fletch's dental records, but she'd just done so, and tears wetted her eyes.

She laid her head on the desk and let them flow. Kelsey had worked all night at the fire scene, and it wouldn't be long before she arrived at the lab with the bones and could compare the dental X-rays to the skulls she'd recovered at the fire.

Would one of them be Fletch?

Maya's tears intensified, and she cried like a wounded child, bawling her eyes out. She really wasn't much of a crier, but since the tears had started falling last night, it seemed like she couldn't control them when they pressed against her eyes for release.

She grabbed a tissue and blew her nose. Grabbed another one and dabbed her eyes. She must look a mess. Which was why she'd insisted on dropping Hunter at Nick's lab to keep reviewing hard drives and making the call in private.

She'd hoped Hunter would have leads to go on from their neighborhood canvass last night, but it had been a bust. The doors that did open were more often than not slammed in their faces. No one was upset about the house burning down. In fact, most were pleased they wouldn't have drug users coming and going and bringing crime with them. Some of the neighbors were so blinded by their hatred of these drug users that they thought the occupants got what they deserved.

Maya sniffled and sat back. She couldn't imagine what it would be like to live in the challenges of the world without faith. To actually believe people deserved to die a horrific death. To not have God to direct their ways.

But you do the same thing. The thought came out of nowhere. *You ignore God when it comes to Hunter.*

She sat straight up, her heart starting to beat hard.

What did that make her? How was she letting her hurt blind her too?

She said she'd put it aside. Given it to God, but she hadn't. Not fully. She was still holding her pain against Hunter. Condemning him just like these neighbors were doing to the drug users. Sure, she wasn't condemning Hunter to death, but she wasn't letting him move beyond his past. The people in the drug house deserved a second chance at life, and Hunter deserved a second chance at happiness too. If she kept him down, he wouldn't forgive himself. Never pursue the happiness he deserved, be it with her or someone else.

She started to get up to go tell him about her discovery when her lab door opened.

Sierra poked her head in. "Got a minute for some results?"

"Of course." Maya took a long breath and let it out.

"You've been crying." Sierra crossed the room. "What's wrong? I mean other than the investigation."

She told Sierra about getting the dental records.

"And then I got to thinking about Hunter," Maya added, surprising herself. She hadn't told anybody about her relationship with Hunter. But Sierra was the perfect person to discuss it with. She'd had to get through a lot with her father to be able to open her heart to Reed, and she might be able to help.

"You two had a thing once, right?" Sierra dropped onto a stool.

Maya gave her friend a quick rundown of her relationship and breakup with Hunter. "I just realized I needed to stop holding it against him. But then I don't know what to do because I'm still attracted to him, and he hasn't changed. I don't want to get hurt again."

"That's rough." Sierra bit her lip. "The heart wants what the heart wants. I know that from Reed. As much as I didn't want to fall for him—did everything not to—I still did. I'm glad now, but at the time it was awful."

"I don't see Hunter ever changing his mind, and I'm spending so much time with him that I have to be careful."

"Can you keep working this investigation without him?"

"Not really," Maya said. "I mean, I can do some things, but like this fire—I could never have gotten on scene without a law enforcement connection."

"Then I say pray about it and go with what you think God would want you to do." Sierra took Maya's hand. "God's got this and everything. I feel like He brought the two of you together for a reason."

"You could be right, but the reason could simply be for me to let go of how Hunter hurt me so I can start dating again. Dating someone else."

"Could be. But your instincts about Hunter could be right. Only time will tell." She squeezed Maya's hand.

Maya waved it in the air. "Enough of this. What did you come to tell me?"

"The fingerprint test for Carson was positive for cocaine."

"So it's official. He did have the drugs in his system." Maya shook her head. "I still don't see him as a user, so it seems more likely that someone made him snort it."

"But why, when your tests confirmed he was also exposed to the toxin through the aerosol release?"

"This could be about someone wanting to discredit Carson and Fletch," Maya suggested. "The cocaine could've been used to make it look like Carson was into drugs and got sloppy. Accidentally released the toxin and died from it."

"That would discredit him for sure."

Maya shook her head. "But it doesn't explain why the cocaine was cut with the biotoxin. That makes no sense in this theory. What else did you find?"

"All the prints on the safe belonged to Fletch."

"Doesn't mean that Fletch wasn't forced to open it by someone else who wanted access to the contents."

"But wouldn't they take the cash too? I mean, if I was this person and got access to the safe, once I saw the stack of money, I'd grab it no matter my reason for wanting the safe open. So maybe our killer didn't need what was in the safe."

"Maybe not," Maya said. "If they kidnapped Fletch, and he had all they'd need in his head, they wouldn't need formulas or data."

"That makes sense." Sierra narrowed her eyes. "Most of the other prints from the lab and office belonged to Carson and Fletch. Plus a few of yours. There was one other set that didn't return a match in AFIS."

Maya was familiar with the FBI's Automated Fingerprint

Identification System as Sierra used it all the time. "It's interesting that you found an outsider's prints in the lab itself. Fletch has often told me that he doesn't let anyone in there but Carson and me. And it's odd too. I'd think whoever released the toxin wore protective gear so they wouldn't leave prints."

Sierra's forehead creased. "That *is* odd, but the prints don't lie. I only recovered one set, and it was on the main lab table. Full set of prints like the person was leaning his or her hands on the metal. Also, the hard drives and papers had both Fletch's and Carson's prints. Doesn't mean Carson accessed the safe, but he probably knew what was in there."

"It would make sense that he handled the drives and maybe even the contract at some point, right?"

Sierra nodded. "I also lifted eight prints from the front door and handle. All but two of them tracked back to you, Carson, and Fletch. The other two didn't return an AFIS match, but one of them matched the unknown print in the lab."

"So we potentially have at least two people—other than myself, Fletch, and Carson—who entered the building," Maya clarified.

"Yes." Sierra looked away for a minute then met Maya's gaze head-on. "Have you stopped to consider that Fletch might have released the toxin?"

Maya crossed her arms. "He wouldn't do that. Ever."

"Don't take this the wrong way, but he's so eccentric. Could he have snapped and done something like this?"

Maya shook her head. "You don't know him like I do. He's innocent. I guarantee it."

"Okay, I trust your assessment, but you should know we recovered Fletch's prints from the canoe. No other prints."

"So Fletch likely left the island via canoe. But again, if

anyone accompanied him, they could've worn gloves. And if it's his canoe, the prints could be from the past."

"Yes." Sierra stood. "I need to get back to processing the evidence from the lab and the fire. I'll let you know what we find."

"Thanks for making this a priority and for trusting my judgment."

"You'd do the same for me."

"I would," Maya said and watched her partner walk out the door and couldn't stop thinking about what Sierra had said about Fletch. Was Maya wrong, believing the best of her friend when he could have gone over the edge?

No. No. Maya was certain he hadn't released the toxin and tied Carson up to die.

She tried to read her email but couldn't concentrate, so she pushed back her chair and headed for Nick's lab. She stepped inside. Hunter looked up from the nearest computer and smiled at her.

Prior to her conversation with Sierra, Maya would have frowned at him, but instead, she smiled back, letting him know in no uncertain terms that she was happy to see him too. A flash of happiness lit his eyes, and he arched a brow. His joy at seeing her radiated through her body.

"You two need a moment alone?" Nick smirked.

Piper socked his arm. "Talk about pointing out something we could be accused of at any given time."

"You're right." A sheepish look erased Nick's smirk.

Maya stepped toward the computers. "Any word on the subpoena yet?"

Piper shook her head. "If I don't hear back from the judge's clerk in an hour, I'll give them a call."

"I have a bit of news to report." Maya shared the information she'd just received from Sierra, and they held a similar discussion to the one she and Sierra had held.

"It's all speculation," Maya said. "We need to find concrete evidence."

"We've made some progress in reviewing Fletch's files." Hunter pulled out the chair next to him and patted the seat. "Nothing that helps, though. The checklist will show you where to start."

Maya kept her gaze on his for a long moment while Piper and Nick were busy. She gave Hunter another smile but suddenly felt awkward displaying her feelings, so she scooted in her chair and logged onto the network. She opened the next file which contained a daily backup. As a scientist herself, she hoped to find something to move them in the right direction.

She opened email files dated years ago, when Rudy Roper was Fletch's assistant. He'd only worked for Fletch for a few months, and Maya had forgotten all about him.

"This might be something." She looked at Hunter. "I totally forgot about Fletch's former assistant. Name's Rudy Roper. Maybe we should consider him. He left a year or so ago. Said he was moving on for a better opportunity. Our community is small, and it didn't take long for word to get out that his claims about the new job weren't true. Fletch said that Rudy's new position was far less autonomous, and he did lower-level research."

"So why did he really leave?" Hunter slid back and propped a leg on his knee, giving her his undivided attention.

She had to work hard to ignore his focus and keep her mind on her work. "Fletch thought it was for more money, but I can't be sure. Fletch was often closemouthed about his work, and I might not know the whole situation."

"Higher pay isn't much of a motive for murder," Piper said. "Tons of people leave their jobs for more money."

"Agreed." Maya swiveled to face Piper. "But if Rudy's

motivated by money, he could've somehow learned about the toxin and planned to sell it."

Piper cocked her head. "Then why release it?"

Nick looked at her. "Maybe as a test to prove it works, and maybe he filmed the exposure and Carson's death."

A deep frown marred Piper's face. "That's extremely cruel. Did you know Roper? Was he capable of something like this?"

Was he? Maya thought about the man. "I didn't know him well enough to say. He was a character who often pushed Fletch to let him do more. That caused some tension, but he wasn't likely holding a grudge. I could be wrong, though and he might be worth looking into."

Hunter met her gaze. "So you think it's possible that he could've done something this cruel?"

She shrugged. "Who knows what a person is capable of?"

Piper considered Maya, her mouth tight. "As a former lab assistant, he has full knowledge of how the lab operates and their security. He might even have the entrance password, if Fletch was lax about changing it."

"With his paranoia, I'm guessing he'd be on top of that," Hunter said.

"Never know." Nick gave Hunter a grim look. "If I go back to the lab, I can log into the system to see if it was changed after Roper left."

Piper's eyes narrowed, her gaze pinned to Nick. "And you're willing to risk going back there?"

Nick faced her and took her hand. "I have to, honey. You know that, right?"

"I do." She kept her gaze riveted to her future husband. "But I don't like it. Not at all."

Maya glanced at Hunter to try to determine what he was thinking. He shared a look she couldn't read. Was he thinking about how he would feel if she were the one going back to the lab? Or was he thinking about Piper and Nick? She just couldn't tell.

"You'd do it if you were in my shoes," Nick said, drawing Maya's attention again.

Piper nodded. "I would."

Nick squeezed her hand and released it to look at Hunter. "We need to talk to this guy."

"Not yet." Hunter's firm tone brooked no argument. "Not when we don't have anything other than an unsubstantiated theory. We have nothing to ask him at this point, and if he is our guy, we risk spooking him. Better to wait until we at least run a background check on him."

"I'm on it." Nick swiveled back to his monitor. "I have a standard algorithm that I just need to plug a few variables into, and I can search the drives from the safe for any mention of this guy."

"Hurry." Maya packed her tone with a sense of urgency. "This could be the lead we've been looking for."

Hunter wanted to tap his foot. To find a way to make Nick and his algorithm work faster. Something, anything, that would give them the lead they so desperately needed.

"Okay." Nick leaned back and ran his hands through his hair. "Got a couple of emails here between Fletch and Roper. One from Roper asking if he could come over to the lab. Seemed he had a proposition for Fletch."

"Did Fletch agree to let him visit?" Maya slid her chair closer to Nick and looked up at his screen.

"No, but there's a follow-up email saying that Roper went anyway, and Carson let him in."

"When was this?" Hunter asked.

"Four months ago, which was after Fletch was awarded the research grant."

Maya paused as if pondering the news. "Rudy might know enough about grants to be able to fake the paperwork."

Hunter nodded. "Still, we're just speculating again."

"We can still get eyes on him, though." Piper perked up. "I'll do it. I'd be glad for a break from these files, even if it *is* sitting in a car."

"I can come with you." Nick grinned at her.

Hunter looked at Nick. "You were going to go to the island, right? And I was hoping you'd do a deep dive on Roper, including his financial situation."

"Yeah, sure." Nick looked disappointed at not getting to go on the stakeout but rested his hands over his keyboard.

"Since we have unknown prints from the lab, we need to figure out how to recover Roper's prints without him knowing it," Piper suggested. "That could rule him out or give us leverage when interviewing him."

"Maybe you could get something when you surveil him," Hunter suggested.

Piper's phone dinged, and she pumped her fist up. "Yes! Finally. We have the subpoena for Peggy."

"Print it, and I'll go serve it." Hunter looked at Maya. "I figure the subpoena is going to make her mad, so you should come with me since she seemed to be more amenable to talking to you."

"Glad to go," Maya said enthusiastically.

He grabbed the subpoena from the printer and opened the door for Maya.

In the car, she looked at him. "How can it take so long to get warrants and subpoenas?"

He merged into traffic. "That's a long discussion, but often it has to do with having enough probable cause. Then finding an available judge and impressing a sense of urgency on their clerk so they can get it before the judge. And on and on."

She shook her head. "I appreciate our legal system, but sometimes it overcomplicates things. Especially when it comes to acting quickly at times like this."

He nodded and turned his attention to the drive under drizzly skies. He found a space right in front of the business and looked at Maya as he pulled the key from the ignition. "Ready to do this?"

"Am I ever." She opened her door and slid out, meeting him at the front door.

He pulled it open, releasing that same lavender smell he'd noticed on their last visit. Peggy was behind the counter again, today wearing a flowery blouse and long skirt. She looked up and instead of the frown Hunter expected, she looked happy to see them. "I left Greg a message to call you. Has he called?"

"No," Hunter said. "Why do you ask?"

"He didn't come into work last night or today, and he's not answering his phone." Desperation raised her voice.

Hunter shared a worried look with Maya. "Has he ever done this before?"

"No. He's very dependable. I called his roommate. He said Greg told him he was going to some dude's island."

"Island?" Maya asked. "When was that?"

"He wasn't positive but thought it was Monday."

Something sounded odd to Hunter. "Wasn't the roommate worried when Greg didn't come home all this time?"

"No, because he was on vacation." She let out a breath that went on and on. "Do you know about this island he's talking about?"

"Likely," Hunter said. "Are you willing to give me Greg's

last name and phone number now so I can get a search going for him?"

"Uzzell." She added his phone number.

Hunter tapped the information into a notes' app on his phone. "Is there anything else you can tell us about him that might help us find him?"

Peggy shook her head. "I wish I would've given you his information the first time and you could already be looking for him."

"You did what you thought was best." Maya offered Peggy a comforting smile.

"If he comes in or you hear from him, call me right away," Hunter said.

"Sure. Sure." Peggy clutched her hands together. "And you do the same thing."

"Of course." He stepped outside and dialed Greg. The call went straight to voicemail.

He looked at Maya. "Peggy's right. Greg's not answering."

"I can text Nick with Greg's full name, and he should be able to find more information about him."

"And I'll get a warrant for his phone records and have it pinged."

He opened the SUV door for her, and after getting inside, she took out her phone and started her text while Hunter called Adair to place the request and also to ask him to forward Greg's driver's license information.

Hunter started the vehicle. "Adair promised to handle it."

"How long will that take, do you think?"

"He'll try going straight to the phone company and hope to find someone who will cooperate without a warrant."

"Is that likely?"

"It can happen."

"But it didn't for Fletch."

"No, it didn't."

Maya fell silent for the rest of the drive, and Hunter had to assume she was wondering where Fletch and Greg might be.

Hunter parked out front of the center, and Maya's phone buzzed. She glanced at the text then looked at Hunter. "Clay's here to talk to you."

Clay. Not good. "Could be because I stepped on his toes about being read in on his investigation. Or maybe he's discovered that our investigations are related."

Hunter opened the SUV door for her. They walked toward the building, and he directed his focus at her. "If Clay is here to read me in on his investigation, you know that you can't sit in on the meeting, right?"

Maya nodded, "But I'll have to get someone to remain outside the room since both of you need an escort while in the building."

"That must get tiring when you know the people you're escorting are on the up-and-up." Hunter pulled open the door to the building.

She frowned. "It's more annoying that I can't know what Clay's about to tell you."

"You know I'd include you if I could."

"I know." She stepped into the lobby that always smelled like calming vanilla.

Clay wasn't calm though. He was dressed in tactical clothing looking fierce, a security badge hanging around his neck, and a scowl on his face as he marched over to them.

He eyed Hunter. "I'm here to read you in, but I don't much appreciate you going over my head to DHS."

Hunter folded his arms over his chest and widened his stance. "I have to do what's right for my investigation. Admit it. You'd have done the same thing."

Clay planted his hands on his hips. "Doesn't make this any better."

Maya didn't want them to argue in the lobby. Better to do it in private or not at all. "Why don't we go to the conference room?"

Maya didn't wait for them to agree but led Hunter to the desk to get a pass then escorted the pair to the glass-walled room just down the hall. She opened the door and stood back. "I'll be right outside unless I can find someone to relieve me."

Hunter stepped to the door and mouthed, "Sorry."

She shrugged, and got out her phone as if she wasn't bothered by being left out of the conversation, but he knew she was curious.

In the room, Clay dropped into a chair and fisted his hands on the table. "You could've just come to me."

"And what?" Hunter asked, making sure the door closed behind him. "You would've laid all of your cards on the table?"

"You know I wouldn't have."

"Exactly. So go ahead and tell me about your investigation," Hunter said to move them along instead of continuing to argue about how they got to this point.

Clay blew out a breath, and Hunter glanced out the window at Maya. She wasn't the kind of person who willingly waited on anyone. She was a take-action kind of woman, and Hunter loved that about her. Matched his personality so well. He felt bad for leaving her out there. She glanced up from her phone, and he gave her an encouraging smile.

She looked like she was going to roll her eyes, but Kelsey stepped into the hallway, drawing her attention.

Hunter sat forward, trying to read Kelsey's lips, but Maya blocked her partner's face.

Had Kelsey identified the victims? If so, Hunter wanted to know about it. Kelsey suddenly took off for the elevator, and Maya turned back, tapping her watch.

She clearly wanted him to hurry up. Even if she didn't, he'd like to know what Kelsey had to say. He looked back at Clay, who was watching him. Hunter twirled his finger, telling Clay to get started.

"Here it is in a nutshell." Clay leaned forward. "We've had intel that a weapon of mass destruction is going to be used in Oregon soon. No details on the weapon. That's what I was supposed to get from my informant who's gone missing."

Hunter's heart dropped at the news of the weapon. Was the toxin part of that plan? Only one person could tell them. The missing informant. "You think your informant died in the fire?"

"I do."

"Do you have dental records for your guy?"

He gave a sharp nod. "Emailed them to Kelsey about an hour ago."

Could that be what Kelsey was talking to Maya about? He'd find out soon enough. "Tell me about your informant."

"Guy's name is Jason Vernon." Clay leaned his chair back. "He's this weird combination of a guy. He's into drugs. Makes him unreliable, but it also puts him in places to keep his ear to the ground and hear things, you know? He needs cash for his habit and knows if he feeds me bad intel I'll stop using him. So I can't count on him to show up all the time, but I can count on his intel. Lately he's started selling for one of the big cartels. Not street-level sales, but larger quantities to dealers. That somehow put him in contact with a guy in the Muslim community who's active in Al Qaeda."

Terrorists? Weapon of mass destruction? Hunter's gut churned. He swallowed hard to keep his emotions from showing. "And you think they might be the ones behind the plans to use a WMD?"

Clay gave a resigned nod. "I doubt our investigations are linked. I mean, you're not dealing with such a weapon, are you?"

"My investigation is classified," Hunter said. "So—"

"No way." Clay snapped his chair forward. "After going above my head, you're going to hold out on me?"

"No, I was going to say this intel doesn't leave this room."

Clay let out a long breath. "Good. Good. Got it."

Hunter explained about the toxin, and that right now, Fletch's former assistant was under scrutiny. "We have no idea if Roper is involved or not. Nick is doing a background check on him, and Piper has him under surveillance. If they've unearthed anything, we'll move on him."

Clay pinned his narrowed gaze on Hunter. "I want in on the arrest."

"I can't authorize that."

"Then get it authorized." Clay's gaze tightened, reaching laser focus. "He might've killed my informant in that fire, and I want to take him down."

Despite his adamant look, Hunter wasn't eager to capitulate. "Tell you what. Let's go see if Kelsey has identified the victims. If your informant is one of them, and we go for Roper, I'll get approval for you to join us."

Clay shot to his feet. "Don't just sit there. This news could break both of our investigations wide open."

14

Maya glanced back at the two men in the stairwell and wished she was alone. If when they got down to Kelsey's lab Maya learned that Fletch had died in the fire, she knew she would fall apart and didn't want to do so in front of Clay. But she couldn't very well deny them the information that their investigations needed.

Correction—that Hunter's investigation needed. She had no idea what Clay was working on. And wished she'd been included in their meeting. She had top clearance with the Feds to work sensitive investigations, but that didn't mean she had cause to be read in here.

At the basement, she tugged open the stairwell door. "Last door on the left."

In the hallway, Clay looked around. "I don't know how Kelsey works in a basement all day. It would drive me crazy."

"*That's* what would drive you crazy?" Hunter glanced back at Clay. "I can't imagine doing her job at all."

"Well, yeah, but that's a given, right?" Clay asked. "Not many people want to deal with bodies that have decomposed to the level that requires Kelsey's involvement."

Maya agreed, but she wasn't going to continue the conversation as it just reminded her of how Fletch might've died. She stepped past the men and pressed her fingers on the keypad for the osteology lab entrance. The door popped open, emitting the hint of an odor that Maya knew was coming from the inner lab, where Kelsey boiled bones in large pots to clean them. Maybe today the pots were filled with Fletch's bones.

That thought made her stomach roil, and she stepped into the cool lab. It didn't help calm her to see three stainless steel tables with bones laid out in anatomically correct order. Not all the bones were present for each person, and Maya had to wonder if Kelsey hadn't been able to recover them or if they were in the big vats in the next room.

Kelsey stood at the far table and looked up. She wore a white lab coat over a paisley dress with a full skirt and a plastic apron over that. "Oh, good. You brought Clay. Saves me having to call you."

He stepped over to her, looking kind of queasy. "Whatcha got?"

"Two males." She gestured at the far tables then looked down at the one nearest her. "One female."

"Have you identified them?" Hunter asked, lingering near the door.

"I have an ID for one of the men." She yanked off her gloves. "The other two, I have no idea on their identity at this point."

"And?" Maya asked and held her breath.

Kelsey smiled. "Your friend Fletch isn't the man I've identified."

Maya let out a breath, nearly sagging to the floor. She grabbed the edge of a table. "You're certain."

"Positive. His dental records aren't a match."

"Is there a match to my informant?" Clay asked.

Kelsey turned toward Clay. "I'm sorry, but yes. The body on the far table is Jason Vernon. He's the person who sustained the gunshot wound."

Clay gave a sharp nod but swallowed hard. He took a few deep breaths and looked at Hunter. "Get me in on your raid if you go for Roper."

Hunter looked at Clay, and something passed between them that looked like acceptance.

"I'll make sure it happens," Hunter said.

Maya was glad the two of them seemed to have resolved their differences, but she had to wonder how Clay's investigation was linked to theirs. She would press Hunter for information when they were alone.

For now, she would get answers from Kelsey. "Do you have any leads on the other two victims?"

"No." Kelsey smoothed a hand over her curly black hair. "The only way to ID them is DNA and dental records. DNA has likely been destroyed in the fire, but Emory will try that, of course. It'll likely take someone coming forward who thinks a family member or friend died in the fire to provide dental records. That might never happen."

"Because this is a crack house and the people hanging out there might have isolated themselves from others and their family," Clay clarified.

Kelsey nodded.

Maya sighed. "I wish there was something we could do. There are parents out there whose son or daughter has died, and they don't know about it."

"Welcome to my world." A sad resignation darkened Kelsey's unique aqua-green eyes. "This happens way too often, and it breaks my heart."

Maya had known that this was what Kelsey faced all the time—of course she had—but today it hit home, and Maya admired Kelsey all the more for the work she did. "You're a good person, Kelsey. A very good person."

Kelsey waved a hand. "I'm just doing my job."

"But what a tough job you have." Maya squeezed Kelsey's hand.

Hunter tipped his head at the door. "Let's go see if Nick has found anything on Roper that we can use."

"Thanks for your speedy work." Maya smiled at Kelsey then led the two men down the hall to the elevator. Inside the elevator, Hunter took his usual casual stance against the wall.

Clay faced him. "Do you think a full-on raid will be necessary at Roper's place?"

Hunter shrugged. "Again. It all depends on what Nick locates or if we need to get prints first to satisfy a no-knock warrant."

"Is that what it sounds like?" Maya asked. "You can break down a door and not notify the guy first?"

Hunter nodded, and Clay looked like he was jonesing to get after Roper. Maya had the same feeling but for a different reason. Rudy could destroy evidence, and when dealing with a biotoxin, they had to act as quickly as possible. Plus, he could be holding Fletch captive.

They stepped down the hallway to Nick's smaller lab and entered. He turned to look at them from the same chair where they'd left him.

"You know Clay?" Maya asked.

"Sierra's brother, right?" Nick asked. "And if I remember right, she said you're the big idea guy in the family. Sometimes too big."

"Sounds like something she'd say." Clay chuckled and shook hands with Piper then Nick. "And speaking of big, I heard you're the big-headed guy on the Veritas team."

"Touché." Nick grinned.

Hunter moved into the room and rested against the counter across from the computers. "Clay's working an investigation that might be connected to ours. So go ahead and talk freely in front of him."

"What's your investigation about?" Nick asked.

"All I can say is I'm working terrorism."

Nick narrowed his eyes. "So we have a deadly toxin and you work terrorism. Tells me the toxin might be used as a weapon."

Clay took a wide-legged stance and rested his hands on his hips. "Something like that."

Nick gritted his teeth. "If it helps, I was able to remotely prove that Fletch had changed the lock combination at the lab, so Roper didn't have access. I also just learned that he's up to his eyeballs in debt but recently began depositing cash each week into his account just under the Fed's reporting threshold of ten grand."

Hunter let out a low whistle. "Any sign of where the money's coming from?"

Nick shook his head.

"Still, it's not anywhere near enough money for selling the toxin." Maya settled in the chair next to Nick. "That would be a huge number and would draw the Fed's interest so it would likely come via wire transfer to a foreign account."

"Maybe he hid the money in offshore," Clay said.

"Seriously, dude. You should know there's no hiding things online from me." Nick laughed.

Clay rolled his eyes. "I forgot I was talking to the wonder guy."

Maya loved that Nick could be lighthearted most of the time, but she was desperate to locate Fletch and didn't want to waste time joking. "Did you find anything else of interest?"

"Yeah, and so did Piper." Nick smiled, likely at the thought of his fiancée. "She said he's carrying. Handgun in a holster at his waist. Not something the average citizen needs to do."

"So he's armed and dangerous," Maya said, thinking about Hunter bursting into the guy's house and being shot.

"And you?" Clay asked. "What else did you find?"

Nick leaned back in his chair and propped his hands behind his head. "Roper has an account on the dark web. Looks like he's been trying to get a website set up. No clue on what for at this point, but there's no reason to be active there unless you're up to no good."

Maya might not be a computer person, but she knew the dark web was a place on the internet that had to be accessed by a special browser and where criminals did business because it provided anonymity.

Clay turned to stare at Hunter. "So, are you going to go after him?"

"It would still be better for the warrant if we had his prints and they matched the ones lifted at the lab, but the dark web account and the fact that he's carrying could help us get a warrant. Let me run it up the flagpole." Hunter dug out his phone and tapped the screen. He lifted it to his ear and stared at the floor.

Maya looked at Nick. "Anything else of interest?"

"Possibly. Roper lost the job he left Fletch's lab to take. He's been unemployed for months, which could be the reason for his debts. But I haven't ruled out the usual causes like gambling and drug abuse. Still working on that."

Maya found all of this interesting, but... "If he does have the toxin, could he have set up the spoofed contract, and how would he have found out about the toxin in the first place?"

Clay raised an eyebrow, looking so much like Sierra that

it was uncanny. "The email said he went to the lab. Maybe he saw it firsthand."

Maya leaned her chair back so she didn't have to crane her neck to see him. "I can't see Fletch being careless enough to share anything about the toxin, but if Carson let Rudy in, and Fletch was working on the toxin, he would be using his biocontainment cabinet, so that might've raised Rudy's interest. And I suppose if Fletch stepped out of the room, Carson might've let it slip."

Clay's eyes glinted. "Do you really think that's possible?"

She shrugged. "Rudy could've started to complain about when he worked with Fletch to get Carson on his side. Then, once he established a rapport with Carson, Rudy might've gotten Carson to tell him what they were working on."

"That makes sense," Nick said.

Clay firmed his stance. "Even more reason to bust this guy's door down."

"I'm just getting started on Uzzell," Nick said. "I'll let you know when I have anything on that."

"Uzzell?" Clay asked.

Maya explained. "It's odd that he seems to be missing too, but then he might be fine."

She looked at Hunter to see how his call was going. He'd taken a steady stance, his hand clamped on the back of his neck, and he continued to look down at the floor. She'd been so focused on finding the toxin and Fletch that she hadn't thought about the weight Hunter was carrying on his shoulders. His shoulders might be broad, but that didn't mean he didn't bend under extreme pressure like this.

"I'll get the information to you the minute we hang up," he said, then listened a moment. "I don't like it, but I get it."

He shoved his phone into his pocket and turned, a deep frown marring his handsome face.

She didn't like the look of that at all. "Everything okay?"

He gave a sharp nod. "I need to send the information to my supervisor, and he'll try for a warrant. He thinks, under normal circumstances, it would be denied, but due to exigent circumstances with the toxin, we have a chance."

"So why the frown?" she asked.

"He wasn't real encouraging about the chance of our success in securing the warrant." He gritted his teeth.

"Need any help with getting it?" Clay asked.

Hunter shook his head. "And by the way, my supervisor is putting an assault team on standby for Roper, and you're approved to join. They'll meet us at a nearby grocery store parking lot to review the plan."

"Good." Clay gave a serious nod. "I want this guy alive. If he started this house fire, I want to look him in the eye and make sure he pays for what he did to these victims."

Maya watched Hunter as he talked with the FBI assault team on a video call while Clay continued to hover over Hunter's shoulder. She appreciated that Hunter had taken the time to plan and to instruct the rest of the team on items to bring to the pre-raid party, which they were calling the meetup in the parking lot.

Maya could easily imagine their meeting. The agents dressed in tactical gear, their focus intense and adrenaline making them jumpy. Piper holding her own with all of the testosterone in the air from the assault team.

And Maya here waiting. Hoping. Praying. That no one got hurt. That they found Fletch at Rudy's house alive and well. That they recovered any missing toxin and the investigation would be over. Life could go back to normal.

Or could it? She didn't know. Not after spending time

with Hunter again. One thing was for sure. She now knew she wanted more to life now than her work. More than managing this business and running her lab. She still wanted her work. Of course she did. But a relationship was now something she could see for herself. A home. A family. A long-term commitment.

But who with? Hunter? Maybe. Sure, just the thought of losing him on this op told her how much she still loved him, but he had to change. To learn to want the same thing bad enough to make a change. To let God work in his life and give up control.

She closed her eyes and prayed. Eagerly. Enthusiastically. With her whole heart, pouring her desires out to God.

She looked up, half expecting a change in Hunter right there. Like God might've flicked him on the head and said *Get with the program*, and that would be all it took. She knew that was wrong. That Hunter had to first embrace the desire to change, which she didn't think he really had. He was still so hurt from all of his losses that his poor heart was torn into bits. He had a Humpty-Dumpty heart, and God needed to put it back together again.

Please.

"We'll be there in thirty." Hunter closed the video call and pushed his chair back.

Clay jumped out of the way. "I need to make a quick call, and then I'm ready to roll."

He stepped to the other side of the room, and Maya saw the break as an opportunity to share some things with Hunter, but not in front of Clay.

She crossed her lab to him. "Can I talk to you in the hallway?"

He lifted a shoulder. "I'm not going to change my mind about you coming along."

"It's not about that." She opened the door and waited for him to join her.

His forehead furrowed. "What is it?"

She let the door close and stepped closer to him. "I just wanted to tell you to be careful."

He tilted his head, his eyebrows raising. "That goes without saying."

"Does it?" She held his gaze.

He didn't respond.

"I know you can't share what Clay is working on, but it's a big deal, right?"

He nodded.

"You're working so hard to resolve this investigation that it seems like now that the toxin has been confirmed that our worst fears might come true, and I don't want you to take any chances. I couldn't bear to lose you."

"You..." He looked up and shook his head. "You know nothing has changed for me, right?"

"I'm praying it will." She wouldn't hold back now, not when he was headed into danger. "I just want you to know I'm no longer carrying any hurt for the way you ended things, and I'm here. Waiting."

His mouth fell open, and he eyed her. "You're serious? You would give us a second chance?"

She nodded.

"I..." He moved closer and tenderly touched the side of her face. "I love you, sweetheart. You know that. But I can't promise anything."

She leaned into his hand. "I know. I want a husband and a family. I know that now. You helped me see that. So I'm going to go after it."

"In the usual Maya way. Attack it full force." He smiled fondly at her.

She chuckled. "I guess I will. When I want something, I go out and get it."

"And if you can't have the something you want?"

"Then I reevaluate and choose again."

He didn't say anything for the longest time. "What you're saying is that, if I can't commit, you're going to move on."

It sounded so harsh when he said it, but... "It's not that simple, but yeah, that's it in a nutshell."

He closed his eyes for a long moment. "Then let's hope I can change because the thought of you with another man tears me up inside."

"Don't think about that now. I'm not ready to move on. Not by a long shot." She lifted his hand and kissed it. "I love you too, Hunter. Now, go bring in our suspect, and let's end this investigation."

He drew her in close and clasped his arms around her back. "No matter what happens, never doubt my love for you. Never."

15

Hunter fastened the last Velcro strap on his body armor and grabbed his rifle. He could count on his fingers the number of times he'd had to carry a rifle in his career. People often thought that FBI agents went busting down doors all the time when, in fact, a lot of the job was sitting at a desk doing paperwork. Or sitting in a vehicle surveilling someone for days on end. He sure didn't see the kind of action they portrayed in books, movies, and TV shows. Neither did his fellow agents suiting up alongside him. So when an op like this one to bring Roper in came up, the other agents were more than happy to get in on it.

He looked at his team. Clay, Piper, and three experienced agents chosen by Adair. Their vests and rifles might be overkill, but they needed to be safe. They'd secured a no-knock warrant, meaning they could bust down the door without announcing themselves.

Normally, they'd watch this guy for longer, get more of a feel for what he was up to, but with a deadly toxin potentially in the hands of others, they had no time to waste.

"Roper is armed, and we need to be careful. Let's not

turn this into a bloodbath." Hunter ran his gaze over the others. "Any questions?"

"No questions," Clay said. "I want this guy alive. So don't get trigger happy." He ran his gaze around the group and received don't-tell-us-how-to-do-our-job stares in return.

"Keep that in mind," Hunter said. "But take no chances with your own life to make that happen. Understood?"

The others nodded.

"Then we're a go." He spun, marched down the street and up to the ranch house with chipping blue paint above a skirt of red brick. A light shone from the family room picture window, and Roper's older model Buick sat in the driveway. A TV played loudly enough for them to hear a McDonald's commercial. Hunter hoped Roper was relaxing in front of the TV and would be so shocked by them breaking down his door that this would be an easy takedown.

Hunter looked over his shoulder at the team stacking behind him. He gestured for Clay to come forward and break down the door.

Clay hefted the battering ram and slammed it into the wood. It shattered and pushed open. Clay dropped the ram and lifted his rifle.

"FBI," Hunter shouted and charged into a minuscule entryway that led to an empty family room.

"Clear," Hunter called out and moved into a hallway. He glanced both ways.

A man carrying a can of beer and bag of chips stepped toward them from the left. "Who are—"

"FBI, down on the floor!" Hunter trained his rifle on the guy. "Face down."

"But I—"

"Down. Down. Down," they all called out.

He dropped to his knees, flashed Hunter a terrified look,

then went prone on the wood floor, spilling the beer and chips around him.

"Cuff him," Hunter said to Clay.

Clay stepped through the beer and crunched over the chips.

Hunter kept his rifle trained on Roper while Clay snapped on cuffs.

"Ouch," Roper whined. "Not so tight."

Hunter could see Clay wanted to fire off a retort but held back. Once Roper was cuffed, Clay searched him and removed his gun. Clay looked up, his face tight with rage.

"I've got him." Hunter gestured with his rifle. "Clear the rest of the house."

Clay looked like he wanted to stay. Like he wanted to argue. But he nodded instead. He tucked the gun in his waistband and led the others down the hall to where Hunter suspected the bedrooms were located.

"What's going on?" Roper asked. "Why are you here?"

Hunter didn't answer him. He wouldn't talk to the man until a witness was by Hunter's side to hear anything Roper said.

Footfalls sounded from each room, and Clay called out clear. "No sign of Fletch or our target item."

"Fletch?" Roper asked. "Does this have something to do with him?"

Again Hunter remained silent and listened to the team moving through the kitchen and dining room.

"Clear." Clay shouted and came back into the hallway shaking his head.

"Let's get this guy into the family room," Hunter said.

Clay shouldered his rifle and jerked Roper to his feet then directed him into the next room and onto an easy chair covered in a plaid fabric. "We still have the garage to clear."

"There's nothing out there," Roper said quickly.

Too quickly, which meant there was *indeed* something out there, and Hunter was going to find out what that something was.

≈

Maya paced her lab. Back and forth. Back and forth. Her work outside of their search to find Fletch, was starting to pile up, and she should be running some tests. Sure, she had capable lab assistants, and she'd assigned most of the tasks to them, but she still had to sign off on reports and process several difficult samples herself. And then there was the business of running the Veritas Center. Tasks galore awaited her.

She loved her work, even the mundane tasks, and would jump right in, but she couldn't work. Not with Hunter risking his life. Not after he told her he loved her and said he hoped he could change. That implied that he wanted to change, and that he was going to do something to make it happen. Could that happen? Could they be together?

Not if he was injured and bleeding out.

She glanced at the clock. He should've broken down Rudy's door by now. Perhaps he was questioning him. Or searching his house.

Oh, Hunter, please call.

Tears stung her eyes, and she clasped her hands together and pinched them until they hurt to take her mind off her emotions. How had she gone from being a workaholic—a woman who could work through anything—to a woman so fraught with worry that she couldn't concentrate?

She had to let go of the worry and leave Hunter in God's hands.

Her phone dinged, and her heart lurched. She jerked

the phone from her pocket. But her heart fell when she saw Emory's name instead. Maya read the message.

DNA results are in for samples recovered at Fletch's lab. Match to Fletch and Carson and one unknown profile. No match in CODIS.

Maya thumbed in a quick thank-you. She *was* thankful, even if the results didn't tell them anything yet. The unknown profile might not have returned a match in the FBI's Combined DNA Index System, but it might match Rudy's, which the deputies would take when he was arrested. Assuming he hadn't managed to evade arrest. Or wasn't killed in the raid, though in that scenario they would still get his DNA but from the medical examiner instead.

She shook her phone as if it would make something happen. "Come on, Hunter. Call me. Please. I need to hear from you."

Hunter and Clay marched through the small kitchen, out the back door, and over a weedy lawn to the detached garage.

Hunter stopped at the side door and peered through the window. He spotted acetone and Ephedrine packets sitting among glass beakers, measuring cups, and jugs with rubber tubing. "You gotta see this."

Clay stepped up to the window then shot Hunter a shocked look. "A meth lab? Roper's cooking meth?"

Hunter was just as shocked as Clay. "We need to get Maya and Sierra out here to process the garage and confirm, but it sure looks like a meth set up. Roper would definitely have the skills to operate one."

Clay shook his head. "Guess that's where his money's coming from."

"Likely. Let's go talk to him about it, and then I'll call Maya." Hunter led the way back inside.

When he reached the living room, Piper met his gaze. "Check out the coffee table."

Hunter looked at the glass table to find a hint of white powder. "Cocaine?"

Roper shook his knee, moving it as fast as a hummingbird's wings. "Nah, I wouldn't—"

"Baggie's on the floor under the couch."

Roper looked up, and Hunter noticed his dilated pupils. "You're using right now."

"Nah, man…I—"

Hunter held up his hand. "Save it. Your eyes say it all. I'm surprised you're still buying cocaine when you're making meth in the garage."

"He is?" Piper asked.

Hunter nodded.

"Nah, not me. I don't use the garage."

"Then your prints won't be in there when our team processes it."

"I might have gone in there when I first moved in." He shifted in his chair, looking like he needed to get up. Probably the cocaine making him jittery.

"Since it looks like he's not going to cooperate, I'll call county to arrange transport." Clay stepped away with his phone.

Roper flashed his gaze to Hunter. "Transport? What do you mean?"

"We're arresting you for making the meth, but also for the murder of Carson Delvalle."

"Carson's dead?" His wide-eyed gaze suggested he was legitimately surprised at their news. Or maybe he was just a good actor.

"He was found dead in the lab on Wednesday."

"But I didn't kill him."

Normally the first question Hunter would ask in a murder investigation was for an alibi, but from Maya's exposure to the toxin, he knew that it could have taken days for Carson to die. Roper would have to account for days of his time if he remained at the lab, but he could've just come and gone for those days too.

Hunter looked at Roper. "When was the last time you saw Carson?"

"I haven't been to the lab for, I don't know, four weeks, maybe five."

"But you admit to being at the lab?"

Roper nodded. "Once. To ask Fletch for my old job back."

From the email, Hunter thought his visit entailed more than a job, but he would circle back to that. "Why not just call?"

"I tried." Roper clasped his hands together and fidgeted with his fingers. "He didn't answer or return my calls. Sometimes he gets so into his work that you have to physically get in his face to grab his attention."

"Did you still have access to the lab?"

"No. No." Roper pressed his hands on his knees. "My password didn't work anymore. But I kept buzzing until Carson let me into the main lab. Fletch was working on something that Carson said he was about to have a breakthrough on, and he wouldn't like being disturbed. Carson suggested I come back another time, but I really needed a job. I was going to lose this house."

Hunter thought the guy admitting he was in debt was in his favor, but still, it could all be a planned strategy. "Did you talk to Fletch?"

"Sort of." Roper frowned. "He looked up from his work for like a second, and I told him what I needed. He said to get lost. That Carson was an excellent assistant, and he didn't need me."

"Is that when you made your proposition?"

Roper flashed a shocked look at Hunter. "How do you know about that?"

"Fletch's emails."

"I wanted him to let me use his lab to do testing for private companies. I didn't really work out the details of what but figured together we could come up with tests needed in the area." His lips flattened into a grim line. "But I didn't even get to mention it to him. He told me to leave. He was too busy."

"Did Fletch tell you what he was working on?"

Roper shook his head. "But he was using the containment cabinet, so it had to be a high-level toxin of some kind."

"But you don't know what?"

Roper shook his head. "Is Fletch okay?"

Hunter met and held the guy's gaze. "He's missing."

Roper's mouth formed an O of surprise. "You think we're working together on something, and we killed Carson?"

"Something like that," Hunter said as he wasn't going to share their theory. "When was the last time you talked to either Carson or Fletch?"

"That day at the lab. I left a few messages for Fletch after that, but he never called me back." Roper let out an exaggerated sigh. "I need to find work, and now you're arresting me for the meth. Just when I didn't think my life could get worse."

"Trust me," Hunter said. "If we find out you had anything to do with what we're investigating, your life will get worse. A whole lot worse."

~

Maya's phone rang in her hand, and she jumped.

Hunter. It was Hunter. She answered. "Are you okay? Did everything go all right?"

"We're all fine." His voice was calm and assured.

The sound of his soothing tone calmed her nerves, and she let out a relieved breath. "Was Fletch there?"

"No, but Roper was. We arrested him. He's cooking meth in his garage. I need you and Sierra to come out here and process the space." He gave her the address.

She memorized it. "Sure, sure. I'll call Sierra, and we'll get there as soon as we can."

"See you then."

"Yes," she said. "And Hunter. I'm so glad you're okay. I—" She clamped down on her lips before she told him she loved him again. She couldn't make that a habit. Not when she didn't know if it would go anywhere. "See you soon."

She disconnected and entered the address in a map program on her phone before she forgot it. She called Sierra, and they agreed to meet at their van. Maya packed a few items she would need in her field kit and hurried to the parking garage, where Sierra was already climbing into the driver's seat.

Maya dropped her kit in the back of the large forensics van lined with shelves and bins holding tools needed to process a scene. She double checked that there was enough protective clothing for the two of them to safely enter a toxic building. Satisfied, she closed the back door and joined Sierra.

Maya plugged her phone into a dangling USB cord and brought up the address. "Not too far away."

Sierra started the van, the big engine rumbling to life in a loud throaty hum in the concrete structure. She wound out of the parking garage and onto the main road. "Did Hunter say if he thought Roper is our guy?"

"No." Maya thought about the call. "He was actually kind of abrupt. Not in a mad kind of way. Just short and to the point."

Sierra stopped at a red light and glanced at Maya. "Any change in what's going on with him since we last talked?"

Since Maya had already told Sierra about Hunter, she didn't feel a need to hold back. "He just admitted he's still in love with me but nothing has changed."

Sierra glanced at Maya, her eyebrow raised. "And you? Are you still in love with him?"

Maya nodded. "For all the good it does me."

"I'd like to say it's going to work out. I mean, look at all the rest of us. We had obstacles and we overcame them, but this is different. Hunter's losses go so much deeper and make them harder to recover from."

Maya hated hearing the blunt assessment, but Sierra was right. "God is the only one who can work this out."

"Then I'll pray for you and Hunter. And you should ask the rest of the team to pray as well."

Maya clasped her hands together. "I don't want to tell them about Hunter."

"You don't have to." Sierra clicked on the blinker and merged onto the freeway. "Everyone can see you two have a thing. Just ask them to pray that it works out."

"I can do that," Maya said, feeling a bit encouraged. "So how's married life? Everything you thought it would be?"

"It is and more." Sierra got a dreamy smile on her face. "Of course we have to adjust to living together. It's only been two months. That's a bit different but still very nice."

"I'm so happy for you two."

Sierra smiled. "I want the same thing for you."

Maya smiled back, but decided to change the subject before she got all emotional and seeing Hunter again was difficult. "Do you want to handle this meth lab the way we have in the past?"

Sierra nodded, and they spent the trip discussing their plan of action so that when Sierra pulled the van up to Roper's house, they knew exactly what they were going to do.

They slid out of the van, and Hunter jogged down the front steps to meet them. Since she'd last seen him, he'd changed into khaki cargo pants and a navy polo shirt. He still wore his body armor, and, of course, his sidearm was strapped to his belt. He looked like a fierce warrior, and Maya's heart started to gallop. His gaze sought her out, and she smiled at him while pulling her protective suit from a tub in the back of the van.

"Thanks for coming so quickly," he said, as if he'd called a colleague, not the woman he loved.

Where was this professional formality coming from? Was he just in his crime scene mode or did he regret telling her he loved her?

He shoved his hands into his cargo pockets. "We also found cocaine inside the house. Hopefully you can check to see if it's pure and the same stuff that was used to cut with the toxin."

"That's a surprise." Maya slid a leg into the suit. "Let me confirm we have meth, and then while Sierra processes the garage for prints and DNA, I'll take a sample of the cocaine."

"Sounds like a plan."

She finished putting on the coverall and fastened the Velcro openings. "Rudy inside?"

"County already picked him up."

She reached for a respirator and goggles. "Did you question him?"

"Yes, but he denies killing Carson and doesn't know where Fletch is."

"Do you believe him?" She settled the goggles on her forehead.

"Unfortunately, I do." A frown marred his handsome face. "Especially with the meth lab. Would explain where the cash deposits were coming from."

"That's true."

"He did admit to recently visiting Fletch's lab, so his prints could be the set in question." He looked at Sierra, who was donning the same gear. "I'll get a copy of the prints they take at booking, and I'm sure you can recover his DNA from the house."

"I'll use his toothbrush." Sierra settled her goggles over her eyes and picked up the respirator. "And the place is bound to be loaded with his fingerprints."

Maya looked at Sierra. "Ready to take the first look?"

Sierra nodded.

Maya gritted her teeth. "Then let's do this."

Hunter and Maya finished up at the crime scene and now he anxiously waited in her lab for results for the cocaine. Even at seven o'clock at night, two staff members were still working, but she had a singular focus and didn't seem to notice them. Or him either. That was fine. The very last thing either of them needed after declaring their love was to be noticing each other.

What had he been thinking in blurting out his feelings for her? Nothing smart. That's what. He'd let his emotions take over. Forgot his past for a moment. Then he'd left for the raid, and reality had come crashing down again. As he'd suited up in tactical gear, he was reminded of how quickly someone could die.

He shifted his attention to her work. "What exactly are you doing?"

She looked over her shoulder at him, a test tube in her hand. "It's pretty technical. Do you really want to know?"

"Sure," he said. It would be good to keep his mind off what he really wanted to talk to her about.

"I just dissolved what we think is cocaine into an organic solvent." She got out a long syringe and poked it into her test tube. "Now I'm going to inject a microliter amount of the liquid sample into the injection port of the gas chromatograph."

She stabbed a frighteningly large looking needle into a port on top of a machine about the size of a microwave. "The sample is immediately volatilized and mixed with the carrier gas. As the machine runs, the different samples will separate based on the volatility and mass. Then I'll run it through mass spectrometry, which will ionize the compounds to generate charged molecular fragments and measure their mass-to-charge ratio. That information is sent to the computer, and it will compare to a database of known chemicals and drugs. If a match is found in the database, the drug and the chemical it was cut with is identified."

"You were right." He smiled. "It's technical, but it's great to see what you do. I knew you were this super-smart scientist, but this is impressive."

A blush stole over her face. "Let me get back to work, and we'll soon know if it's cocaine and if it's pure or not." She turned back to the machine.

An hour later, she looked up and frowned. "Rudy's cocaine isn't pure. It was cut with laundry detergent."

Her statement hung in the air for a moment until he could focus and process it. "So it can't be the cocaine that Carson had in his nostril."

She lifted her face shield. "I can't say absolutely. He or

someone else could've taken the pure cocaine and cut it with the detergent *after* they poisoned Carson, but it's unlikely. If he possessed the pure product, he would want to use that for his high."

"Makes sense." Hunter stood and planted his hands on the table. "Even if Rudy's prints don't come back matching those in the lab, he admitted to being there so he could still be our guy."

Maya swiveled to face him and peeled off her face shield. "I have to agree, and even with the prints, he might not have killed Carson."

"Which means we're back at square one." Hunter's attitude darkened, and he didn't want to bring Maya down with him so he resisted frowning.

His phone buzzed. He dug it out and, seeing the text from Adair, he opened the message. "They have a location on Greg's phone."

"And?"

"And it's pinging from the island."

Maya blinked a few times. "But how is that possible. The prints we haven't identified might be his, but otherwise, there was no sign of him there when we searched before."

Hunter shoved his hands into his pockets. "Searches don't always catch everything. We could've missed something."

Maya raised an eyebrow. "Or he's not there. What do you want to do?"

"I'm going to head to the island."

"If you're going," Maya met his gaze, "I'm going with you."

16

Hunter had a bad feeling in the pit of his stomach as he docked their rental boat at the island and peered through the darkness at the lab. The moon and stars were hiding behind heavy clouds, after the morning rain had given way to sunshiny skies, and the temperatures still hovered near eighty. The only light came from large lightbulbs scattered on posts throughout the property and an exterior light casting a glow from the corner of the building.

A seal affixed to the front door warned people to stay out, but the CDC no longer had a presence on the island. Hunter wasn't worried about exposure. Not when they would be outside. The building had been searched so he didn't think they would have to step inside, but if they did, Maya had brought along protective clothing for both of them.

He slung his and Maya's backpacks onto his back and jumped onto the dock. He tied up the boat and held out his hand to Maya. She took his hand, and the touch of her fingers sent his pulse into hyperdrive. He couldn't lose his focus now. Nor would he let her know how touching her affected him and encourage her to think he'd changed. As soon as her sneakers were solidly on the dock, he let go.

"I'll call Greg's phone. But if he came here to do something bad, he would likely have silenced his phone. Still, listen for it." He got out his phone and made the call.

Silence, save the running water and rustling grass surrounded them. He ended the call and shoved his phone into his pocket.

"We'll do a grid search," he said. "We'll make an outer circle first where the phone pinged from and then work our way inward."

She peered up at him, the hazy glow from a nearby light highlighting her face. "Do you really think we'll find him here?"

He shrugged, the heavy backpacks trying to hold his shoulders down. "I honestly don't know, but let's get started."

They stepped ahead, shining flashlights into knee-deep grass and weeds. Looking. Searching. Hoping to find any hint of Greg's possessions. A strong breeze whisked through the grass, and it swayed in a gentle rhythm. The farther they walked from the lab, the thicker the weeds grew, and Hunter had to bat some of them out of the way to allow them to continue.

Maya pressed down a sapling and stepped over it. "It'd be a lot easier if we could take the path."

"True, but anything in the path would've already been discovered. Besides, the path isn't in our grid at the moment." He stepped over a huge thistle and listened to the comforting sound of the river rolling by, his mind going to the surreal location for their search. "How in the world did Fletch afford to buy a private island anyway?"

Maya glanced up. "Same way I got the Veritas Center. He inherited it."

Made perfect sense. "I honestly didn't even know there were private islands in the Willamette until I met Fletch."

"Me either." Her pant leg got caught on a wild raspberry, and she struggled to move forward.

"Let me help." He stepped over to her and bent down to free her leg. She rested her hand on his shoulder, and that fire lit in his heart again.

The moment she was free, he pushed back and started along the bank to a beach area that led up to a dock and boathouse, keeping his focus pinned on the circle of ground illuminated by his flashlight.

The strong breeze whipped toward him, bringing him to a dead stop. He looked at Maya. "Do you smell that?"

She nodded, her eyes wide. "There's no mistaking the smell of death."

Maya wished she were anywhere but here, doing anything but suiting up to move forward through the scrub to discover who had died. She could hardly breathe for thinking it might be Fletch. Was likely Fletch.

She swallowed away the thought and donned a protective suit, as did Hunter. But these weren't nearly as restrictive as the ones they'd worn in the lab. No need when there was little risk of exposure outside. They settled respirators over their mouths and noses.

She looked at Hunter. "Ready?"

He arched a brow. "Is anyone ever ready to confirm that someone has died?"

She shook her head and marched ahead to the boathouse. She opened the door, and flies buzzed above Fletch's boat covered in a tarp.

"That's Fletch's boat." She glanced back at Hunter, her

mind racing with questions, the biggest one was if they were going to find Fletch under the tarp. Her stomach churned.

"Someone brought it back." Hunter stepped past her.

"Maybe Carson's killer and that's Fletch under the tarp." She swallowed hard.

Hunter undid the straps holding the tarp down, and Maya prayed she was wrong, but she knew that someone had lost their life. If they hadn't caught the decomp odor downwind, she might think the flies suggested someone left fish to rot, but that was a far different odor than the stench emanating from under this tarp.

Hunter lifted the canvas. She swallowed a few times and looked inside the boat. A young male wearing a T-shirt and jeans lay curled on his side. His face was bloated and shaded in various colors of purple. Not Fletch.

Maya sighed out a breath of thanks for that, but her feeling was short-lived. Some poor guy, likely Greg, had lost his life. Despite the body's condition, she was confident a visual identification was still possible.

She stared at the boat, shaking her head. "I guess they brought the boat back to leave Greg's body here, but why take it in the first place?"

"That's what we need to figure out," he said and led her back outside. He stepped away from the building and lifted his respirator then unzipped his suit, likely for some cooling air in the unusually warm and muggy temperatures. "I'll call this in and get the ME out here. And follow up Adair on Greg's DL information. Then I'll cordon off the area."

She pulled down the zipper on her suit to catch the breeze now that they were upwind of the boathouse. "What do you want me to do?"

He got a funny look on his face that she couldn't read. "Get Sierra out here to process the scene."

"Sure thing." She reached inside her coverall for her phone and made the call.

"Maya. Good," Sierra said before Maya could get a word in. "I needed to update you. Rudy's fingerprints don't match any of the prints I lifted from Fletch's lab."

Maya sighed. "We found another body."

Sierra took a sharp intake of air. "Tell me about it."

Maya explained. "Hunter wants you out here to process the scene. Can you come?"

"I have a few things to finish up here, but then I'm on my way."

"See you soon." Maya shoved her phone into her pocket and looked at Hunter.

Even in his protective gear she could see his shoulders were tight, and he was rubbing the back of his neck while he talked. She wanted to help him. To take some of the weight off his shoulders, but what could she do?

She thought ahead to what was going to happen. No one would touch the body until the medical examiner arrived. Maya sure couldn't help there. She couldn't tell by looking at the body if he'd been exposed to the toxin, and she had no idea how she could use her toxicology skills to help. In the lab, sure. She'd run his bloodwork, but just looking at a body? Not really.

So what then? Nothing came to mind. She'd just have to be in tune with Hunter's moves so she could pitch in wherever possible. No hardship for sure. She'd been in tune with his moves since she'd laid eyes on him. That was part of her problem if she wanted to keep her emotions in check around him. Still, she could always swallow them down like she'd done for years and provide moral support.

He ended his call and got out a roll of crime scene tape from his backpack. "ME's office will send someone right out, and Adair promised the DL info in a few minutes."

Hunter fixed the end of the bright yellow warning tape to a tree and started unraveling the roll.

"Sierra said Rudy's prints don't match any found at the lab," Maya said.

"Not unexpected." He was so calm about the news. Unbelievably calm. He just kept unrolling the tape and affixing to trees to secure the scene.

She stared at him, trying to get a read on his mood. "So you don't think he's involved?"

He ripped the tape in two and tied the end to a light pole. "My gut says no, but I'm not ready to rule him out."

"Is that because you don't have another suspect to take his place?"

"I forget how well you know me." He ran a gloved hand over his head, pushing his sweaty hair back. "I'd like to continue the grid search until the ME gets here, but you can wait here if you want."

"I'll help." She started off.

They'd gone nearly a mile when a boat motor hummed in the distance.

Hunter looked up, perspiration dotting his forehead. "We should head back so we're at the boathouse when the ME arrives."

Maya turned back. "I hope it's Dr. Albertson again. She's always been open to our team's help and sharing information."

Hunter cocked his head. "You all walk a pretty fine line with law enforcement, don't you?"

"They either love our help or think we're interfering. The good news is the list of those who love us is growing."

He swept his flashlight over the ground in front of him. "I think a lot of the negative feelings are over how much you all charge."

"We aren't cheap, but we do try our best to keep costs

down for law enforcement." Something shiny caught her eye, and she squatted to free it from the grass. "A belt buckle."

Hunter used his phone to take a photo of the buckle then picked it up. "Looks like it's from a man's belt. Nothing unusual about it." He grabbed a nearby stick and stuck it in the ground. "A marker for Sierra so she knows where we found it."

He bagged the buckle and pocketed it. His phone buzzed. He glanced at the screen and held it out to her. "Greg's photo."

She took a good look at it, and then conjured up the deceased's face. "The victim is Greg, all right."

"I agree."

The boat roared closer, and she peered ahead to see Dr. Albertson and Josh pulling up to the dock in a small aluminum boat piloted by a county deputy. Maya and Hunter continued to search the ground but moved steadily toward the boathouse and had their respirators back in hand when the ME and her assistant arrived at the boathouse.

Dr. Albertson planted her feet. "What do we have?"

Maya explained. "Young male in a boat. He was covered with a tarp that we removed. No obvious sign of how he died so could be the toxin."

"Let's take a look." She donned her respirator and entered the boathouse.

Josh followed her, as did Hunter and Maya.

Dr. Albertson switched on the single bulb dangling above, casting eerie shadows around the space. Maya shuddered. Dr. Albertson didn't seem to be bothered by anything, but quickly climbed onto the boat.

She reached down, touching the victim's neck. "Been here a few days. Looks like strangulation marks."

"Strangulation?" Maya shot Hunter a look. "The belt buckle."

"Could be," he said.

Dr. Albertson looked at them. "What buckle?"

Maya explained. "Does it look like he could've been strangled by a belt?"

"Maybe, but I can't say for sure until I get him on my table and do a complete exam." She lifted his eyelids. "No petechiae—pinpoint hemorrhages—of the eyes."

Hunter stepped closer and looked up at the doctor. "Is the lack of hemorrhages what you would expect to find if he was strangled with a belt?"

"Yes." She stood, the light casting a shadow over her narrow face. "The petechiae requires sustained force to form like you receive from manual strangulation, and is rarely present when a ligature is used."

"What about ID?" Hunter asked. "Can you check for a wallet so we can confirm?"

She shifted the body and withdrew a worn nylon wallet. She removed a driver's license and took a long look at it. "Greg Uzzell."

"Anything else in his pockets?" Hunter asked.

She pawed through them and brought out a picture that she handed to Hunter. It was of Fletch and Greg outside the escape rooms. Hunter flipped it over, but nothing was written on the back.

He passed it to Maya. "I wonder why he's carrying this around."

She studied the picture. "Nothing unusual in the photo."

Maya gave the photo back to Hunter. He used his phone to take a picture of it and handed it back to Dr. Albertson as she was responsible for collecting Greg's personal effects.

"Any sign of cocaine use like with Carson?" Maya asked.

She bent closer and shook her head. "I need better lighting to see that."

Maya pointed her flashlight at the victim's face.

Dr. Albertson leaned closer. "Nothing here but a dead mosquito."

Maya's interest perked. "As in a mosquito with its stinger stuck in the body?"

"No. Just lying on his skin."

"It could've bitten the killer, he swatted it, and it fell on Greg." Maya started to get excited about the potential lead. "We need to collect it."

"Why?" Hunter asked.

"Emory can check the mosquito for the killer's DNA. "

Hunter stared at her, and she suspected his mouth hung open under his respirator. "You've got to be kidding me. She can get DNA from a mosquito."

"That she can." Maya pointed at the insect. "And if this little thing stung the killer, in twenty-four hours, we'll have his DNA for comparison."

17

Hunter would like to say that being back in the morgue the next morning was easier, but it wasn't. The day an autopsy became routine was the day he had to quit his job because it would mean he'd lost all emotion. Plus, he was still unsettled after the death notification call to Greg's parents. The loss of life was always difficult, but when someone met a violent end, it was even harder to accept. And more so when a parent had to deal with the loss of a child. Even an adult child.

He shrugged his shoulders to shift on the biohazard suit and approached the table. Thankfully, Dr. Richards wasn't present today. Just Dr. Albertson and her trusty sidekick, Josh.

"Find anything yet?" he asked loudly to be heard over his respirator.

She looked up, her eyes narrowed. "No sign of cocaine use, but see here." She pointed at purple striations circling the victim's neck. "He was definitely strangled. Not sure yet if it was the cause of death, but judging by the thickness of the bands, a belt or something thick and heavy like a belt was used."

She moved back. "You should also know lividity indicates the body was in a different position than you found it in. See how the blood is pooled on his backside and feet? If he'd died in the prone position like you found him, it would have pooled evenly along the entire side of his body except where he connected with the boat's seats."

Hunter thought of Maya's supposition that Greg had gone up to the lab and interrupted Carson's murder. "So Greg was killed elsewhere and moved to the boat."

"Exactly." She looked up. "He was sitting up for up to six hours after death."

"Six hours?" Hunter asked.

She nodded. "At that point, the lividity is fixed, as blood vessels begin to break down within the body and it won't change. Before that, if he'd been laid down in the boat, the blood would have shifted."

Hunter could imagine Greg arriving at the lab. The killer seeing him, jerking his belt from his pant loops and strangling Greg, then setting him aside to be dealt with later. Problem was, Sierra hadn't found any trace evidence to suggest the body had sat anywhere for hours. But he would have her go back and do a closer look because she wouldn't have been focusing on that and could've missed hair or fibers.

"I'm going to start the cut now." Dr. Albertson picked up a scalpel. "Feel free to take a seat."

Hunter pulled a stool up to the table and watched her dissect this twenty-five-year-old man whose life had just been beginning when he was brutally murdered. Hunter didn't often deal with murder investigations, but each one hit him hard. He didn't know how the partners at the Veritas Center dealt with death on a regular basis. Especially Kelsey. And police detectives. Hunter may be an FBI agent, a position often touted as a hero in the law enforcement community, but local police were the real heroes in his book. They faced more difficult things on a regular basis. Unless you were in the FBI behavioral unit. That was a whole other story.

Dr. Albertson looked up, grabbing his attention. "The hyoid bone's intact. I'm guessing you know it's the U-shaped bone of the neck."

He had indeed heard of the bone on many occasions, so he nodded. "I thought they were most often broken when someone was strangled."

"In manual strangulation, yes, but not so in a ligature strangulation or hangings. It happens, but isn't as common." She looked down at the body again. "There are pinpoint hemorrhages—petechiae—in internal organs of the neck located above the point of constriction."

Okay, now she lost him. "And that means?"

She met Hunter's gaze. "He was indeed strangled."

"Not the toxin then?"

"Could be both, and I can't rule out toxin exposure without the blood tests. But let me look inside his lungs too." She sliced open one of Greg's lungs and shook her head. "No inflammation. Still not official proof though."

Hunter wanted an answer far faster than the standard forty-eight hours. "Can I take a sample back to Maya to run the rapid test?"

She took an exaggerated look around the area. "I don't see anyone here to stop you."

She laughed behind her respirator, and so did Hunter. It felt good to release some of the tension. That was only possible because Dr. Richards had returned to Atlanta.

"I'll need a set of Greg's fingerprints too," Hunter said.

"Way ahead of you." She tipped her head at her assistant. "Josh, give him the set we took for them."

Josh went to a nearby counter and came back with a

fingerprint card holding ten perfect prints. Hunter held onto the card for now. Once out of his protective suit, he would put it in his cargo pocket. He waited through the entire autopsy and then looked at Dr. Albertson. "Can I get that sample for Maya?"

She turned to Josh. "Take one, will you?"

Josh nodded, and Hunter was struck by the fact that this guy never spoke nor did his expressions change very often. But he seemed to be a good assistant and had been with Dr. Albertson for years. She had exacting standards. If he wasn't capable, she would've let him go.

Josh handed over the sample, and, back at the Veritas Center, Hunter dropped off the fingerprints with Sierra and gave the sample to Maya. She donned her protective gear and moved over to the cabinet.

He took a seat at a lab table.

Maya looked back at him. "So if Greg died of strangulation, who do you think did it?"

He stowed his phone. "I've had those same questions running through my head since I left the morgue. What if Fletch called Greg to come to the island like he did you? Maybe Greg showed up after they'd released the toxin. He discovered the murder and their plot to do something with the toxin, and they had to get rid of him."

"It's really the only thing that makes sense, right?" She sat at her containment cabinet. "Unless Greg just decided to go to the island on his own, and he killed Carson. But then who killed him?"

Hunter had no idea. "His phone might've told us something. We know it's on the island, but Sierra's team hasn't located it yet. They're still searching with metal detectors and should eventually find it. In the meantime, I've requested his records so we can review his calls, but that could take some time too."

"Something we don't have if the killer has some of Fletch's aerosolized toxin."

"Or even has Fletch and is forcing him to create more of the aerosolized version."

Hunter nodded. "How much more toxin? That's the scary question."

"It wouldn't require much to out a large number of people." Maya's eyes narrowed, and she turned back to her work.

He took that to mean she didn't want to talk about this anymore. He didn't blame her. It was scary to think about what someone could do with the toxin and probably did neither of them any good to ponder it. He opened his laptop and caught up on the reports from DHS, which didn't give him any new information.

Maya removed her arms from the cabinet and turned to look at him

"This needs time to sit, and then we'll know if Greg was exposed to the toxin." She went to the sink. "I wonder—"

Her phone buzzed on the stainless steel table, cutting her off. She dried her hands to look at it. "Sierra says most of the prints from the boat match Fletch. A few from Carson. And a few that match the unidentified print on the lab's front door."

Hunter internalized the information. "So the person who went into the lab also touched the boat?"

Maya nodded. "Greg's prints don't match the ones on the boat or the front door to the lab."

Interesting. "Do you think he landed on shore and was killed right away?"

"Seems like it, but why was he even there?"

"While you finish up here, I'm going to call Nick to see what he has on Greg. And if he doesn't have the roommate's number, I'll get it from Peggy to see if I can get anything else out of him." Hunter made the call.

"Hey, man," Nick answered.

"What did you dig up on Greg Uzzell?"

"He lives not far from Float Away in a two bedroom with a roommate named Tyce Umstadt."

"Lived," Hunter said. "I'm sorry to say he's dead."

"Man, that's rough. How?"

"That hasn't been determined," Hunter replied. "He was strangled, but he also might've been exposed to the toxin. Maya's testing now."

"Guy looks like he might've had a drug habit. He's broke and his credit cards are all maxed out. And his landlord said he was behind in his rent."

"I was hoping to talk to his roommate. Do you have the guy's cell number?"

"Yeah, sure." He shared the phone number. "No landline."

Hunter noted the information on his pad. "Anything else I should know about him?"

"No, but the roommate works in a gun shop. If you question him, you should be careful."

"Thanks," Hunter said and ended the call to tap in Tyce's number.

"Yo," he answered.

"This is Agent Hunter Lane with the FBI," Hunter said. "Are you Greg Uzzell's roommate?"

"Yeah, man. His dad called. Told me about Greg. What happened to him?"

Hunter wasn't going to share the details. Not only wasn't the cause of death official at this point, but it didn't do Tyce any good to know Greg had been strangled. It was such an ugly, violent way to die, and Hunter wanted to spare him from dealing with such trauma. "Tell me about the last time you spoke to him."

"Sure. Sure." He paused as if thinking. "It was Monday afternoon. He was heading to some island to see a friend he did escape rooms with."

"Did he say why he was going to the island?"

"Nah."

"And you didn't ask?"

"Nah. We weren't like close, you know? Just shared a place. Didn't keep track of each other. Still, I figured since he was on vacay he was going for fun."

His statement tracked with the information Peggy had shared, and Hunter didn't think he sounded in the least bit worried about this call, suggesting he was on the up and up. "Would you mind if I came by and looked at Greg's room?"

"Like now?" His tone skated high.

"If that's okay."

"I...well..." He cleared his throat. "The place is kind of a mess."

"I don't mind. What's the address?"

Tyce offered it, but reluctance lingered in his words.

Hunter didn't want to make things worse for Tyce, but Hunter was going to take a look at Greg's room. "Should be there in ten minutes."

"Okay...yeah...sure."

Hunter hung up, but, before he could stand, he got an email with Greg's phone records.

"Phone records are here," he told Maya, opened the file, and looked for calls on Monday and the week before that. "Lots of texts in the days before he went missing, but none to or from Fletch. Greg only made one phone call, and it was to his work."

Maya looked over her shoulder at him. "So Fletch didn't ask him to come to the island?"

"At least not via Greg's cell. I suppose Fletch could've called Greg at work. I'm heading over to his apartment. I'll have Piper request the call log for Float Away and have her track down these text numbers."

He forwarded the call log to Piper along with instructions and stood.

"Can I come with you?" Maya asked.

"What about the test?"

"I don't need to babysit it. I can have my staff watch it and report any findings."

"Then let's go."

Hunter drove them to Tigard, a suburb of Portland, his mind lingering on why Greg would go to the island without an invitation. But he pulled up to the older apartment building where Greg had lived without any answers.

He turned off the engine and looked at Maya. "There's no reason to suspect this roommate is involved, but Nick said he works at a gun shop. So he could be armed. Keep your eyes and ears open for any sign of danger."

"Will do." She slipped out.

They took the sidewalk under the relentless sun, and Hunter pounded loudly.

A blond guy sporting a neatly trimmed goatee opened the door. Hunter put Tyce in his early twenties, and he was dressed in skinny jeans and a black T-shirt. He doubted he was hiding a gun in those pants or under the T-shirt.

He swiped his hand over his sweaty forehead. "You the FBI dude?"

"Agent Hunter Lane." Hunter displayed his credentials and introduced Maya as an associate.

"Never talked to an agent before." He gave Hunter a wide-eyed appraisal and seemed to find him lacking.

"Can we see Greg's room please?" Maya asked.

"Sure. No sweat. But remember I warned you about the mess." He turned and sauntered through the living room, which was littered with empty beer bottles and pizza boxes. A couple of vaping pens lay next to the boxes, and the strong smell of marijuana permeated everything.

Pot was legal in Oregon, but as a federal agent, Hunter could arrest him, though he wouldn't. He did consider warning him about the dangers of vaping, but that could make the guy belligerent, and he could deny Hunter access to Greg's room without a warrant.

Tyce entered a hallway with stained carpet and stopped outside a closed door. "This's it. You can let yourself out when you're done."

"Thanks." Hunter stepped into the stifling room. The apartment didn't have air conditioning, not unusual for this part of Oregon where it wasn't needed very often.

Maya closed the door behind her. "Tyce doesn't seem too broken up about Greg's death."

"I noticed that too. He said they weren't close, but still, you'd think he'd show a hint of sadness."

"Yeah." Maya stepped to a small desk covered in mail and took gloves from her pocket before pawing through a stack of envelopes. "Greg has some past due notices here."

"Fits with what Nick said." Hunter put on his own gloves and picked up a few of the envelopes. "Utilities. Phone. Credit card. Looks like he definitely needed money."

She gave him a knowing look. "Maybe he *is* involved in stealing the toxin, and we just haven't found out how."

He tapped an open laptop. "We should get Nick to image this."

The screen woke up and displayed a map program showing Fletch's island and another open tab for a boat rental business.

Hunter leaned closer. "So he was last looking at how to get to the island. He had to have a boat to get there and was checking out rentals. He couldn't have returned it."

"Why didn't the rental people call him?"

Hunter shrugged. "I'll have Piper run that down."

Hunter got out his phone and thumbed a text to her.

"So we have a broke guy who spends whatever cash he has on a boat rental." Maya tapped her finger on the desktop. "Either he was truly going to the island for a vacation to escape his problems, or he was expecting the island visit to pay off in some way."

"The only way I can see it pay off is if he's involved in the toxin theft. Maybe not involved as in a partner with whoever killed Carson, but he knew about the toxin and planned to steal it for himself. Or he was hoping to get money from Fletch for another reason. Blackmail maybe?"

Maya's tapping finger picked up speed. "I can't imagine Fletch doing anything that's blackmail worthy. Unless you think Fletch was knowingly making toxin for a terrorist. But then how could Greg even know that?"

"Maybe it has to do with that picture that Greg had in his pocket."

"We need to see the original copy to get a good look at it again."

He dug out his phone. "Let me call Dr. Albertson to see if she's transferred it to evidence or if she still has it with his belongings, and we can pick it up on our way back to the lab."

He made the call and arranged to get the photo from her. They continued searching, and Hunter got down on his knees to look under the bed. He pushed a football and pair of dirty sneakers out of the way to get to a shoebox. He dragged it out, and the heavy weight told him it didn't hold shoes.

He lifted the lid and let out a low whistle. "Will you look at this?"

Maya rushed across the room and stared down on the box. "That's a lot of cash."

Hunter riffled through it then sat back to peer up at her. "Looks like twenty grand to me. We need to get Sierra out here to process this and take it into evidence."

She met and held his gaze. "So where does an hourly employee get twenty-thousand dollars in cash?"

He shook his head. "I don't know, but I can pretty much guarantee most of the options aren't legal."

∼

Maya had stared at the photo they'd picked up from Dr. Albertson all the way back to the center and up to Nick's private lab. But she didn't see anything suspicious no matter how many times she'd looked at it. She did have hopes that Nick could scan and enlarge it. Maybe enhance it.

He peered at the picture. "I can't guarantee it'll be clear, but I'll try. Hold on, and I'll have it up on the big screen in a jiff."

"Just do your best," Hunter said from where he'd leaned a shoulder against the wall.

Nick focused on his computer, and Maya watched him work with the pixels in a video editing program.

Piper was once again sitting beside Nick, going through the multitude of Fletch's computer files, and she met Hunter's gaze. "I got the call logs for Float Away. No calls from or to Fletch. And I had an analyst look up all the texts made from Greg's cell."

She handed a paper to Hunter. "Nothing stands out to me."

Hunter ran his finger down the page, and Maya peered

over his arm at the list of names matched up to the text numbers.

He looked up. "I don't see anything odd here, either."

Piper frowned. "I can't see how Greg was involved in the toxin release."

"Maybe he wasn't," Hunter said. "Maybe it was just a case of being in the wrong place at the wrong time."

"But how do you explain the cash, then?" Maya asked.

"I can't."

Hunter looked at Piper. "Are you guys not finding anything in Fletch's files, either?"

"Still working backward in time, but no." Piper turned back to her computer.

Maya faced Hunter. "Could Greg have saved the money?"

"Not likely on his salary."

Maya gave it some thought. "The weird thing is that he didn't use it to pay off those bills."

"Maybe he just got the money and hasn't had a chance to deposit it. Or we just didn't see the confirmation of him bringing his bills current."

"Which could again point to involvement in Carson's murder or the toxin." Maya's phone dinged, and she glanced at the screen. "The toxin test completed. Greg wasn't exposed to the toxin."

Hunter frowned. "So maybe he never made it inside the lab, or if he did, he was protected from the toxin. He could've been the person who killed Carson."

"Or he didn't get up to the lab, but then he wouldn't have seen Carson or know about the toxin release." Maya tried to figure out what this meant, but she really had nothing to go on.

"Check out the screen." Nick leaned back.

The photo opened on the large TV mounted on the far wall.

Maya stared at the image of Fletch and Greg and scoured the background. "Nothing. There's just nothing here."

"I agree," Hunter said. "And yet, Greg was carrying it. Why?"

Maya shrugged. "It's certainly not blackmail-worthy, so the cash didn't likely come from using this picture."

Hunter looked at her. "Maybe Greg had something else he was blackmailing Fletch on. Something that happened at Float Away or the escape rooms."

"But what?" She lifted her hands in frustration. "This is going nowhere fast."

"I might have something here," Piper announced. "Not related to Greg, but a few terse emails with a former subordinate who claims Fletch blackballed him and he can't get another job. It was when Fletch worked at a USDA lab."

Maya thought back to Fletch's time at the USDA. "He hasn't worked there for nearly five years. Why is this subordinate coming forward now?"

Piper leaned back in her chair to look at Maya. "After Fletch fired him, he decided to travel. Now he's looking to get back to work and claims Fletch ruined his reputation. He says Fletch badmouthed him with others in the industry while taking credit for research this guy did."

"Talk about motive to want to get back at Fletch," Hunter said.

"What's this guy's name?" Nick asked.

Piper faced her fiancé. "Eshan Assad."

"Let me see what I can find out about him?" Nick looked at Maya. "And while I do, go ahead and search the drives for his name. Let's see if it comes up in other places."

Maya took out her phone. "I'll also text Blake so he can see if this guy has a record." She tapped in the text then went back to the computer, the only sound in the room the machines humming on the floor and fingers clicking over keyboards. Maybe the silent sound of desperation, too.

Her search returned several terse emails between Fletch and Eshan. "Says in an email here that Eshan was going to sue Fletch. This is from a month ago."

"I've got one from last week," Hunter said. "Eshan seems to be all bluster and no action. He hasn't gone through with the lawsuit. Fletch calls him out on it, likely adding fuel to the fire."

The excitement of a potential lead built in Maya's stomach. "We need to bring this guy in. Anyone have a home address?"

"Yeah," Nick said. "Got his current address. And more. He's a conspiracy theorist. Goes by the name of HoaxBuster online, and I found several posts about stockpiling weapons and talks about using them on people who've wronged him."

Hunter's face lit with eagerness. "Sounds like he could be our guy."

"Oh, man," Nick said. "He's affiliated with Al Qaeda."

Maya's heart dropped. If Assad was affiliated with them and handed over the toxin to the group, she couldn't imagine the toll.

She pushed back her chair. "We need to talk to him. Give me his address."

"Hold on." Hunter grabbed her arm. "This guy could be a killer, and we need to do a threat assessment before rushing in. And even then, this is a law enforcement issue, and you can't be involved."

It was *so* like him to be cautious when all she wanted was to move forward. "I'm going to talk to him."

"Maybe." He locked onto Maya's gaze, and the force of his intensity felt like he'd physically shoved her. "After we bring him in for questioning, and he's secured. Only then."

18

Hunter informed his supervisor about the terrorist threat so he could update DHS, but they both agreed they couldn't wait on bringing Assad in. The threat was too big. So Clay and Piper and three additional agents followed Hunter through Assad's broken-down door and into a living room filled with ratty old furniture. There was a strong chemical smell in the space, and Hunter did a fast assessment for danger. He found nothing but Assad sitting in a recliner, his legs up and crossed. He turned to gape at them.

"Hands!" Hunter shouted. "Let me see your hands."

Assad reached down to the side of his recliner.

"Hands in the air, now!" Hunter yelled.

Assad flashed an angry dark-eyed gaze at Hunter but complied. "I was just going for the lever."

"Keep your hands up." Hunter moved in closer. "Nash, release the chair lever."

Piper came forward and used her foot to kick it down. Assad was catapulted forward but he kept his hands up.

"On the floor," Hunter commanded. "Face down."

"But I—"

"Do as I say. Now!" Hunter shouted.

Assad dove to the floor and kept his hands above his head.

"Hands behind your back," Hunter said. "Slowly."

He complied.

"Cover me while I cuff him, Nash."

"Roger that," she said, her rifle aimed at Assad.

Hunter slung his rifle over his back and grabbed his cuffs to secure Assad. He was wearing sloppy sweat pants and a T-shirt with few places to hide anything. Hunter found a ring of keys, a wallet, and some change in the guy's pockets. He stood to look through the wallet and found the usual items but also located a white electronic keycard with no markings on it.

He bent down far enough so Assad could see the card and held it out. "What's this for?"

"You can't just come busting into my house like this and demand answers," Assad said.

"We have a warrant that says we can," Hunter informed him.

"But why? I haven't done anything wrong."

Hunter looked at Piper. "Help me get him back into the chair."

They lifted him by the arms and settled him in the recliner. Hunter took a good look at the guy. He was geeky looking with out of control mousy-brown hair that needed to be cut, thick black glasses, and a full beard. Hunter had no problem thinking of this guy as a scientist. Perhaps one who killed another person. Maybe the reason for the strong chemical smell.

Hunter looked at Piper and the other agents. "Clay, you stay with me. The rest of you secure the house and start the search."

"Secure and search?" Assad stared wide-eyed at Hunter. "But why?"

Hunter ignored his outrage. "Where were you on Monday?"

Assad shrugged. "Here probably. Watching TV. It's pretty much all I do these days."

"Don't you work?" Hunter asked, though he knew the answer.

"I want to. Need to. But I can't find a job."

"Why's that?" Hunter played along.

His eyes tightened into slits of anger. "A guy I worked with was threatened by my intelligence. Stole my work and then blackballed me."

Hunter assumed he was talking about Fletch but wanted to hear Assad say the name. "This guy have a name?"

"Fletcher Gilliam," Assad nearly spit out. "A weasel of a man who parades in sheep's clothing. Hiding his true nature and getting others to believe in him."

"Seems like you're mad at the guy," Clay said. "Maybe want to take it out on him."

Assad's mouth fell open. "Are you kidding me? Of course I do, but what can I do? I tried to get lawyers to sue him, but no one would take my case. Said I couldn't prove what he'd done."

Clay kept his focus pinned on Assad. "That had to make you mad."

"Totally." He narrowed his eyes. "Fletch is going to pay for this. You can be sure of that."

Clay raised his eyebrow. "Maybe you already took care of it."

"Say, what's this about anyway?" Assad blinked dark eyelashes at them. "Did something happen to Fletch?"

"You tell us, Mr. Assad," Hunter said.

Assad frowned. "I didn't hurt him, if that's what you mean."

Piper stepped back into the room. "No sign of Fletch, but we did find a biohazard suit and respirator."

"Why do you have the suit?" Clay asked.

"I have a lot of survival gear."

Clay looked at Piper.

She shook her head. "Didn't see anything else."

"It's not here. I keep it in my storage area."

"So why's the suit in your house, then?" Clay asked.

He shrugged.

Clay got in the man's face. "You're keeping things from me, Mr. Assad, and I don't like it when people keep things from me."

Assad lifted his chin, a smirk on his face.

Clay planted his hands on the chair. "Where's the storage unit?"

Assad shrugged, his smug expression making Hunter take in deep breaths and let them out slowly.

Clay pulled back to look at the others, his eyes filled with anger. "Tear this place apart until we find the key and address for the storage place. No worries about being careful. Clearly, Mr. Assad doesn't care about his things, or he would cooperate."

After the team departed to the other rooms, Clay walked to a bookshelf and swept the items onto the floor. "Let's see what we have here." Clay squatted by the items, a few of them broken.

Assad glared at him. "You will pay for this."

"Actually, you're the one who's going to pay if you don't start giving us information."

"What do you want to know?"

"Tell us about the last time you saw Fletcher Gilliam," Hunter said.

He shrugged. "When I came back from traveling overseas, I found out no one would hire me, and I went to see him. I'm not sure what day that was."

Clay watched Assad carefully. "What did he say to you?"

"Say?" Assad interlaced his fingers and squeezed. "He told me I deserved to be blackballed."

"He give a reason?" Hunter asked.

"The same one he gave others." He scoffed. "Said I was the one who tried to steal *his* work and pass it off as my own."

"Did you?" Hunter asked.

That earned Hunter a menacing glare. "You're just like everyone else. Believing him over me. It's because of my race. I know that. You know that. But someday, I will get revenge. On you. On him. On everyone who has wronged me or inflicted their prejudice on me."

Clay shared a worried look with Hunter then turned his attention back to Assad. "Sounds to me like you have something planned."

A sick smile crossed the man's face.

They weren't learning much by antagonizing the guy, so Hunter decided to take a different tact. "I suppose it's something grand. A sharp guy like you wouldn't do things halfway."

He lifted his chin. "You're right. I wouldn't."

"You might be talented, but if you're planning to take out so many people, you probably have some help."

His chin lowered a fraction, but the haughty look remained on his face. "No man is alone. We need help to eradicate the infidels."

Now they were getting somewhere. "Aren't you afraid these people will turn on you like Fletch did?"

"No. Never." Assad shot up higher in the chair. "We are brothers in faith. We will prevail."

Hunter's phone vibrated in his pocket, and he got it out.

He read the text from Nick saying that Assad had a past association with Fadhil Yasin. The guy was connected to Al Qaeda and wanted for a car bombing in New York that had killed ten people.

Shock traveled over Hunter, but he worked hard to hide it. Assad was clearly more involved in terrorism than they'd first thought, and it was now seeming like their greatest fear was coming true.

He made sure he appeared calm so he didn't give away the fear eating at his gut. "Does the name Fadhil Yasin mean anything to you?"

Assad paled, telling Hunter he'd finally pierced Assad's armor, and they were indeed getting somewhere.

But Hunter was wrong. Way wrong. Assad clammed up, and Hunter stepped out of the room to text Maya and assure her all was well. He wished he could call her, but talking to her might distract him when he needed to be on his game with Assad.

He also called in Sierra, Nick, and Ainslie to process the scene and deputies to pick Assad up and take him to the Multnomah County Detention Center. Hunter believed he had a better chance of getting Assad to talk once in custody. At least Hunter hoped that was true.

Hunter went back into the room. Assad glared at him from the recliner. Clay leaned a shoulder against the wall as if he didn't care about Assad, his phone out researching the guy. Piper was searching the house for any lead, and the other agents had gone back to the office.

Hunter sat on a worn chair, not speaking in hopes of causing Assad's anxiety to grow. The clock Clay had swept to the floor ticked down the time, the room filled with uncomfortable silence.

Through the open front door, Hunter heard footsteps on the walkway. Nick stepped inside. He scratched his short reddish beard and looked around, his gaze connecting with Hunter.

"Thanks for coming." Hunter stood and handed the keycard to Nick. "Any ideas what it might be used for?"

Nick turned it over in gloved hands. "Not from looking at it, but I'll take it back to the lab to see what I can find on the magnetic strip."

"That is mine!" Assad shouted and bucked forward in his chair.

Clay looked up from his phone. "It's evidence."

Hunter focused on Nick. "Be sure to take his phone too. It's on the table by the wallet. No landline, just a cell."

Wearing a white Tyvek suit, Sierra arrived at Assad's doorway, her kit in hand.

Nick faced her. "Can Ainslie shoot the guy's card and cell so I can take them back to the lab?"

"Sure." She turned and called out to Ainslie, who came into the room dressed in similar attire to Sierra. Ainslie had pulled back her long dark hair into a ponytail like Sierra. They both wore booties and latex gloves and sharp expressions.

Sierra looked at Hunter. "Where did you find the card?"

"In the guy's wallet. I took it from him when I searched him and laid it on the table over there." Hunter gestured at the small side table by the recliner. "Shoot the keys too. Looks like there's one for his storage unit. Piper's searching for the address in his office so we can check it out."

"Will do." Ainslie took the card from Nick and stepped over to the wallet. She placed a numbered tent marker by it and started taking pictures while Assad looked on in disgust. If the guy bothered Ainslie, she didn't show it. She was a total professional. All the people on the Veritas team were. Hunter only wished he could have found a reason to call Maya out here too. He was getting used to having her around. How was he ever going to say good-bye to her again?

"Where do you want me to start?" Sierra asked Hunter.

Hunter snapped his focus back to where it should be. "We found a biohazard suit and respirator. Take samples in case he didn't decontaminate it thoroughly."

"You're wasting your time," Assad said. "It hasn't even been worn."

Hunter ignored the comment. "I also spotted a drinking glass in the kitchen with lipstick. Be sure to swab that."

Sierra nodded. "Depending on the sample, I should be able to recover DNA and tell you brand and color. Maybe that will lead to whoever was here."

Assad scoffed at them. "You cannot possibly discover that information."

Sierra looked at him. "Actually, I not only can, but I will. And then it's only a matter of time before we find out where that brand is sold. If it's unique enough, we should be able to get video from the store showing who bought it."

Hunter knew that was a huge long shot, but Assad paled telling Hunter he bought Sierra's explanation. And he clearly didn't want them to know the identity of the woman who'd been at his house.

Clay looked up from his phone. "You could just save us all the work and tell us who was here with you."

"I will not."

"No worries." Clay looked at Hunter and held up his phone. "I just discovered Assad has a sister. She belongs to a young progressive women's group that's known for activism. She lives just down the street. What say we pay her a visit?"

"No! Please. She is not involved in this." Assad shot his gaze from person to person.

"Involved in what?" Clay asked.

"You know." Assad glared at him.

"No." Clay's face morphed into an iron mask. "You tell me."

Assad jutted out his chin. "I'm not saying anything."

Clay pushed off the wall. "Then we'll visit your sister."

Piper entered the room, an envelope in her hand and a satisfied smile on her face. "Storage rental papers."

"Perfect," Hunter said. "We'll tear apart the storage unit and then talk to the sister."

"I..." Assad bit his lower lip.

"Something you want to tell us before we go?" Clay asked.

Assad lifted his chin. "May the wrath of Allah be upon your heads."

Hunter wanted to shoot back a sharp comment but held his tongue.

Ainslie finished her photos and stepped out of the room.

Nick bagged the card. "Anything else?"

"Yeah, a word outside." Hunter looked at Clay. "Keep an eye on this guy for a minute, will you?"

"Glad to," Clay said, eyeing Assad.

Hunter followed Nick outside and down to the walkway. "I assume you ran a background on Fadhil Yasin already, so tell me about him."

"Interesting guy."

Hunter didn't know what to make of that comment. "Interesting good or interesting bad?"

Nick's eyes narrowed. "Definitely bad. He was an Iman in New York City for a fairly large Muslim mosque. In the last year he was there, he turned into a fanatic. Hating and calling out people who openly sinned, like drug addicts, prostitutes, gamblers, et cetera. He totally lost it and that's when he set off the car bomb."

"Wow, you weren't kidding." Hunter shook his head. "Interesting guy. Any idea why the change?"

"Turns out the woman he was engaged to fell in with a bad crowd. Got addicted to crack and got pregnant. He decided the people who did this to her had to pay, which is when he set the car bomb. What he didn't know was this woman snuck out of the house that night to join her buddies."

"She was killed in the bombing?"

Nick nodded. "Yasin really lost it then, and he bailed before he could be arrested. He's been lying low. No one's seen him since then."

"How did you find this information on him?"

"Assad posted a picture with him on a forum. He didn't post his name, but I matched it through facial recognition."

"Can you text me his picture?"

Nick peeled off his latex gloves and got out his phone. "Coming your way."

Hunter's phone chimed, and he looked at Yasin's photo. He had dark wavy hair with a chin covered in a full black beard. He wore black-rimmed glasses with thick lenses, but they didn't hide the anger and pain in his eyes.

Hunter looked up. "Looks like a guy filled with hate."

"My take too."

Hunter held up his phone. "Thanks for this and for finding this guy."

Nick nodded. "Just be careful. As you said, he looks like a guy filled with hate, and men like that are dangerous."

19

Hunter got out of the SUV with Clay at the storage facility, the hot sun beating down on them. The place was located in a sketchy neighborhood on the east side of Portland. The units were rusty metal and the security lax without any sort of gate at the entrance.

Clay inserted Assad's key in the lock, and it dropped open. "Bingo."

Hunter grabbed the hot metal handle and rolled up the door, then found the overhead light and switched it on. He didn't know what to expect, but he hadn't imagined finding sealed boxes stacked to the ceiling.

He stepped into the sweltering unit, and sweat instantly beaded up on his face. It was eighty-five outside but felt like one-hundred-twenty inside. A musty smell clung to the space. Not unusual if the contents had been stored over the rainy Portland winter and spring.

"Looks like merchandise," Clay said. "And a lot of it for someone who doesn't own a business."

"It's a lot of merchandise even *if* he has a business." Hunter got out his pocketknife and sliced open the first box. Mounds of respirators filled the box.

Hunters gut tightened and sweat formed on his forehead, not only from the heat, but from the realization of what Assad might have planned. "He only needs a large quantity of respirators like this if he's planning to be exposed to something that might kill him. Or he could've been hoarding for the pandemic."

Clay tapped a label. "Look at the dates on these boxes. They were shipped long ago."

Hunter sliced open the next box. "Biohazard suits."

Clay scowled and swiped an arm over his sweaty forehead. "He's into something big."

"Something that could very well involve botulism toxin. Maybe there's a lead in one of these boxes." Hunter ripped open the next one. "More respirators. Has to be a hundred in this box alone."

Clay's scowl deepened, and in the next stack, he rested his hand on a case of latex gloves. "There's enough stuff here to keep a large number of people safe for a very long time."

Hunter paused in cutting another box open. "Like Assad said, he's not alone in whatever he's planning. We need to figure out if Yasin is part of the group."

"Maybe Assad's sister can shed some light on that."

Hunter nodded and closed the box. "The rest of these boxes are likely the same items. We can lock up and get Sierra's team out here to go through them so we can go see the sister."

Hunter climbed into his SUV. "Also means they're going to release the toxin in such a way that they won't need to protect their living environment."

Clay buckled his seatbelt. "So either they're leaving the area immediately after release or they're releasing it in a limited way. Like targeting certain audiences."

"If he's working with Yasin, Al Qaeda might be behind this plot." Hunter got in his car, cranked the engine, and headed out of the storage facility. "So who does Al Qaeda hate most besides all Americans?"

Clay narrowed his gaze. "Their goal is to move all Americans out of the Middle East. They might target our leaders who supervise overseas politicians."

"Or companies operating over there," Hunter said. "When we finish talking with Assad's sister, I'll ask Nick to look for likely targets."

"I'll check in with my supervisor to see if he's heard anything new about imminent attacks." Clay got out his phone and made the call.

Hunter drove the route to Sakina Assad's house and listened to Clay's side of the conversation.

As Clay talked, his frustration matched Hunter's over this investigation. He was still struggling to believe Carson's death and Fletch's disappearance might lead to terrorism—lead to a plot that could kill an incredibly large number of people.

Clay shoved his phone into his pocket. "He didn't have any additional intel, but he'll run it up the flagpole to D.C. to see if they have any."

Hunter shook his head. "Wonder how long that's going to take to get back to the DHS contact my supervisor is working with."

Clay frowned. "You think he's going to butt in when we interview Assad?"

"It's possible, and certainly if we fail to get any information from Assad."

Clay crossed his arms and frowned. "We need some proof that our investigations are connected. Which means finding Jason's killer."

"Or Fletch." Hunter pulled up in front of a small complex of townhouses with neat landscaping and freshly painted buildings. He shifted into park and pointed out the window. "She's in the second building."

They made their way to a black door holding a red flowery wreath. Matching flowering plants and tall spikes of green foliage spilled out of large containers on both sides of the entrance. Clay pounded on the door, and it rattled under his fist.

Hunter wished for a strong breeze to cool the area and moved to a shaded spot to get out of the sun.

The door opened, and a woman resembling Eshan minus the glare peered at them. She wore black slacks, a colorful blouse covering her neck and arms, and a black hijab over her head, leaving her face exposed.

Clay and Hunter flashed their credentials, and Clay introduced them.

Sakina's eyebrow went up, but that was her only response, as if she was accustomed to law enforcement coming to her door.

"Can we come in, Ms. Assad?" Hunter asked. "We have some questions for you regarding your brother."

Her large brown eyes narrowed. "I don't think so."

"I would much rather talk to you here than to take you downtown for a formal interview," Clay said, his tone much more congenial than when he'd interviewed her brother.

She looked between them, then stood back without speaking. Hunter didn't give her a chance to change her mind and stepped into a two-story foyer. Clay joined him.

"The living room is straight ahead," Sakina said.

Hunter strode past a steep stairway leading to the second floor and down a hallway that opened up into a great room with an open kitchen. The scent of incense lingered in the air, and Hunter saw a stick smoking from a holder on the coffee table. He glanced back and noted that

Sakina had left the front door open. Her distrust was evident in her look and in her actions.

"Please sit." She gestured at a beige sofa loaded with colorful pillows.

Hunter found a spot among them and sat. Clay perched on the arm.

She settled on a matching easy chair and folded her hands on her lap. "What is it you want to know about my brother other than he is a law-abiding man?"

Clay shifted to face her. "Are you aware of his affiliation with a man called Fadhil Yasin?"

She shook her head, and, if she was lying, her expression didn't give away her thoughts. "Should I have heard of this man?"

Hunter decided not to pull any punches. "He's wanted in a car bombing that killed ten people."

She jerked back and clasped her hand on her chest. "My brother would not associate with such a man."

Clay shifted. "He admitted to knowing him."

Her mouth fell open. "Have you tortured him to get the information?"

Hunter narrowed his gaze. "Of course not."

"Has he been arrested?"

"Yes."

She crossed her arms, resignation tightening her face. "Then he will be tortured."

"I know there are stories of such a thing happening," Hunter said. "But trust me. We won't harm your brother."

She rolled her eyes, and her arms tightened.

"Do you know Eshan's whereabouts this past week?" Clay asked.

She tipped her head. "He wasn't with me, if that's what you're asking. I've been home alone except for when I was with my women's group."

The group Clay mentioned, which seemed odd considering she still wore a head covering when many progressive Muslim women had stopped wearing them.

"Does he belong to any men's groups?" Clay asked.

She nodded. "He is involved in our local community center."

"Where's that located?" Hunter asked.

She gave him a nearby address, and he jotted it down in his notebook.

Clay pinned his focus on her. "Were you aware that he's been unable to find a job?"

She gritted her teeth. "Yes. Some person he worked with blackballed him. Of course he didn't do what this other person said, but he is a Muslim, so it is easy for people to believe negative things about him."

"I'm sorry that kind of prejudice happens," Hunter said.

She arched an eyebrow but said nothing.

"Are you aware of any terrorist activities in the Portland area?" Clay asked.

She clasped her hands on her lap. "This after you say you are sorry for your prejudice? We are not all terrorists, you know."

"I *do* know that," Hunter said. "But your brother is affiliated with one, so I must ask if you are involved with them in their cause."

She didn't look like she believed him, and she stood. "I am not, and it is time for you to leave."

Maya blew out a relieved breath, and her feet stuttered to a stop at the sight of Hunter talking to their night guard, Pete, in the lobby. They were probably talking law enforcement as

Pete was a former police officer, and he looked the part with his buzz cut and wide stance.

She wanted to race across the room and throw her arms around Hunter. To hold him and never let him go. Especially never let him go on another dangerous op. But that was his job —his world—and he loved it, so she would never ask him to change. Just like he would never ask her to leave a job she loved.

Listen to her. Thinking that they might someday be in a position where a discussion like that would be relevant.

She shook off her thoughts and calmly crossed the spacious lobby, letting the cool blue and beige colors calm her nerves. By the time she reached Hunter, she was able to conjure up a serene smile. "Glad to hear your op was a success."

He responded with a sharp nod.

She couldn't tell what he was thinking. Which was fair when she was hiding her emotions from him. "We'll be meeting with the partners in the conference room for an update, but we have time to grab a snack first. You hungry?"

"I could eat."

She nodded. "I made some fresh hummus this week. Let's head up to my condo."

"Yum. Your hummus is the best."

Pete rubbed his belly. "Aw, take pity on a guy stuck down here for the rest of the night and bring me just a little, won't you?"

She chuckled at his pitiful tone and look. He reminded her of a sweet puppy begging at the dinner table. "You know I will."

His hangdog expression was replaced with a beaming smile. "This is why I love working here. Fine people, all of you."

"Right back atcha," Maya said and headed for the elevator. She punched number six then looked at Hunter, who was leaning against the wall. "I really am glad things went well with Assad. And that no one got hurt."

He leaned back, but tension clung to him. "Yeah, me too."

"You don't sound so thrilled about it."

"No, I am, it's just I wanted to get more out of Sakina and her brother."

"So what are you going to do?"

He let out a long breath. "Let him sit in lockup for a while to understand the reality of prison life. Clay, Piper, and I are going to take another run at him tonight."

Maya could easily imagine the three of them questioning Assad. "I wish I could be there. Look the man in the eye and tell him how much Fletch means to me and get him to talk."

Hunter frowned. "He's not the sort of guy who's going to take your feelings into account."

"Yeah, I suppose not."

The doors opened at six, and she stepped out. Hunter came up beside her and twined his fingers with hers. He didn't say a word, just kept walking.

Shocked, she didn't know what to say, if anything, but one thing was clear. She loved holding his hand. She felt like it held a promise for something he wasn't quite ready to commit to. But wasn't she a fool for even thinking this way? He wasn't ready to commit years ago and look how that ended. He likely wanted to change then too, and yet in six years, he hadn't. So what was different today?

Nothing. Except her heart. And she was putting herself in a position to be hurt.

Thankfully, they reached her door, and she had to remove her hand to unlock it. She nearly sighed over the loss. Over the potential that might never be realized between them.

She swallowed her feelings. She would stick to her guns. Keep things professional between them. If he tried to hold her hand again, she would refuse no matter how much she wanted it. That was the only answer until he was ready to commit to her.

She went straight to the kitchen that held a lingering smell of coffee from the maker she hadn't emptied that morning. "Go ahead and have a seat. What do you want to drink?"

"Water is great, and I can get it myself. Just tell me where the glasses are." He joined her in the kitchen that normally felt just the right size, but his presence seemed to take up every square inch of the space.

"Top right by the fridge." She scooted to the end of the kitchen even though everything she needed was in or near the refrigerator.

"Is something wrong?" He grabbed a glass and filled it with water and ice through the refrigerator door. "You seem jumpy all of a sudden."

"Just thinking about the investigation," she said, hoping she could ignore him and make that a reality.

He took a long sip of the water, and she watched his tanned throat as he swallowed. "Do you want me to update you on the leads we found or wait until the meeting?"

"What do you want to do?" She got the hummus and carrots from the refrigerator.

"Wait, so we can have a few minutes to enjoy the hummus and each other's company."

"About that." She set the items on the island. "I know we both laid our feelings out there, but since nothing has changed, maybe we should stick to the investigation and sort this out later."

He set down his glass and clamped his hands on the countertop. "I thought we were just starting to get along again. Like we used to."

"Yeah, but again..." She shrugged and went to grab crackers and plates.

"You don't think I'm going to change."

She had to work hard not to stop walking at his comment, but she got out the plates and looked at him. "I don't see what's different now."

He dropped onto a stool and stared into his water glass. "I never wanted anything as badly as I want to be with you."

"Wasn't that true in the past?" She scooped a large dollop of hummus onto her plate.

"Yes."

"So what's different now?"

"I can't put it into words but it *is* different." He reached for the spoon then let his hand fall. "Maybe seeing you again after all these years has made me realize what I've given up. Maybe seeing Piper so happy with Nick is showing me what I'm missing. I don't know. It's just different."

She dipped a carrot into the spicy black bean hummus and chewed. The flavors exploded in her mouth, and she almost groaned over the melding of the garlic and adobo peppers.

"And yet." He locked eyes with her. "You still doubt me."

She swallowed the spicy bite. "I'm sorry. I don't want to."

"I get it. I haven't given you any reason not to." He got up and came around the island. He took her hands and looked her in the eyes.

Her resolve evaporated at the power of his gaze—the touch of his skin. Her heart thundered in her chest. How she wanted to keep holding his hands. To do more. Maybe have him lean down and kiss her again.

"I'm not going to hurt you this time, sweetheart. I promise." His tone was adamant. Sure. "I'm going to figure out how to get over this and do everything I can to make you the happiest woman in the world."

She looked into his sincere gaze and remembered what her father always told her. If something seemed too good to be true, it probably was. Despite Hunter's sincerity, she thought this might be one of those times when things were too good to be true.

20

Clay, Piper, and Maya's partners were clustered around the conference room table with drinks in hand by the time Maya and Hunter got down there. At her distrust of him, Hunter had wanted to bolt from the condo. But he deserved it. And then he went and made a promise that he didn't know if he could keep. So maybe she was right. Maybe they needed to focus on the investigation. That was safe and wouldn't hurt her. She was the most amazing woman. He was rediscovering that with every minute spent in her presence, and she sure didn't deserve to be hurt again.

"Go ahead and start with an update," she said to him.

He remained standing at the head of the table, looking at the very talented partners and suddenly feeling inadequate. Could be because of the conversation upstairs or could be over his failure to get Assad to talk. Either way, he had to shrug off the emotions and get to it.

He took several deep breaths and started. "As some of you know, we arrested an Eshan Assad this afternoon. He and Fletch had a falling out in the past." He explained their disagreement. "Assad admits to wanting to get back at

Fletch, and he admits to going to Fletch's lab a few weeks ago."

Kelsey set down her mug of tea. "But not this week?"

"No. Not this week," Hunter said. "At least that's what he claimed. But we found a biohazard suit and respirator at his home. Sierra is processing those."

Sierra sipped from a silver travel mug. "I found particulates on the suit, but testing to identify the swabbed samples will take time."

"We also found a blank keycard in his wallet," Clay said. "Nick is reviewing it."

"It's a basic magnetic stripe card," Nick said. "You run the stripe over a sensor that reads the contents of the stripe. A central system holds data that the card is then compared to. It could be a hardwired connection or work on radio waves. We're determining which one this card is now. In either event, we hope it will lead us to the central system that should give us some valuable data."

"Like what?" Hunter asked.

"Like what the card unlocks."

"That would be valuable indeed." Hunter smiled. "And what about his phone?"

"It's password protected, so my guys are using an emulator to crack the password. Should have something soon."

Hunter nodded. In his job on the local FBI elite cyber squad, he was very familiar with the difficulty in cracking passwords. "Nick also discovered that Assad is connected to Fadhil Yasin."

"A nasty dude," Nick said and shared Yasin's past.

Maya clasped her hands together. "Do you think terrorists are actually behind the toxin release and Carson's and Greg's deaths?"

"I'm beginning to."

"Me, too," Clay said. "Especially with what we found in the storage unit."

Hunter shared about the boxes of supplies.

Maya gasped, and the others stared at him.

"It's clear they're gearing up for something big," he said bluntly because there was no way to sugarcoat this news. "Which even more increases our need to find Fletch."

"I've got my feelers out for any hint of an impending terrorist event, and so far nothing." Nick placed his hands on the table. "And I can't push my team any faster on that card and phone. They're already working at top speed."

Maya joined Hunter at the head of the table. "What about other leads we're running down?"

"I still have forensics to process from the boathouse and now Assad's place," Sierra said. "Though I can assume the large number of prints I lifted from his house belong to him, it would be good if I could get his actual prints ASAP to compare."

"I'll make sure that happens," Hunter said. "But go ahead and compare the ones you have to the ones from the lab to see if we can physically connect him to Fletch."

"I'll do that the minute I get back to my lab and let you know what I find." Sierra took a sip from her mug. "Do you want us to process the storage unit?"

Hunter nodded. "I've got the keys, but they're booked as evidence, so I'll need to get you to sign off before I give them to you."

Sierra set down her mug. "I'll send Chad out to the scene so I can keep working the samples."

Emory swiveled in her chair to look at Maya, the movement slow with her advanced pregnancy. "I have several DNA processes still running. Rudy's, Greg's, the buckle, and the mosquito."

"And these were good samples, so you expect results?" Maya asked.

Emory nodded. "We'll get DNA profiles for sure, and I'm just starting the samples from Assad's place. The DNA from the bones was a bust, though."

Hunter had hoped to be able to ID the other people, but now they were going to have to rely on dental records for that. "Let us know the minute you have information on these outstanding items."

"Of course. And in case I go into labor, I'll make sure my team knows to report to you." She shared a shy smile with Blake.

His downcast expression brightened, and Hunter could easily imagine him as a proud dad.

Blake cleared his throat. "On another note. I checked into known drug dealers who might have had contact with Carson but came up empty-handed."

"At this point, I don't know what to make of the cocaine," Maya said.

"Intelligence agencies have documented links to illicit drug activities for many of the terrorist organizations." Clay looked around the table. "It's called narco-terrorism, and they derive much of their funding this way. Though usually, we're dealing with opium and its derivatives like heroin."

"The toxin is meant to kill people so it doesn't seem like drug sales for funding," Maya said. "Unless, of course, they're going to sell it."

"Still, it could give them connections for a ready supply of drugs," Clay said.

"What about the sister?" Nick asked. "Does it seem like she's involved?"

"From our interview, not really," Hunter said. "But she could be."

Nick narrowed his eyes. "I'll work on finding a connection between her and Yasin."

"We're finished with the hard drives," Piper said. "I can help with that."

Grady leaned forward. "I've finished analyzing the bullet I recovered in the fire rubble. It's a 9mm, but it's in such bad shape, I doubt we'll be able to match it to the weapon."

Clay slammed his fist on the table. "Let's hope you're wrong about that."

"I could be," Grady said. "But it's unlikely."

"We have to figure this out," Clay snapped.

"There's just so much we don't know." Hunter shook his head. "And the only way to find out the answers is to get after it. Starting by doing our best to make Assad talk."

In the parking lot under starry skies and a refreshing breeze carrying the smell of sizzling beef from a nearby restaurant, Maya wished they had a strong lead to find Fletch. Something stronger than this interview that she couldn't even be part of. "I still want to come along to interview Assad."

Hunter gave her a tight smile. "And I'd like to take you with me, but it would be improper. I've probably already involved you in way too many aspects of the investigation. And I sure can't afford to have you there if our DHS contact shows up."

"I get it. I just don't like it."

He lifted a hand as if he planned to touch her face but let it drop. "I gotta go. Clay's waiting for me."

She suddenly didn't want him to go at all. "Call me when you have any information."

"I can't take my phone into the jail with me, so it won't be until we conclude the interview."

"I know." She squeezed his arm. "Just call as soon as you can."

He eyed her. "You sound worried, but Assad can't hurt us."

"True, but if Yasin knows you arrested him..."

"Assad couldn't have notified Yasin of his arrest."

"But his sister could have, right?"

"Yes, if she knows Yasin, but we haven't found a connection between them."

"Doesn't mean she doesn't know him." Maya shoved her hands into the pockets of her lab coat. "And Nick might find that connection in his research."

"Let's hope he does."

"Coming?" Clay called from where he stood by Hunter's SUV.

"Gotta go." Hunter squeezed her hand and took off across the parking lot. She stood in the lot watching until his SUV disappeared then took one more look at the clear sky filled with millions of sparkling stars before heading indoors.

"Nice night out," Pete said from behind the desk. "Would be a perfect night for a date."

She shook her head. "You are so not a subtle matchmaker."

"I know, but then, you need more than subtlety." He grinned. "You're the only one I need to work on these days. All the rest are paired up. Means all my attention is devoted to you."

"Gee thanks." She laughed. She knew he meant well. He thought of all the partners as his kids and treated them as such.

"Just don't let Hunter get away again."

She wanted to tell him she never let him get away in the first place, but maybe she had. What would have happened if she'd gone after him when he'd walked out? Would she have been able to convince him to work on his fears? Might he have done so, and they'd have stayed together?

"Aw man," Pete said. "Did what I said put that look on your face?"

She knew what look he must mean. Sad. Tired. Frustrated. All wrapped up with longing for a man she couldn't have. "I'm fine. Just tired. I'm headed up to my lab to catch up on everything I've neglected this week."

"Most everyone else is working too." He frowned. "I worry about Emory though. She should be taking it easy."

"She's not taking any chances with the baby. She'll rest if she needs to." Maya started for the elevator.

"Let's hope you're right," Pete called after her. "I've delivered a baby before, but I sure don't want to do it here."

Maya stepped into the stairwell, her thoughts on Emory. She doubted Pete would have to deliver her baby. If she somehow went into labor and couldn't leave, Blake would take care of her. He'd likely delivered a baby or two when he was in law enforcement.

She pushed open the door to her lab, taking a moment to look around for the first time in days. Her staff had left the place neat and tidy as always, and there was a faint hint of bleach lingering in the air. She was so thankful for her assistants. But they couldn't do everything, so she headed to her desk.

She sat down to the stack of reports for law enforcement and spent hours signing off on them.

Her phone rang, and she glanced at the clock. Seven. Had to be Hunter. She grabbed her phone but an unknown number appeared. The call could be about the investigation, so she answered. "Maya Glass."

"Hi." The woman's high-pitched voice wasn't immediately recognizable. "It's Lucy Karl, the escape room manager."

Maya sat forward, her mind racing over why Lucy might be calling. "Yes, Lucy. What can I do for you?"

"Fletch called me. He said he wanted you to meet him here in fifteen minutes."

"Fletch? Really? He called?" Maya's heart raced at the good news.

"Yeah."

Maya took a calming breath. "Did he say where he was?"

"No. He just said to meet him here."

Maya wanted more details. "What about the phone number he called from? Can I get that?"

"No number."

Odd. "Didn't it show up on caller ID?"

"We don't have that on our work phones. Look. I gotta go. Busy night here. See you soon."

"Sure, I'll—" The call went dead.

Maya continued to hold her phone, her thoughts racing over the good news. She got out her phone to call Hunter, then remembered he couldn't take his phone into the jail. She could call the jail, she supposed, but Fletch wanted to see her in fifteen minutes, and she had no time to wait for a deputy to locate him and interrupt his interrogation.

She tapped his number, left him a detailed message, and took off running, her hopes soaring. Fletch was not only alive, but she was going to see him in fifteen minutes, and she wouldn't be late.

"Go ahead, Assad." Hunter leaned back in his chair and casually crossed his leg in the small room that was starting to feel airless and stuffy. "I can sit here all night if I have to."

Assad glared at Hunter in the same way he'd been doing since Hunter and Piper had entered the interrogation room at the Multnomah County Detention Center in downtown Portland. Clay was watching from behind the glass because the room was so small. The space was only big enough for a small table, four chairs, and video recording equipment.

"I'm sorry you're finding yourself in this situation," Piper said, playing her role as the good cop. "Yasin has threatened you if you speak. I get that. He's a killer. You don't seem like one to me. But you're trying to stay alive by not talking to us."

He focused on her, his gaze remaining hard and challenging. "I do not wish to speak with a woman about business matters."

"Would you like her to leave?" Hunter asked.

"I would."

Hunter looked at Piper. "Will you go and send Clay in?"

Piper clenched her hands under the table for a moment then smiled at Assad. "I'll leave, but not because you want me to. I'll do it out of respect for my fellow agent who has asked me to go."

She stood and pulled her shoulders back, eyed Assad for a long moment, then gracefully exited the room. Hunter was proud of her for remaining so calm and not letting this creep's prejudice get to her. Clay shot in before the door even closed.

He straddled a chair and pinned Assad with his gaze. "Thanks for tagging me in, Assad. I'm glad to be here."

Assad tried to cross his arms, but the cuffs wouldn't allow it, and he dropped his hands to the table. "It will not matter. I am not speaking."

"So you've said. But like my buddy here mentioned." Clay jerked a thumb at Hunter. "We have all night. Shoot, we have days if it comes to that."

Clay tightened his hands on the back of the chair and leaned forward. "But here's the thing, Assad. I've been interviewing guys like you for a long time, and you will talk to us. I guarantee that. So do us all a favor and quit wasting our time."

~

Maya hurried through the sultry night and into the escape rooms where the tantalizing scent of fresh popcorn saturated the air. The place was jumping, just like Lucy had said, and Maya had to wait in a line to get to the counter. The same teenage boy from their last visit was signing teams up for their rooms. An excited buzz filled the space, and Maya felt it clear to her toes.

She checked her watch. Three minutes.

Come on, come on, come on. Fletch could be waiting for me. She moved up in line and checked her phone to see if Hunter had tried to call back. Nothing. No call or text. So he was likely still in the interview.

Father, please let Assad talk tonight so we can finally find out who killed Carson.

"You again," the boy behind the counter said in an accusing tone. "Fletch hasn't been here, and Lucy said she'd call if he showed up."

Maya stifled a need to snap back at the kid. "Actually, Lucy called me to come down here."

"Really?" His bushy eyebrows rose. "She's, like, been locked in her office for the last few hours and told me not to bother her."

"I need you to get her for me."

He chewed on his lip. "I dunno."

Maya got out her phone and showed him the call. "This's your number here, right?"

"Yeah. Sure...okay. Let me buzz her." He picked up the phone's handset and pressed a button. "The lady who's looking for Fletch is here."

"My name is Maya," she said.

"Maya's her name." He listened but looked totally bored with the conversation. "If you say so."

He settled the handset on the cradle and lifted the end of the counter. "She said to go on back. Down the hall, last door on the left."

Maya scooted through the opening and nearly ran to the office. She took a moment to take a few breaths to calm down and knocked on the closed door.

The door opened a notch, and Lucy, her eyes wide, peeked out.

"It's just me," Maya said.

Lucy pulled the door all the way open and stood back but didn't speak. Maya expected Lucy to be cheerful, but the woman had acted odd when they interviewed her, so Maya wasn't concerned at her quiet mood.

Maya stepped into the room. Lucy quickly closed the door. Two men with inky black hair and dark skin stood behind Lucy.

The shortest one, dressed in a crisp black suit, lifted a handgun and pointed it at Maya. "Welcome, Dr. Glass. So good of you to join us."

21

Hunter felt like they were finally wearing Assad down. His posture was sagging, his eyes less alert. And yet, he hadn't said a word to help them find Fletch. But Hunter wasn't giving up. Not with so much at stake and no other strong leads. He really did have all night.

Hunter fixed his focus on Assad. "Tell me one thing. Then we'll take a break. Do you know if Dr. Fletcher Gilliam is alive?"

Assad rolled his eyes. "As I have said, I do not know anything about that."

Hunter curled his fingers under the table and tried to come up with a new way to get the information they needed out of this man.

"Okay, let's look at this hypothetically," Clay said, sounding as frustrated as Hunter felt. "Hypothetically, a scientist has gone missing along with his formula for aerosolizing a certain toxin. Hypothetically, you know someone who might have abducted him. Hypothetically, could he still be alive and is being held against his will?"

Assad gave the slightest of nods but didn't speak and

Hunter's hope perked up as Clay could be on to something here.

A broad smile crossed Clay's face. "Well then, we're getting somewhere."

"This is all." He planted his hands on the table, the chains holding his cuffs jingling. "I am not saying another word."

"Actually, you didn't say anything," Hunter said. "So when we find Yasin—and we will—he can't blame you for talking."

Assad lifted his chin, his expression haughty. "He knows I am loyal and would never give away his confidences."

"Here's the thing, Assad." Hunter stood. "Whether you say anything or not, he's going to think you talked. And then he's going to arrange to have your life snuffed out while in prison. Or even take your sister's life."

"But I—"

"You haven't told us anything," Hunter said. "I know that. But *he* doesn't know that, does he? And we can make sure word gets back to him. But we can also make sure you're protected."

He scoffed. "He knows I am loyal. Knows that you are liars."

"Then why do you look so worried?" Hunter smirked. "My associate and I are going to take a break. You think on that while we're gone."

∾

Maya wished she hadn't come alone, but with the business open and in full swing, she didn't expect danger. And even if she had brought someone along, it wouldn't change anything. They would just be in danger too. Besides, Hunter knew where she was, and she just had to stall to buy time until he got there.

The short man waved his white plastic gun at the chairs by Lucy's desk. He held the small weapon that looked like a toy in gloved hands. Maya knew it wasn't a toy, though. He was using a 3-D printed gun. In her experience, they were often used because the person in possession of the gun thought they were untraceable. He obviously didn't know that her team had the skills to trace such guns back to the printer they were made on.

"Have a seat." The man had a thick Middle Eastern accent, a wide jaw, pockmarked skin, and full lips. But most importantly, he matched the photos she'd seen of Fadhil Yasin, and his expression said he wasn't used to people ignoring his commands.

Lucy hurried to the chairs and sat, clasping her hands on her lap and looking terrified.

Maya remained standing and took a moment to think about her next move. Did she acknowledge right off the bat that she knew who he was or wait to see if he brought up his name? She'd never come face to face with a terrorist before and didn't know what to do. Best to take clues from him.

He gestured at the taller man whose burly arms were crossed, his gaze pinned on Maya. She assumed he was the muscle brought along to keep her in line. She was going to think of him as Igor until she learned his real name.

He came toward her and unfolded his beefy arms, releasing a strong body odor that nearly made Maya gasp. He was going to shove her onto a chair.

"What do you want with me?" she quickly asked Yasin.

"Sit, and I will tell you." He waved the gun again.

She didn't want to be at a disadvantage, but she also needed to know what was going on, And Igor was reaching out for her anyway, so she perched on the edge of a hard backed chair, ready to escape if the opportunity presented itself. Igor stepped back.

She set her purse on her lap and took some comfort from the feel of her Glock 43 sitting in the bottom of her bag. Hopefully they wouldn't even begin to suspect she might be carrying and she could get to it and use it.

She met Yasin's gaze. "Okay. I'm sitting."

He moved closer to her but left too great of a distance for her to spring on him. "I need your help."

Not at all what she expected him to say, but she wouldn't show her surprise. "With what?"

"Not what, who. Dr. Gilliam. He's refusing to reproduce the aerosolized toxin for us. So I need leverage to convince him."

Her pulse shot up at the news that Fletch was alive, but she wasn't going to show Yasin that either. "And I'm that leverage."

"Exactly." He smirked. "Once I threaten to kill you, the stubborn Dr. Gilliam will do as I ask."

"Or not," she said, though she knew he was right.

"Come now, Dr. Glass. You know your friend. He will capitulate."

"Not if he thinks you're going to kill countless people with the toxin."

"Of course I am. He knows this already. But my mission is one of mercy."

She forgot about hiding her emotions and shook her head over his absurd comment. "How can that be?"

"You will soon see." He smiled, but it was dark and dangerous. "Now come. We will leave to meet with him."

"How do I know he's really alive?"

His smile evaporated into a cold line. "You need not know anything." Yasin pointed his gun at Lucy's temple. "Come along with me and she lives. Refuse and she dies."

Lucy clasped her hands tightly on her jeans and met Maya's gaze, her eyes pleading. "Please. Please. I don't want to die."

"Did you hear that?" Yasin asked. "She needs you to come with me."

"Fine," Maya said, trying to come up with a way to buy some time for Hunter to listen to her voicemail. "I'll come with you, but not until I know your name."

"Oh, right. We haven't been properly introduced. I am Fadhil Yasin." He cast her an arrogant look as if he thought she should be duly impressed.

"You're friends with Eshan Assad," she said, making sure her tone was emotionless.

"Ah, so you know this. It does not matter." He glared at Maya. "We have talked enough. It is time to go."

Evil burned from his eyes, but she looked right back at him so he didn't think she was intimidated. "And what happens to Lucy now?"

"I can't trust you, so she'll have to come with us too." He looked at Igor. "Come. Take her. And, Dr. Glass, you will come with me."

She stood, praying, Hunter would pick up his voicemail and come looking for her. The kid up front would tell him she'd arrived on her own and came to the office to meet with Lucy. Hunter might think she'd gone to meet Fletch as her message had indicated and that Maya was fine.

But her situation was so far from that. She needed to leave some sort of clue that told him she wasn't fine. She looked around. Down. Spotted the ring her mother had given to her before she died. Hunter would know Maya would never leave her mother's ring behind for any reason. She stood, shouldered her purse, then slipped her hands behind her back and tugged off the ring.

She started for the door and casually set it on the desk

behind her, making sure to block Yasin's view of the desk with her body as she walked toward him. He didn't notice her furtive actions and shoved the gun in her back.

"Remember," he said. "Lucy's life depends on you not trying to escape."

She understood his warning, but if the opportunity presented itself to get away, she would take it. He'd told them his name and didn't bother to hide his face. He would kill them both when he was done with them.

He pushed her down the hallway and into the dark alley. Igor had already gotten Lucy into the large SUV and was waiting by the open door.

"Inside," Yasin said. "Quickly."

She took her time walking toward the vehicle, knowing the moment she got inside the SUV that her life expectancy would be cut short. At the door, Yasin pulled back the gun from where he'd shoved it in her back.

Perfect. Now! Act now!

She jerked her elbow back. Knocked the plastic gun from his hand. It skittered across the pavement, coming to land under the dumpster. She turned to run.

He grabbed her upper arm, his hand biting in like a vise. The pain took her breath and thoughts for the briefest of moments. Enough time for him to shove her inside.

"The gun," Igor said.

"Leave it. It can't be traced to me, and I have other weapons." Yasin held out his hand to Maya. "Your phone."

She'd hoped he wouldn't have thought about that, but she dug it from her purse and gave it to him, holding out hope that he didn't know about the gun concealed in the bottom. He ripped off the phone's protective case and threw her phone against the brick wall. It shattered into tiny pieces. He stomped on it, the grinding sound confirming he'd destroyed it.

"Now the purse." He flapped out his hand.

Silently crying, she gave it to him. He set it in the front seat and tossed her phone case on top of it. "Now, we must move."

He climbed in beside her. Igor closed the door and jogged to the driver's seat. He got the SUV going, and Maya looked back, wishing, wanting someone—anyone—to step out the door to save them.

~

Hunter was true to his word, and he stepped into the hallway to give Assad a break. More than honoring his word, he wanted to check in with Maya to see if the partners had learned anything new that might help when they went back to Assad.

Clay exited the room and closed the door.

Hunter looked at the deputy standing guard outside the door. "We'll be back in a few."

The young guy with his thumbs hooked in his uniform waistband nodded, and Clay set off. Hunter followed him, and after picking up their phones, they stepped into the empty lobby with wet floors, the strong odor of the disinfectant they'd used filling the air. Hunter stopped and looked at his phone. Maya had called an hour ago and left a voicemail, plus he had a text from Sierra.

He quickly checked the text first. "Sierra says Assad's prints don't match the unknown prints at the lab."

Clay scowled. "So he wasn't likely there when Carson was killed."

"He could still be our killer if he wore gloves the entire time," Hunter said.

"Yeah." Clay ran a hand over his hair. "That's a good possibility for sure."

"Maya could have something that will help us get him to talk." Hunter started playing the voicemail and held out the phone so Clay could hear. Her excited voice came over the speaker.

"Fletch contacted Lucy at the escape rooms. Asked me to meet him there. Headed out now. Pray that he's really waiting for me."

The call went dead, and instead of a jubilant feeling, Hunter's heart sank.

"You don't look so thrilled about the news," Clay said. "You think it's a set up?"

Hunter stared at Clay. "Don't you?"

"Yeah."

Hunter tapped Maya's phone number and held his cell to his ear. The call rang and rang and rang, then voicemail finally picked up. He left a message to call him. "Assad can wait. Let's go."

Hunter and Clay retrieved their weapons and bolted from the detection center. Hunter raced his vehicle over the busy Portland streets, his heart beating hard. At the escape rooms, Hunter charged out of his SUV. He tried the front door. It was locked, but lights remained on inside. He banged on the door and kept pounding until the teenage kid they'd seen on their first visit came to the door.

"We're closed," he said through the glass.

Hunter flashed his badge. "Open up."

The kid twisted the deadbolt and stood back.

Hunter pushed past him. "The woman I was with the other day. Maya. Did she come in tonight?"

"Yeah. Went to talk to Lucy in her office." He jerked a thumb over his shoulder. "They both must've split out the back door because I didn't see them again."

"Were they alone?"

"I think so."

Not good enough. Not by a long shot. "No one else with them? Not a guy with red hair?"

"Not that I saw, but I suppose he coulda come in the back."

Hunter wanted to drag information from the wishy-washy kid, but better to see for himself. "Take me to the office."

The kid ran a hand over his messy hair. "I don't know. Lucy doesn't let me in the office."

Hunter fired him a this-isn't-optional look. "Don't make me arrest you for impeding an investigation."

The kid stepped back and looked at Clay.

"If he doesn't, I will." Clay's eyes were narrowed and icy, his body immovable.

The kid glanced at the door. "I gotta lock up, though."

Clay spun and twisted the lock. "Go."

The kid went through a lifted section of the checkout counter and marched down a dark hallway. He stood outside the last door and pointed. "Lucy's office."

Hunter twisted the knob, thankful to find it unlocked. He rushed in and scanned the room. Every inch of the space. His gaze landed on the desk. Froze on Maya's ring on the laminate wood. He picked it up. Clasped it tightly in his hand, his heart twisting.

"What is it?" Clay asked.

He unfurled his fingers to display the ring. "This belonged to Maya's mother. Maya would never leave it behind."

Clay arched a brow. "Unless she wanted to draw your attention to it."

"Exactly."

Hunter shoved the ring into his pocket. "We need to assume she didn't leave here of her own accord."

Hunter turned to the door where the kid was biting his lip. "Do you have security cameras?"

The kid shook his head. "Just fake ones to make people think we do."

Hunter stifled a curse and pushed into the hallway. He looked both ways and swallowed hard to keep the rising panic from taking over. He rushed into the alley and looked around. Searching for a lead. Anything to tell him where Maya might be. His gaze landed on a smashed phone.

An iPhone. Maya had an iPhone, but without a case he had no idea if it belonged to her.

He dug his phone from his pocket and dialed Nick. "I'm assuming you have a way to track Maya's phone?"

"Sure thing."

"Then do it. Now! I think she's been abducted."

22

Maya blinked in the dark room located in a large manufacturing business. She was glad to be out of the vehicle that had taken on Igor's unpleasant scent. This business carried the smell of chemicals, which she was used to.

She swept her gaze around the space that was about ten by ten. Very little light came in from the door, and she couldn't make anything out but shapes. Her kidnapper gave her a shove, but she only stepped into the room far enough for a clear view of Fletch tied to a chair in the shadowy corner. He looked up. His face was haggard, and dark circles hung under his eyes. His pale yellow T-shirt was stained, his jeans torn.

He blinked a few times, his jaw dropping. "What are you doing here?"

Yasin gave her a shove and lifted a knife to her neck. "She is your motivation. Work or I will kill her."

"But I..." Fletch said, sounding hopeless.

Maya met his gaze and held it. "Don't do it. I will willingly die to stop the toxin from being produced for this lunatic."

Yasin poked the knife into her throat, slicing her skin.

Pain arced through her body, and she felt the trickle of blood running down her throat. "Let's see how long you last."

He released her and pushed her ahead toward another chair. He shoved her onto it. "Tie her and the other one up."

Igor hurried across the dark room, moving fast for such a big man and dragging a terrified Lucy with him. He settled her on a chair and then coiled ropes around her upper body and secured her hands behind her back. He moved to Maya next and tied her up the same way.

Yasin stepped closer and tugged on the ropes. He looked at Igor. "Good work. Nice and tight."

Igor beamed like a child receiving praise from a parent.

Yasin collapsed his switchblade and shoved it into his pocket.

"Come," he said to his associate. "Let's give them a few minutes for Dr. Gilliam to decide to do the right thing."

He spun and Igor followed, a smirk on his face.

"Can we have the light on?" Maya asked.

Igor grunted, but Yasin flipped on the switch for a single bare bulb hanging from the ceiling. He closed the door behind himself. Lucy stared at the door, terror in her eyes.

Maya knew nothing she would say could calm the woman so she didn't try and faced Fletch. "Are you okay?"

"I'm fine." Tears wet his eyes. "Did you go to the lab? Find Carson?"

She nodded. "I'm so sorry, Fletch. What happened?"

"Yasin and his gorilla broke in and tied Carson up in the main lab. Then he had me dress in biohazard gear, and so did they. That's when he..." Fletch's voice broke, and he gulped air. "He mixed the toxin with cocaine and made Carson snort it. Then Yasin sprayed the toxin and set up a camera to film Carson's death. He wanted to be sure the toxin worked before we left the island."

"And Greg?" she asked. "How does he fit into this?"

His expression perked up. "Did you find him? Is he okay? They said they'd let him live if I went with them."

"They lied."

"They killed him?"

"Yes. We found him in your boat."

"No. Oh, no," Lucy cried out. "They're going to kill us too, aren't they?"

"We'll be fine," Maya said to calm herself, though she didn't believe it in the least. She looked back at Fletch. "So why Greg?"

"Yasin found out Greg was my friend. He also found out Greg was in debt up to his eyeballs and needed money. He got him to spy on me. To make sure I was working. So Greg kept asking me to go with him to the escape rooms, and he quizzed me on the progress I was making in my work. He didn't ask for details, and he was subtle." Fletch shook his head. "But when I think back on it, it's so obvious. When I succeeded, he told Yasin."

"But why did Greg come to the island?"

"He got greedy. He figured if Yasin was willing to pay him so much money just to keep tabs on me, that whatever I was working on had to be worth big bucks. He was going to steal it. Unfortunately, he ran into Yasin and the gorilla before he even got to the lab."

Maya was thankful to finally have some answers, but she still had plenty more questions. "And your call to me? What was that about?"

"When I finalized the project, instead of sending an email to Eberhardt, I decided to call him. But I got his assistant, who said he knew all of Eberhardt's projects and mine wasn't on his list. He thought I was some lunatic calling him. I could never have imagined someone could pose as Eberhardt convincingly enough to fool me. Me, of all people!" He shook his head.

"If only the assistant had told Eberhardt about the call, things would have gone very differently." Fletch squirmed in his chair. "Before I could figure out who was behind the subterfuge, Yasin showed up and explained everything he'd done. I was shocked beyond words."

"He's a worthy adversary for sure." She held Fletch's gaze. "I don't know how we're going to get away from him, but we have to try."

~

"No!" Hunter snapped at Nick on the phone as he paced the alley. "You have to be able to track Maya. We have no other way of finding her."

"Her phone's been disabled, and it's not pinging."

Hunter looked down at the crushed iPhone. "Disabled means destroyed, right?"

"With an iPhone, probably."

Hunter held his breath before he said something he shouldn't. "Let me get back to work. Maybe we'll recover something to help."

He ended the call. With a shaking hand, he shoved his phone into his pocket. He was losing it. His brain turning to mush when he needed to be the sharpest he'd ever been. Maya needed him. Was counting on him. Just like everyone else he'd lost had been. He'd failed them. He wouldn't fail her.

He marched toward the door. The tip of something white poked out from under a dumpster, catching his eye. He bolted across the alley toward the object. "Clay, get out here!"

Clay rushed out the back door and looked over Hunter's shoulder.

"It's a 3-D printed gun," Hunter said.

"Could belong to whoever took Maya, I suppose, but why leave it behind?"

"No telling." Hunter picked up the gun in his gloved hands and stood. "If he wore gloves, we won't be able to tie it to him."

"I don't know about that," Clay said. "I heard Sierra once traced a gun like this back to the printer it was made on. It's an expensive printer, and they're not that common yet. We might be able to find out who bought it and track the gun holder that way."

"Then let's get back to the lab." Hunter ran for his vehicle and didn't care if Clay kept up with him.

But he did, climbing into the passenger seat while Hunter shoved the gun into an evidence bag. He got his vehicle running, floored the gas pedal, and tore out of the lot.

"Hey, man, take it easy." Clay clicked on his seatbelt. "We can't find Maya if we crash."

"I know my driving skills." Hunter desperately wished the FBI's vehicles had lights and sirens like local police, but they rarely needed them so the agency didn't fork out the extra money.

"Call Sierra. Tell her to be waiting for us and to gather the partners." Hunter swerved around cars and trucks, horns honking.

"Seriously, dude, I'd like to live." Clay grabbed onto the dash and held on while he lifted his phone to his ear.

Hunter eased up a fraction but sped the remaining distance to the center. He parked in front of the door, and Sierra stood waiting for them. When they ran toward her, she held out a gloved hand. "Give me the gun and get your passes from Pete."

Hunter handed it over, and she led them to the counter where Pete waited. Maya might be missing, but protocol still had to be followed for safekeeping of all evidence in this building. Still, Pete worked at lightning speed, and the three of them were soon on the elevator.

"How can you tell which printer this was printed on?" Hunter asked, hoping details would keep his mind from going to all the terrible places it wanted to travel.

She looked at the bag, then back at Hunter. "The 3D printers work in a similar way to inkjet printers, using a back-and-fourth motion. But instead of ink, the 3D printer nozzles discharge a filament in layers, creating a three-dimensional item. Each layer contains small wrinkles called in-fill patterns. In an ideal world they would be uniform, but they aren't. The printer's model type, filament, and nozzle size can cause slight imperfections."

"So it's kind of like how a person's fingerprints are unique," Hunter said.

She nodded. "The patterns are unique and repeatable, which means I can ultimately trace them back to the original 3D printer."

The doors opened, and she led them down the hallway to her lab. The partners stood waiting for them. It struck him then. He wasn't alone. He didn't need to find Maya on his own. Not by a long shot. Not when he had so many capable people behind him. Beside him. Eager to enter the search.

Hunter was so filled with gratitude that he was too choked up to speak.

Thank you, Father, for providing. Now please help us find Maya.

Clay stepped forward and got out his phone. "Once we

know where Maya's located, we'll need tactical support on a moment's notice and can't wait for a warrant to act. I'm going to call in my brothers. Have them bring assault equipment and standby in the lobby."

"I'll have Grady add to the stockpile," Sierra said.

"Do it. Both of you." Hunter got out through a throat that was fast closing on him. He might lose his job over this but time was of the essence.

He'd planned to call Adair, but having the Byrd brothers standing by would allow them to react faster than going through proper channels with the FBI SWAT team. Something Hunter knew they might need if they were to bring Maya home alive.

Maya's mouth was getting dry from the fear eating away at her gut, and she swallowed hard as she looked at Fletch. She lowered her voice in case their abductors were listening. "I can't let you give in to them."

"And I can't let them kill you or Lucy," he whispered but firmed his sagging shoulders, looking renewed. "It will take me a full day to create the toxin again. I can stretch it out to take even longer. That'll buy time for you to figure out a way for us to escape."

"And if I can't find a way?" Panic hit her hard. "Then they'll have toxin to kill so many people. I can't be responsible for that."

"You won't be." His eyes tightened with resolve. "I'm the one making it."

"No. No." She shook her head and tried to come up with an alternative.

"I have to do it. Don't you see? It's the only way." He took a long breath and let it out. "Worst case, if I finish and we don't have a plan to escape, I can release it and expose us. That will stop Yasin too."

"The toxin doesn't kill right away." She locked gazes with him. "He'll live long enough to expose other people."

"Yes, but not the number of people he ultimately wants to kill." Fletch lifted his jaw. "It's the only way to keep you and Lucy alive."

She opened her mouth to argue, but the door flew in and a shaft of light cut across the floor like a hot knife slicing through butter.

Yasin stood in the shadow of the doorway, a sinister look darkening his face. "Well?"

"I'll do it," Fletch answered.

Maya stifled a gasp that wanted to come flying from her mouth. The die was cast, and without a miracle from God, their fate was sealed.

~

Hunter felt helpless in the conference room with the Veritas partners, Clay, and Piper. Sierra had determined the printer's make and model and just needed to talk to the manufacturer to find out who they'd sold it to, but the company was closed for the day, so they were at a standstill. They didn't even know if the company sold printers direct to consumers or through third-parties.

"There." Nick closed his laptop. "My algorithm is running on the internet for any company that sells this printer. I don't expect many hits, but it's still going to take time to run a thorough search."

Hunter clenched his hands. "What else can we do?"

Blake got to his feet. "Review the outstanding leads."

"But—"

"But nothing." Blake picked up a marker. "We calm

down and work the investigation like we'd do for anyone else."

"Right." Hunter scoffed. "Calm down. Like that's even possible."

Kelsey pressed her hand on his arm. "Maya needs you to do it."

She was right, but nothing had worked so far. His body was covered in sweat. His mind in a fog. And his faith that God would spare Maya when He'd allowed so many in Hunter's life to pass on? Nearly nonexistent.

All eyes focused on him, and panic swamped him. He took long breaths. *In. Out. In. Out.* One after another, praying as he did so, until he could breathe almost normally.

"Pray with me." Kelsey grabbed his hand, and the partners followed suit. She offered a heartfelt plea for Maya, Fletch, and Lucy.

Guilt jumped on Hunter's back like a tiger seeking prey. He'd been so focused on Maya that he'd failed to even consider Fletch and Lucy. He had to do better. Be better.

He took another breath, and, when the prayer ended, he squeezed Kelsey's hand, firming in his mind that he could do this. Could find all of them.

Blake looked at Nick. "Once that algorithm returns files, is there any way you can get access to the sales information for these retailers?"

"Not legally, but..." He shrugged.

Hunter didn't care if Nick broke every law on the books right now. "Do what you have to do."

Nick grinned. "You got it."

Blake tapped the words *Fletch's Hard Drives* on the whiteboard with the end of a marker. "You said you finished these. Should we go back through them?"

"Yes," Piper said. "But I think at this point, finding

anything is a long shot. And I need to mention that I checked into Greg's boat rental. The company had one boat that wasn't returned, but if Greg rented it, he didn't book it under his name. He also gave them a bogus phone number, which is why the company never followed up."

"So he didn't want the rental to be tracked back to him," Hunter said. "Means he was trying to hide something, but what?"

Blake tapped the board again. "What about forensics?"

Sierra sat forward. "My team and I are working several scenes right now. The lab. The fire. Items from Assad's house and the storage unit. The boathouse. Greg's room. Rudy's place, though, honestly, I've put that on the back burner."

"Do you think you'll find anything useful?" Hunter asked.

"Other than prints and DNA, nothing else is obvious to me at this point. And you should know, we finished Assad's biohazard suit. The particulates were plastics used in making the suit, so no lead there."

Blake looked at his wife, and his gaze softened. "What's happening with DNA?"

"Rudy's and Greg's DNA completed," Emory said. "They didn't match the unknown DNA profiles we've recovered, and neither did the blood from the mosquito. Assad's DNA is still running. Sorry. I wish I could be more helpful. Oh, and we also swabbed the lipstick for DNA."

"I've matched the color on that," Sierra said. "It's Revlon Pink Truffle."

Hunter thought about his visit to Assad's sister. "Sakina Assad was wearing lipstick. A light pink. Kind of barely there."

"Sounds about right," Clay said. "And it would make

sense that she would visit her brother and that he would claim it wasn't her so we'd leave her alone."

"Makes sense, sure, but it's not helpful." Hunter was growing restless, and he had to do something other than sit in a meeting. He stood. "I'll leave these follow up items to you all. I'm going to go back to talk to Sakina. Play on her sympathies. See if I can get her to tell me something. Report any new findings to me."

Clay got up. "I'll go with you."

Sierra stood. "I'll walk you out."

She led them back to Pete, where they handed over their badges. Hunter half expected the other four Byrd brothers to be camped out in the lobby, but they hadn't arrived yet.

Hunter looked at Sierra. "Call me the second you have anything."

She firmed her shoulders. "You can count on it."

He could feel her narrowed gaze tracking them as they exited the building.

Needing to burn off some adrenaline, Hunter jogged through the mild night with clear skies and stars sparkling overhead. He unlocked the doors to his SUV with his remote, the sharp beeps ricocheting through the air. Once Clay climbed in, Hunter peeled out of the lot, tires screeching, and got them on the road.

"I want to live," Clay said, but before Clay could say anything else, his phone rang.

"It's Aiden." Clay answered the call from his oldest brother on speaker.

"We're on the way to the center." Aiden's deep voice boomed through the speaker. "You need anything at the moment or should we just hang out in the lobby?"

"Hang out for now," Clay replied without asking Hunter's opinion. "Hunter and I are on the way to lean on an uncooperative suspect's sister."

"We're pretty good at leaning on people." Aiden's confidence rode through his tone. "You sure you don't want us to come along?"

"We want her to cooperate, not die of shock." Clay chuckled.

Hunter might normally laugh with him, but nothing was funny right now. Nothing! He pressed his foot on the gas pedal and careened around a corner.

Clay fired him a testy look, but Hunter didn't care.

"Okay, we'll hang tight," Aiden said. "We have our assault gear and are prepared. Just give us a call if you need us."

"Roger that." Clay hung up.

Hunter glanced at him for a brief moment before putting his focus back on the road. "Must be great to have such support."

"Yeah, sure." Clay sounded anything but sure. "I mean, they can all be a pain in the butt at times. Still, I'd rather have them around than not. You have family?"

Hunter shook his head but wasn't going to get into his losses.

"Too bad. There are things in life you just can't do alone."

"You talking about God?"

"Nah. I mean, sure, we need God." He shifted in his seat to face Hunter. "Absolutely. But I'm talking about other people. No one can exist on their own. Like now. We all have to band together to find Maya."

Hunter was about to respond when Clay added, "At least not thrive on their own. You know, to be the best they can be."

Hunter pulled up to Sakina's house. Maybe later, long after he had Maya safely in his arms, he would think about Clay's comments.

A light shone through the family room window, illuminating the darkness, but there wasn't a car in the driveway.

"I can't tell if she's home or not." Hunter killed the engine and hopped out. He went straight to the door and rang the bell. Clay joined him on the small porch as he had on their earlier visit.

Hunter tapped his foot until he heard footsteps inside.

Thank you, God. Thank you.

"Yes?" Sakina's voice came through the door.

Hunter swallowed to be sure he wouldn't sound panicked. "It's Agents Lane and Byrd with more questions for you."

She cracked the door and peeked out. "I've said everything I'm going to say to you."

"Things have changed since we've last talked. One of our colleagues has been abducted, and we have a few more questions." Hunter did his best to remain calm and took a step forward. "Please. Won't you let us come in?"

"Fine." She pulled the door open.

Hunter raced past her before she changed her mind, hurrying into the space that smelled of a tangy spice mix, likely from her dinner. Trying his best to act casual, he leaned against the wall in her living room and waited for her to take a seat. Clay stood next to him, his focus intense. Hunter gave Clay a look to take it down a notch, and he relaxed his shoulders.

Sakina perched like a bird on the edge of the sofa. "What do you need to know?"

"We know your brother didn't take our colleague because he's behind bars," Hunter stated right up front to disarm any animosity she might have when they mentioned the terrorism. "But we think he's connected to the person who did."

268

She looked at Hunter then at Clay. "And who do you think this person is?"

"Fadhil Yasin," Clay said.

"Him again?" She rolled her eyes. "I already told you I do not know him."

"But do you know *of* him?" Hunter asked.

"No." She clasped her hands together and fired him a resolute look, making it clear that, if she did indeed know something, she wasn't going to talk.

The snippet of calm Hunter had maintained evaporated.

"Please," he said. "The woman who was taken is very special to me, and I've lost everyone I was close to. I can't lose another person in my life. Help me. Please." The panic in his tone scared him. On the other hand, if he heard such a plea, he would help.

"I would tell you if I knew anything, but I know nothing about this man." She lifted her hands, palms up. "Nothing. Please believe me."

"Are you close to your brother?" Clay asked.

She nodded.

Clay held her gaze. "Do you want him to be released from jail?"

She nodded.

"Then help us, and we promise to do our very best to get him released."

"I am sorry. I want Eshan freed." Her eyes darted between them. "But I do not know anything."

Disappointed and frustrated at this hopeless interview, Hunter pushed off the wall and headed for the door. He spotted a framed photo of Ehsan, Sakina, and another man. Hunter's mouth fell open. He quickly recovered and picked up the photo to show to Sakina. "Who's this man with you and Eshan?"

She stared at the photo for a long moment. Too long in

Hunter's mind, as if she was making up a story. She finally looked up. "That's Zahid. Zahid Noori. Eshan's friend and business associate."

Hunter worked hard to hide his surprise at the different name for Yasin. "How long have you known him?"

She tapped her chin. "Eshan met him first. Maybe two years ago. I guess I have known him about a year."

"What kind of business are they in?" Hunter demanded.

"Manufacturing. Toys."

"Do you have an address for him?" Clay asked. "Or know the business name?"

"Women are not included in business discussions." Her eyes narrowed. "Why all the questions about Zahid? He is no guiltier of breaking the law than Eshan is."

She was right. They were both equally guilty. Yasin, Zahid Noori, as he was going by now, was very guilty. He'd committed one act of terror already, and Hunter knew that, if they didn't find him soon, he would certainly take more lives. Including Maya's as he had to be the person who had taken her.

23

Maya returned Yasin's stare and tried not to be intimidated, but her knees were shaking. She searched her brain for a way to intimidate him back, but she knew very little about him and his cause. "Why are you doing this?"

Yasin looked like he wanted to sigh, but took a few breaths. "You will know when you will know."

"What's that supposed to mean?" Maya lifted her chin, pointing it at him like she might her gun if she were still in possession of the weapon. "You're standing right here. You could just answer my question."

"It is not my answer to give."

"Wait. What?" She blinked hard. "You're not the mastermind behind all of this."

"I am not."

She tried not to react but her mouth dropped open, and she eyed him as she worked to process the news. "But who is?"

"Like I said. You will know *if* and when they want you to know. Now, I must get your friend moving here." He looked at Igor. "Untie him and escort him to the work area."

Fletch was wobbly when Igor got him to his feet.

"Make sure you get him some water," Maya said before they could leave the room. "Maybe electrolytes. Keep up his strength."

Yasin turned to look at her. "You care about your friend. That is admirable, but perhaps you need to start caring about yourself too."

"I'm unimportant," she said, as she would willingly sacrifice her life to save so many others.

Fletch met her gaze from the doorway. "Don't say that. Don't ever say that. You're important to me. My best friend who keeps me sane. I need you."

"Oh, how touching." Yasin clasped a hand over his heart.

Fletch spun on Yasin. "She's my friend, and you killed my only other one."

"Ah, Greg. Greed can often take people out." Yasin didn't deny killing Greg, and if Yasin was their murderer, he didn't sound the least bit upset about killing Greg.

"Greed didn't do it," Maya stated with force. "You did."

Yasin smirked, his dark eyes alight with insanity. "Technically, it wasn't me."

Maya jerked her head at Igor. "Then your goon did."

Yasin frowned. "We're getting off track when we have such important things to take care of." He took his knife from the sheath on his belt and rubbed his finger along the edge of the blade. "Remember, Dr. Gilliam. If you balk or try anything foolish, I will slit the good Dr. Glass's throat, and then you'll have zero friends left."

Back at Nick's lab, Nick's calm tone grated on Hunter. Clay had called Nick from the car to get him searching for information under the name of Noori, and Hunter had hoped he would have something already. But nothing yet.

Hunter nearly went over the edge and lost it. "Hurry, Nick! Hurry!"

Nick pointed at the screen. "Look at this. A guy named Noori owns a design-your-own fashion doll business. Customers can choose all the doll's features, and the doll is then custom printed from thermoplastic."

"The kind of plastic used in a 3D printer." Hunter's panic ebbed into excitement. "Sakina said her brother and Noori were in toy manufacturing. Are there any pictures of the owner?"

"None returned with the search, but let me go to the company website." Nick typed in the company's name, and the site loaded, displaying a variety of doll faces and clothes. He clicked on the *about* section.

When it opened, Hunter scanned the page. "Not only no picture, but nothing about Noori, at all." He looked at Nick. "Where did the listing that mentioned the company link to?"

"Wayback Machine."

Hunter was familiar with the internet archive site where you could view old versions of websites.

"Let me open that page to see what we can see." Nick clicked on the link, and an old version of Noori's company website dated five years earlier filled the screen.

"Can we find the about page for this date?" Hunter asked.

Nick clicked around. "Here it is. Noori is listed as the owner, but still no photo."

Hunter stood back. "So at some point he felt comfortable with listing his name with the company, and then he decided to take it down. In any case, this information doesn't prove it's our guy. There's no way I'll be able to get a warrant to raid the business. Or even to compel them to let Sierra evaluate their printer."

Clay stepped forward. "Then there's only one thing to do. We head down to the lobby, grab my brothers, and hit this place."

Hunter agreed, but... "We could all lose our jobs."

"So what?" Clay planted his feet. "A job loss is far better than Maya losing her life."

"Then let's move."

"I'll escort you out." Nick jumped up and grabbed Piper's hand. They all raced down the steps to the lobby.

"Follow us," Clay yelled to his brothers as he checked out with Pete. "I'll update you by phone once we're on the road."

Hunter got behind the wheel of his SUV, and Clay rode shotgun. Piper kissed Nick good-bye and took the backseat.

The Byrd brothers, Aiden, Brendan, Erik, and Drake, loaded into their vehicle. Hunter got on the road, thankful for support from these men. He wished he'd had time to do recon of the building so he knew what they were up against. At least Grady had offered many of his gadgets, which would help with surveillance, and the brothers had brought an assortment of equipment along as well.

Clay called Aiden to update him on the warehouse and told him they'd talk further once they reached the place. Thirty minutes later, Hunter drove into a manufacturing district on the east side where the doll manufacturer was located. He pulled into a nearby parking lot with a full view of the business but a thick tree line that provided cover for their vehicles.

Clay lifted his binoculars. "Two cars outside the building. Too far away to make out the plates in the dark."

Hunter glanced at Clay. "Let's go meet up with your brothers and get closer to the building to do an assessment."

He slipped out of the vehicle and went to the other SUV, Clay and Piper in step with him. The four brothers had climbed out and were assembled around their open tailgate. They were all wearing Kevlar vests and comms units, as were Hunter, Piper, and Clay. All the brothers were fit and fierce, and Hunter couldn't ask for a better team to rescue Maya. If indeed she was in this building.

"There are two cars out front," Hunter said. "We have no idea of how many captors we're facing."

Aiden scratched his wide jaw. "One of us needs to get up to that building with the Range-R system. See how many heat signatures we're dealing with and where they're located in the building."

Hunter had been thinking the same thing and was glad to hear that the brothers had brought a handheld radar device so they could better plan the assault.

"Agreed," Hunter said. "I'd like—"

"I'll go," Erik interrupted. "I'm the youngest and can move quicker than you old dudes."

His brother, Brendan, socked Erik in the arm. "I agree that you should go. Your marksmanship is the worst of all of us. You need to be close up for any shots you take."

Erik rolled his eyes.

"Go for it, Erik," Hunter said, not wanting to mess around with jokes at a time like this. "Unless there's action near the building, we'll stand down until we hear back from you."

"Don't let us down, kid," Aiden said as Erik took off. "Maya's life could depend on you."

Maya twisted her arms, trying to free herself. Had been trying for three hours now. Her arms ached from the ungainly position, and the scratchy rope bit into her wrists, exposing raw skin. But she wouldn't give in to the pain and moan. She wanted to. How she wanted to. But Lucy was already so fragile that Maya's suffering would add to Lucy's discomfort. Maya didn't want to do that to her.

Lucy sighed. "Do you think they'll leave us here until Fletch finishes whatever they need him to do?"

"It's likely, yes."

"But he said that might be twenty-four hours or more."

Maya was fully aware of that fact. Twenty-four hours to find a way out of this windowless room out in the middle of nowhere. A business where Hunter would never think to look.

"I'm sure they'll give us restroom breaks if we ask. And —" Maya heard footsteps coming their way, they stopped.

"Someone's coming," Lucy whispered, her eyes wide. "I hope Fletch is working, or they're going to hurt us."

The door opened, and Igor shoved Fletch into the room and onto the chair.

"You're back already?" Maya asked.

"He was not working. Mr. Yasin did not like this. Said to teach him a lesson." Igor grabbed the ropes and secured Fletch to his chair.

"What? You're going to beat him up now?" Maya asked. "How will that help?"

Igor moved behind her. "It is not him I will teach. It is you."

He started untying the knots in the rope around her chest.

"Fine," Fletch said. "I'll work. I promise."

"You have said this before. I think it is time for the lesson."

Igor jerked Maya up by the elbow.

"No," Lucy said, sobbing now. "Please don't hurt her. Fletch said he would cooperate."

"This is not of your concern." Igor grasped Maya's arm

276

and started for the door. Maya tried to drag her feet and slow him down, but he just tightened his grasp and pulled harder. He jerked her down a long hallway to a room at the end, where the door stood open. She heard Yasin's voice but didn't recognize the voice of the woman he was talking to.

He was promising to deliver on the toxin tomorrow and said that they would achieve their revenge and purge the earth. Two things Maya still didn't have any details about.

"I have the doctor," Igor said and shoved her into the room.

Maya quickly ran her gaze around the office holding shelves filled with small dolls on plastic stands. A big desk took up the middle of the space. A take-out container with rice, beef, and carrots that smelled like cinnamon and nutmeg sat uneaten on the worn wood. Behind the desk sat a beautiful woman with a traditional Muslim head covering and black blouse with a high collar, looking very much like a woman in mourning.

She gestured at a nearby vinyl chair. "Have a seat, Dr. Glass."

Igor forced Maya onto the chair, jarring her already raw wrists, the pain excruciating. Maya bit back a painful moan and focused on the woman. "Who are you?"

"That's not important." The woman, whose posture was already good, sat up straighter in her chair. "Just know that I am in charge."

A woman. A Muslim woman by the looks of things. In charge. Maya would never have suspected this, but she was going to take advantage of the time to question the woman. "So you know the reason for wanting the toxin, then?"

"I do."

Maya lifted her shoulders. "The least you can do is share it with me."

She arched a brow and eyed Maya. "You Americans are so pushy and rude. It will be your downfall."

"And is that why you want to kill us?" Maya asked, hoping to prod her into talking.

"Your lack of control often leads to improper behavior. You defile your bodies with drugs and alcohol. Tattoos and piercings. Your morals are loose and corrupt." Her words were coated with hatred. "We have to stop it before you pollute the rest of the world, and, in doing so, put those who are addicted to the drugs out of their misery."

Maya stared at the woman and tried to read between the lines. "You're going to target people who are addicted to drugs?"

"At first." She rested her hands on the desk, her fingers curled into fists. "They will pay for their sins."

"You set the fire at the crack house."

She blinked her long lashes. "We had nothing to do with a fire."

Maya believed her. She would have to ask Fletch about that. "And after you target addicts, you'll stop?"

"Hardly. When your incompetent law enforcement believes they know what we are doing..." She paused and smiled. "...we will move on to Sin City."

That could only mean one place. "Las Vegas."

"An entire city devoted to sinning. We will wipe the place clean with the aerosol that your friend is going to make for us." Hatred and venom erupted from her mouth.

Maya looked at the woman, whose beautiful features were marred with her virulence. Maya couldn't imagine being that angry. It had to stem from something terrible that happened in the woman's past. "This sounds personal."

"It is none of your business." She relaxed her hands. "I have said enough."

Maya felt like she was still missing important details, but

it seemed like she wasn't going to get them. "Why did you bring me in here?"

The woman locked gazes with Maya. "I wanted you to know how serious I am. That I won't hesitate to kill you if I need to. Or kill Lucy. Or abduct more of your partners and kill them too. All to make Dr. Gilliam cooperate."

"You definitely seem serious," Maya said, trying to play down her fear of this woman.

The woman stood. "Then you should tell your friend to get back to work. Or I will begin eliminating everyone you know, one by one."

～

Igor hauled Maya back toward the room. She dragged her feet to check out the building. She saw big windows on one side. If they could get to them, could they break one and escape? A shadow passed by one of the windows, and she slowed to take another furtive look. Could it have been a person darting by? Clouds rolling over? Wind whisking a tree branch that moved?

"Come," Igor demanded and jerked her harder.

At least he didn't seem to notice the person. If it even *was* a person. Could it be Hunter or Piper or his fellow agents? Had they figured out where she was being held?

Oh, Father, please let it be so.

She would keep her ears open for them, but she suspected, if they were coming to rescue her, and if they didn't break down the door and rush in, they would be silent in their approach.

Igor jerked open the door to the small room and shoved her back inside with Fletch and Lucy. Maya tripped, gaining her footing just in time to turn and land hard on the chair.

He tied her up and went back to the door.

"Talk to the doctor like you were told. Fix this or I will." He stomped out of the room and closed the door.

Fletch ran his gaze over her. "You're okay?"

"They didn't hurt me." Maya took a long breath. "He brought me to a woman who threatened me, Lucy, and my partners if you don't work."

Fletch shook his head and tsked. "I'm going to do what they want."

She wanted to argue with him, but she didn't want to be responsible for people she loved being killed. "She told me they're first going to target drug users then move on to Vegas. They want to rid the world of sinners."

Lucy gasped, and Maya forgot how this woman didn't deal with the aftermath of lunatic criminals on a regular basis like Maya did.

Surprisingly, Fletch's expression brightened. "Then they're going to need a lot of toxin. Which means they'll either have to bring someone in to help them continue to produce it or keep me alive. And that means they'll keep both of you alive too."

Maya thought about his statement. She couldn't feel good about remaining alive when so many others were going to die.

A faint scraping noise on the outside wall had her turning that direction. It lasted only a second.

"Did you hear that?" she whispered.

Lucy shook her head.

"Hear what?" Fletch asked.

"Nothing. I'm probably imagining it." She took another look around the room. There was no drywall or insulation, just wooden studs and the exterior wall.

If Hunter was on the other side, he could cut through the wall and rescue them. She knew SOS in Morse code and planted her feet on the floor to scoot her chair toward the wall. She moved close enough to touch it and tapped three short taps. Three long ones. Three more short ones.

No response.

She tried it again. And again. When she got no response, she relaxed her tired arms and tried to come up with a way to escape this place. She had the time while Fletch worked on the toxin, and she would use it wisely.

24

"I'm telling you, it was an SOS signal." Erik planted his hands on his hips, taking a stance Hunter assumed he used in his job as a PPB patrol officer. "I know my Morse code, and I didn't imagine it."

"What did the heat signatures for that area say?" Hunter asked, not sure he trusted Erik's findings or not.

"There are three people. Two of them five feet from the wall and one just two feet from the wall."

"Could be Maya, Fletch, and Lucy," Aiden said, appraising his younger brother with a stare Hunter could imagine him using in his ATF position.

Erik held firm under Aiden's tight assessment. "Maybe, but then in another area of the building there were three more heat signatures grouped in a small space, too, so I can't be certain. Other than the SOS."

"You're sure, man?" Drake asked, and Hunter could easily see him in his role as a US Deputy Marshal questioning suspects.

"Positive." Erik widened his stance and looked each of his brothers in the eye.

Aiden gave a sharp nod. "Then I say we go with the

theory that Maya somehow knew we were here and sent us a signal."

"Back door's right next to where the heat signatures were recorded," Erik said.

"Then we breach the back door," Hunter said. "Silently. Try to move them out of the building without alerting their kidnappers."

"And if we're wrong and it's the kidnappers and they draw down on us?" Brendan, a Multnomah County deputy and SWAT member, asked.

"We return fire," Aiden stated.

Brendan narrowed his gaze. "I get that we have to do this, but I just want everyone to be clear on what firing on these abductors could mean for our careers. Shoot, this could mean prison time."

"Then we better do our best to take them peacefully," Piper said.

"We could talk this to death, and we don't have time for that," Hunter said. "Everyone still in?"

They all nodded.

"Anyone have lockpicking skills?" Hunter asked.

The brothers looked at Brendan, and he tipped his head at their SUV. "Have the tools in the back."

"Then we'll follow your lead," Hunter said.

Brendan grabbed his small tool kit and put it in his cargo pocket. He gave a firm nod and set off.

Hunter fell in behind him and the others after him.

Brendan approached the door and picked the lock while Hunter stood guard. Brendan silently freed the door. Hunter moved in and signaled for the others to follow.

He crept down a hallway and glanced around a corner that led to another hallway. A door was open at the end, light spilling onto the concrete floor. A male and female were talking. Clearly not Maya's or Fletch's voice. To his immediate right was another locked door, which would be where the SOS had originated. He signaled for Brendan to unlock the door.

Brendan swiftly moved forward, silent and deadly looking. He inserted lockpicks and tripped the lockset. Brendan stowed his picks then lifted his rifle. He gave a nod and opened the door. Hunter swept past him and inside the room.

Maya and Lucy were bound in chairs. He locked eyes with Maya, and his heart soared. He wanted to free her and grab her up in his arms, but he had to keep calm and rescue her.

Lucy gasped. Hunter held a finger to his mouth to silence her. Maya remained silent, but tears flooded her eyes and rolled over her cheeks.

Hunter motioned for Brendan to go to Lucy, and he crept over to Maya while Piper covered their backs.

"Is Fletch here?" he whispered close to her ear and untied her.

She leaned into him. "They just took him to make the toxin."

Hunter released the rope on her wrists and had to bite his tongue not to swear at the bloody circles in her tender skin. "Do you know if they have any of the aerosolized form of the toxin from Fletch's lab?"

"I didn't think to ask."

"Do you know what's at the end of the hallway and how many people there are?"

"An office. Two men. One woman. At least that's all I've seen."

He freed the ropes around her body, and she swiveled to face him, her hand reaching out for his. "I don't know if they have many weapons. Yasin has a knife. There's a big guy I'm calling Igor. He hasn't displayed any weapons, but he's definitely their muscle. I figure he'll be with Fletch, and the other two still in the office."

"Thank you. Aiden and Erik will lead you out of the building to safety while the rest of us free Fletch." He kissed her—a short peck that would have to do for now.

She gently touched the side of his face. "Be careful."

He smiled and helped her to her feet. She followed Lucy into the hallway to meet up with Aiden and Erik, who escorted them down the hall. Piper, Drake, and Brendan moved up to Clay. Hunter relayed the information Maya had given him.

"Clay and I'll locate Fletch. The rest of you take the office," Hunter whispered. "Hold outside the office door until I give the signal or if they come to the door.."

"Roger that," Piper said.

The five of them took off, rifles raised. They split at the end of the hallway. Hunter and Clay moved to the large room where the dolls were made. Hunter signaled to hold at the entrance and scanned the space. Seeing no one, he inched along the wall to an open door near the front of the building.

He heard motion inside but no talking. He gestured his intent to breach the room to Clay.

Clay gave a firm nod.

Hunter held up three fingers, then counted them down and burst into the room. A large man sat in a chair facing Fletch, who was working behind a table.

Fletch looked up. His eyes went wide.

The man spun, but by the time he did, Hunter had his gun in his face. "On the floor now. Slowly. Hands where I can see them."

When the man complied, Hunter said, "Cuff him, Clay."

Hunter looked at Fletch. "Do they have any of your aerosolized toxin or did they discharge it all at your lab?"

"Discharged it all," Fletch replied.

Once Clay had the man cuffed, Hunter pressed his mic. "Take the office."

"Roger that." Piper's whispered voice came over his earbud.

"Boy, am I glad to see you," Fletch said.

"Are you okay?" Hunter asked.

He nodded. "Did you find Maya and Lucy?"

"They're safely outside." Relief flooded through Hunter, washing out the adrenaline that had kept him going for hours. His legs felt weak, but he took long breaths to power through it.

Hunter waited to hear the all clear from Drake over his earbud, and, when he did, he looked at Clay. "You got this guy?"

He nodded. "Go on. Check on her."

Hunter didn't have to be told twice. He bolted for the office to make sure the suspects were apprehended. Once he confirmed they were in custody, he would race out of this building to reunite with the woman he loved.

Maya stopped at the edge of the parking lot and looked at Aiden, who seemed to be in charge. "This is far enough."

He shook his head, his dark gaze intense. "I promised Hunter I would take you to his vehicle, and that's what I'll do."

She knew by the fire in his eyes that she wasn't going to change his mind, so she started walking. She wanted to be where Hunter could find her the moment he was free. If he wasn't hurt.

Father, please protect him. I need him. Don't let him be hurt. Or anyone. Not even the vicious people who took me.

"Excellent!" Aiden fist bumped with his brother.

"What is it?" Maya asked.

"All suspects have been apprehended."

Her heart soared. "And no one was hurt?"

"Hunter didn't say."

"But he would have if someone had been shot, right?"

"Likely."

She didn't like Aiden's vague reply, but he couldn't tell her something he didn't know. Anything he would say would be speculation.

They reached two SUVs, and Aiden unlocked the doors of the back one. He helped a shaking Lucy into the backseat and looked down at her. "You doing okay?"

She nodded, but tears were flowing over her high cheekbones.

Maya didn't feel like crying. Not when she was worried for Hunter.

She looked at Aiden. "Do you have binoculars I can use?"

"I'll get them." He popped the back hatch of his vehicle and reached into a large duffle bag. He handed a pair of powerful binoculars to her.

She focused on the building but saw no movement. No one stepping through the door. "If everything's okay, why aren't they coming out?"

"By they, I assume you mean Hunter," Aiden clarified.

"Yes," she admitted, not caring that she wasn't even trying to hide her feelings for him.

"He's in charge and has to make sure everyone's accounted for. Takes a few minutes to do that." He gave her a tight smile.

But she couldn't smile back and wanted to insist he take her back to the building so she could see Hunter with her own two eyes. But she couldn't demand anything. Not when he and his brothers had risked their lives to save her. She hadn't even thanked them.

She met his gaze. "Thank you so much for rescuing us."

"No worries." His nonchalant attitude was typical for a law enforcement officer whose goal was to help others, no matter the risk to their own safety.

"I just want you to know I appreciate it." She shifted her gaze to Erik. "You too, Erik."

"Glad to do it." He smiled, and Maya was once again struck by how handsome these brothers were and how much they looked alike.

She lifted the binoculars. The warehouse door opened, and Hunter stepped out.

Her heart galloped in her chest.

"He's okay," she said on an exhaled breath of relief. "He's coming outside."

"Of course he is," Aiden said when he could've said I told you so.

Hunter cleared the doorway and took off running in her direction. She didn't care if Aiden wanted her by the vehicles. She handed him the binoculars and bolted across the lot. No one was going to stop her from throwing herself into Hunter's arms.

Hunter spotted Maya racing across the parking lot, and he couldn't move fast enough. He kicked up his speed to Olympic-worthy timing and raced for her. She was moving fast too. Her hair flying behind her. She looked amazing. Graceful and gorgeous, even after her ordeal.

They met under a streetlight. He didn't say a word but whipped her into his arms and swung her around. She laughed, her joyful sound bringing a smile to his heart.

He slowed and set her back on her feet to look deep into her eyes. "I was so worried I was going to lose you too."

"But you didn't. I'm fine, thanks to you, Piper, and the Byrd brothers."

"Yeah, they really stepped up." He tucked her hair behind her ear. "Now if you don't mind, I'm going to kiss you."

"I don't mind at all. In fact, I encourage it." She raised up on tiptoes.

He lowered his head, savoring each second before their lips touched. Almost losing her made the kiss more intense. More vibrant. His heart jolted in his chest.

She snaked her arms around his neck. Drawing him closer. Closer. He deepened the kiss. Reveled in it. Wanted it to never end.

And then it struck him. It didn't have to end. She wanted to be with him. He wanted to be with her. There was no reason not to be together.

He drew back. Gulped in a breath. She did too, her chest rising and falling. She'd been as impacted by the kiss as he was.

"I know this is sudden, and I don't have a ring, but will you marry me?"

Her mouth dropped open, and she eyed him.

"I've never loved anyone the way I love you," he explained. "And I think you feel the same way."

"I do, but your commitment issue. What about that?"

"Nearly losing you gave me a serious sense of perspective. You survived. Praise God, you survived."

"Thanks to Him and you all."

"And that's it, right?" he asked, keeping his eyes on hers. "I couldn't have done it on my own. I needed the others and God. I've been believing everything's all up to me. To keep the people I love safe is all up to me. And that's where the fear comes from, because I know I can't do it. But I don't have to do things on my own. I can ask for help from an incredible support network."

She smiled at him. "I'm so happy to hear that."

"We can finally be together." His phone rang. More than anything, he wanted to ignore it, but he was on the job.

"Sorry." He quickly answered the call from Nick on speaker.

"Found something interesting in my search," Nick said. "Sakina Assad killed their little sister."

"Killed her?" Hunter stared at his phone.

"She set that car bomb in New York, not Yasin."

Hunter tried to process the news. "But he was blamed."

"Yes, because he was so angry at the people who got her hooked on drugs and was very public about it. But Sakina wanted revenge too. She didn't talk about it, and no one suspected her because she's a Muslim woman."

"You should know," he said to Nick but looked at Maya, as he didn't know if she knew this. "Sakina is the woman behind the bogus contract and toxin."

"No way!" Nick said.

"I recognized her when I went to confirm Drake had everyone in custody," Hunter said. "And she started spewing her hatred at me and yelling that I ruined her plan."

Maya twisted her hands together. "I talked to her in the office, but she wouldn't say who she was. Just that she was targeting sinners. Specifically drug users. Then, she was going to move on to Las Vegas."

"She wants revenge for her sister," Hunter said.

Maya nodded. "And you stopped her. I'm so proud of you."

"And I think that's my cue to go," Nick said. "Buh-bye. And guys. Time to kiss and make up." Laughing, he ended the call.

Hunter shoved his phone into his pocket and sirens sounded in the distance.

He wanted more time with Maya now for that kissing and making up Nick mentioned, but Hunter would have to wait. "That will be the deputies we called to transport our suspects. I'll need to put my agent hat on again and get to work."

She sighed. "I'm glad this is all over and that Fletch is alive, but I really wish we could just go home and not have to deal with all the follow-up."

"I'd like that too." He cupped the side of her face and grinned. "But the cars are a good mile out yet, and I plan to kiss you senseless in the time it takes for the deputies to arrive. Then you'll have plenty of time to give my proposal some serious consideration."

25

Two weeks later

The escape room private party was getting underway as Hunter stepped inside. He spotted Fletch in the hallway and went to talk to him. Hunter passed the popcorn machine with corn pinging off the glass sides and the buttery aroma firing off his stomach in a loud growl.

He would have to wait until the buffet was served later. He offered his hand to Fletch.

"Thank you, again." Fletch shook Hunter's hand. "For the rescue and all that."

Hunter released his hand and waved him off. "No need to keep thanking me every time you see me."

"You kinda saved the world. I mean if that toxin had been released..." He shook his head. "I feel like such an idiot for falling for a bogus grant like that."

"Don't think that way," Hunter said. "They did a great job of spoofing it. They were sophisticated enough that even with files from your internet provider, Nick couldn't trace their work. It could have happened to anyone."

Fletch ground his teeth together. "But I'm not anyone."

Hunter had spent some time with Fletch in the last two

weeks while they'd wrapped up the investigation, and he'd come to know how highly the guy thought of himself. Not in a conceited way, but in a *setting high expectations for his super intelligence* way.

"It all worked out in the end," Hunter said. "And, on the bright side, you accomplished something that had seemed impossible in the past, and our government can use your research."

"Yeah, that's the bright side." Fletch smiled but then it faded. "Can you tell me what's happening in closing up the investigation?"

"Most of it's classified, but what do you want to know?"

"The DNA findings. Did they prove Sakina was on the island?"

Hunter nodded. "One of the unknown samples belonged to her."

"I still don't get why she had to hide herself from me. Makes no sense. But maybe she thought I wouldn't take a woman as seriously as a man."

"Could be."

"Anything else that will help nail them?"

"Both the mosquito DNA and the other unknown DNA recovered at the lab belonged to the guy Maya was calling Igor. And the keycard we found on Assad is for the doll fabricating place, which ties Assad to the investigation. Plus, Sierra matched one of the 3D printers at the doll fabricating place to the 3D gun Yasin used. So, we have strong forensic evidence, and we think Igor will flip on the others."

"Sounds good," Fletch said. "I just don't want them to get away with killing Carson or stealing the toxin."

"The only thing we're still working on—actually, Clay is, as it's not related to my investigation—is who killed Clay's informant and the other people in the fire."

Fletch nodded. "I can't believe you guys thought I'd been there when I was stuck at the doll place the entire time."

"The witness was so sure it was you." Hunter held Fletch's gaze. "We're all glad they were wrong."

Fletch's eyes watered, and he gritted his teeth. "Thanks for the update. I'm going to go choose a room."

"Just one thing before you go," Hunter said.

"What's that?"

"Don't isolate yourself so much. You need other people. Trust me. I know."

"I get it, and I'll try, but you know..." He shrugged. "Catch you later."

He walked off, and Hunter felt bad for him. His whole conspiracy theory mentality didn't allow him to open himself up to others. Hunter got that. Not the conspiracy part, but the fear of letting someone in. Good thing Hunter had found Maya. She was well worth the risk.

He heard the main door open behind him. Expecting Maya, he turned to look, but it was Aiden, all dressed up in dark jeans and a royal blue shirt. Hunter suspected he would be sought after by every single female here tonight. Or maybe his brothers would be competition.

"Hey, man, don't look so disappointed." Aiden grinned. "I'm gonna assume you were expecting someone else."

"Maya's not here yet."

Aiden nodded. "I left her and the partners about an hour ago. They had some voting to do."

Maya had told Hunter that the Byrd brothers asked to lease space at the Veritas Center for a new investigative agency they wanted to form.

"So you went ahead with the proposal for rental space?" Hunter asked.

"It was a hard decision to leave law enforcement. Hard for all of us. Maybe Erik the most, since he's just getting started, but running that op with you convinced us that we could do some real good if we weren't hindered by all the red tape."

"I hear you on that." Hunter frowned. "I'm still doing paperwork to explain why I called you all in instead of an FBI SWAT team."

"All of us are still explaining, too, but it was worth it." He grinned.

Hunter nodded. "You have a name for this new agency?"

"Nighthawk Security. It was wonder kid Erik's idea. He said that, due to the bird's coloring, it's hard to spot with the naked eye during the day. We figure we're going to be doing a lot of surveillance and protective details and we'll want to blend into the background. Seemed like a fitting name."

"Sounds good to me. I mean, I'd hire you based on that name." Hunter checked the door again.

"I'm sure Maya wanted to get changed after working in the lab all day."

"Probably," Hunter said, but he didn't care if she came in her lab coat. He just wanted to see her.

Aiden clasped his shoulder. "You got it bad, man."

Hunter puffed out his chest. "I know, and I'm proud of it."

Aiden laughed. "Have you done this escape room thing before?"

"Never. I figure the best plan is to get in whatever room Fletch is in. He's a pro."

"Thanks for the tip. I'll go look for him now."

"Don't tell your brothers, or there'll be no room for me."

"Are you kidding and let them win? No way."

Hunter laughed. "I've never met a more competitive group than you guys."

"And we're proud of it." His laughter trailed him down the hallway.

Hunter remained in place, his gaze pinned to the door. It opened, and the remaining Byrd brothers rushed in, all spiffed up for the night out and already trash-talking over the upcoming competition.

"Steer clear of me, little brother," Drake said. "I'm going to wipe the floor with you."

"Says the guy who's never done escape rooms." Erik lifted his shoulders. "I'm an expert at this."

Drake wasn't at all intimidated. "We'll see who wins."

Brendan shook hands with Hunter. "Ignore them. They have no manners."

Hunter rolled his eyes. "Good luck to all of you."

"They're going to need it." Brendan laughed and headed down the hall. The others followed, joking along the way.

Life at the Veritas Center was about to change if the partners agreed to lease space to these guys. A good change, Hunter thought. Having such fine men working together with them would be a huge bonus to the Center. Plus, the Center could use the income from the rent so they could do more pro bono work. A win-win for everyone.

The door swung in, and he held his breath. Finally, Maya stepped through. She wore a slinky red dress that clung to all of her curves and fired his imagination. She smiled, a slow, sultry number just for him, and his heart flip-flopped.

They'd spent every free minute together for the last two weeks, which weren't many. He was looking forward to finishing up all the loose ends on this investigation so he had more free time. But he wouldn't think about that now. He would just enjoy a night out with the woman he loved.

Maya took in Hunter's appearance. They'd all agreed to dress up to celebrate being alive and victorious over Sakina and her scheme. Hunter wore a gray suit with a black knit shirt. The jacket fit him as if tailored for his body and emphasized his muscular shape.

He came toward her, reaching for her hands. "I thought you'd never get here."

She clutched his hands and planned to hold on tight all night. "We had to decide on Aiden's proposal."

"And?"

"The partners agreed to let them lease space and live in the empty condos."

"Sounds like a good decision for all."

"Agreed. But please don't say anything until I can tell Aiden."

"No worries. I'm not leaving your side for even a minute."

"I like the sound of that." She smiled up at him, and he drew her into his arms. Okay, fine, she would let go of his hands to twine them around his waist as he held her close.

"You look amazing," he whispered. "I love the dress."

"This old thing?" She laughed because she'd dropped almost a full paycheck on it this week when she'd gone shopping with Kelsey.

She heard the door open behind her and felt the cool night air waft in and caress her bare shoulders. She didn't want to step out of Hunter's arms, but she released him and grabbed his hand as she turned, struck by how well their hands fit together, as if God had intended it all along. The thought warmed her clear to her bones.

Nick and Piper stepped in, then Emory and Blake. Maya's heart filled with joy when she saw Piper clinging to Nick's arm. They'd been so happy together that Maya couldn't wait until they were officially married.

Hunter shook hands with them. "Glad you could make it."

"Are you kidding?" Blake asked. "We needed one more night out before the baby's born."

Emory ran a hand over her belly. "I can't believe I'm still pregnant. This little munchkin is as stubborn as her daddy and doesn't want to be born."

"Her?" Maya grabbed Emory's hand. "It's a girl."

Emory nodded. "I had an ultrasound today and the tech slipped up and told us."

"I'm having a girl." Blake's dreamy eyes warmed Maya's heart.

"Um, sweetheart." Emory moved closer to Blake. "Technically, I'm having the baby."

Blake slid his arm around her shoulders. "All that matters is we're soon going to have a baby girl."

"Come on," Nick said. "Let's go choose a room so Piper and I can skunk you before that happens."

Emory frowned and swatted her hand at him.

"Not a good idea to mess with a hormonal pregnant woman," Blake warned.

Emory raised an eyebrow. "That goes for you too."

Blake held up his hands. "Wouldn't think of it."

They started down the hall, Emory insisting Blake stop for some popcorn.

Hunter chuckled. "I can't wait until we're at that stage of our relationship."

Maya's gut tightened. This was some serious talk that they'd never had. "We've never talked about kids."

"I just assumed you wanted them."

"I do," she said. "If they're yours."

He drew her close and lowered his head. His mouth inches from hers.

"Way to block the entrance." Grady's voice carried through the foyer from the door.

Maya stepped back to look at him. He'd worn a long-sleeved shirt that coordinated nicely with Ainslie's pale blue skirt and sparkly top. She wondered if they'd decided together on what to wear.

"Glad you could make it," she said sincerely, though she didn't appreciate one more interruption to the kiss she so desperately wanted.

"Way to sidestep my comment." Grady laughed.

Sierra and Reed, along with his sister Malone, pushed through the door, and everyone had to move back. She saw Hunter nod at the dark-haired Reed, a kind of under-standing between fellow FBI agents. Maya took a moment to admire Malone's black dress. It was simple, but the way Malone looked in it was anything but. She was stunning, but Maya knew Malone didn't let her good looks go to her head.

Laughter erupted in a nearby room.

"I hear my brothers are here," Sierra said. "You tell them yet?"

Maya shook her head.

"Mind if I do?" Sierra asked.

Maya squeezed Sierra's arm. "Go ahead. I'm sure they'd love to hear it from you."

"No time like the present." She tugged Reed down the hall.

"I'm drawing up the paperwork for their agency, so I guess I should check in too." Malone smiled and strolled down the hall, her very high heels clicking on the floor.

"Might as well see how they react." Grady looked at Ainslie. "If you're game, that is."

"Of course."

They departed, and Maya looked up at Hunter. "Now, where were we?"

"I was just about to—" He shook his head. "Incoming."

Maya turned to see Kelsey and Devon arrive. Devon wore khaki pants and a knit shirt, and Kelsey had on a frilly dress in a flowery print that was fitted at the top and had a full skirt. Thankfully, they were the last of her partners, and maybe she could get them moving quickly and finally succeed in kissing Hunter.

"Everyone's inside," she said. "Sierra's telling her—"

A joyous whoop sounded, taking away Maya's words.

"I guess they're excited." Kelsey smiled.

Devon frowned. "It's going to be a lot different around the condos with these guys moving in. None of us will get any sleep."

Kelsey touched Devon's cheek. "Oh, you poor baby."

He grinned. "I think I'll milk this for all I can."

"Come on." She grabbed his hand. "Let's go congratulate them."

"We'll be right in," Maya said, turning to Hunter.

When they were gone, Hunter said, "You look amazing, but..." He drew her closer. "Still, one thing you seem to be missing."

She'd carefully chosen even the smallest accessory for tonight, so she arched an eyebrow. "What's that?"

He reached into his pocket and drew out a ring box. He got down on his knee and looked up at her. "I know this isn't the most romantic place to make this official, but I wanted to celebrate with our friends tonight. So, Maya Glass, I'm now officially asking. Will you marry me?"

"Yes. Of course." She fanned her face that was heating up as much as her heart was bursting with joy and excitement over their future together.

He opened the box and revealed a solitaire in white gold, the very ring she'd dreamed of having. He slipped it onto her finger and stood. "I love you, and I promise I'm committed to you for life from this moment forward."

"I love you too." She flung her arms around his neck and drew his head down.

The air fairly crackled between them as his head descended. She couldn't wait and pulled harder, his lips landing on hers. They were warm and insistent. Demanding. Exploring. And she surrendered to it all. To the man she was going to marry—and soon—if she had anything to say about it.

"You guys coming?" Fletch's voice came from down the hall. "Everyone's waiting—oh, sorry. You're um. You're busy."

Maya had never loved the sound of commitment more than she did right now, but she leaned back to look at Fletch. "We'll be right in."

"If you say so." He backed away, his face as red as his hair.

"We embarrassed the poor guy," Hunter said, running his hands down her bare arms, leaving delicious shivers behind, to grasp her hands.

"He'll get over it." She smiled up at the most marvelous man.

"We should go, but I don't want to."

"I know, but we have a wonderful group waiting for us. The most amazing partners with their significant others, their lives just beginning. I want to share our happiness with them."

Hunter released one of her hands and turned to lead her down the hallway. "And what about the Byrd brothers?"

"Those guys?" She thought about them. "Now, they're another story. Five lonely bachelors. I'm going to do my best to change that."

Hunter tossed back his head and laughed. "That's my

go-getter of a fiancée. Never rest, even if it means organizing other people's lives."

"I just want everyone to be as happy as we are, and that's going to take some concerted effort." She winked at him. "Might as well get started on that right after we announce our engagement."

NIGHTHAWK SECURITY SERIES
Protecting others when unspeakable danger lurks.

Keep reading for more information on the additional books in the Nighthawk Security Series where the Cold Harbor and Truth Seekers teams work side-by-side with Nighthawk Security.

A woman plagued by a stalker. Children of a murderer. A woman whose mother died under suspicious circumstances.

All in danger. Lives on the line. Needing protection.

Enter the brothers of Nighthawk Security. The five Byrd brothers with years of former military and law enforcement experience coming together to offer protection and investigation services. Their goal—protecting others when unspeakable danger lurks.

Book 1 Night Fall – November, 2020
Book 2 – Night Vision – December, 2020
Book 3 - Night Hawk   – January, 2021
Book 4 –Night Moves – July, 2021
Book 5 – Night Watch – August, 2021
Book 6 – Night Prey – October, 2021

For More Details Visit -
www.susansleeman.com/books/nighthawk-security/

THE TRUTH SEEKERS

People are rarely who they seem

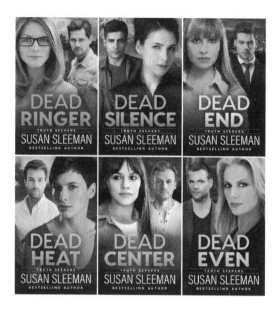

A twin who never knew her sister existed, a mother whose child is not her own, a woman whose father is anything but her father. All searching. All seeking. All needing help and hope.

Meet the unsung heroes of the Veritas Center. The Truth Seekers – a team, that includes experts in forensic anthropology, DNA, trace evidence, ballistics, cybercrimes, and toxicology. Committed to restoring hope and families by solving one mystery at a time, none of them are prepared for when the mystery comes calling close to home and threatens to destroy the only life they've known.

For More Details Visit -
www.susansleeman.com/books/truth-seekers/

BOOKS IN THE COLD HARBOR SERIES

Blackwell Tactical – this law enforcement training facility and protection services agency is made up of former military and law enforcement heroes whose injuries keep them from the line of duty. When trouble strikes, there's no better team to have on your side, and they would give everything, even their lives, to protect innocents.

For More Details Visit -
www.susansleeman.com/books/cold-harbor/

HOMELAND HEROES SERIES

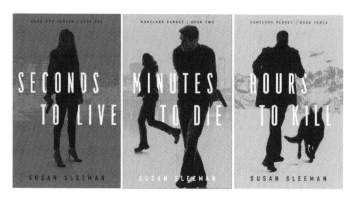

When the clock is ticking on criminal activity conducted on or facilitated by the Internet there is no better team to call other than the RED team, a division of the HSI—Homeland Security's Investigation Unit. RED team includes FBI and DHS Agents, and US Marshal's Service Deputies.

For More Details Visit -

www.susansleeman.com/books/homeland-heroes/

WHITE KNIGHTS SERIES

Join the White Knights as they investigate stories plucked from today's news headlines. The FBI Critical Incident Response Team includes experts in crisis management, explosives, ballistics/weapons, negotiating/criminal profiling, cyber crimes, and forensics. All team members are former military and they stand ready to deploy within four hours, anytime and anywhere to mitigate the highest-priority threats facing our nation.

www.susansleeman.com/books/white-knights/

ABOUT SUSAN

SUSAN SLEEMAN is a bestselling and award-winning author of more than 35 inspirational/Christian and clean read romantic suspense books. In addition to writing, Susan also hosts the website, TheSuspenseZone.com.

Susan currently lives in Oregon, but has had the pleasure of living in nine states. Her husband is a retired church music director and they have two beautiful daughters, a very special son-in-law, and an adorable grandson.

For more information visit:
www.susansleeman.com

Made in the USA
Middletown, DE
15 July 2021